Traders

of the

Ancient Seas

JAMES FARRIS

ISBN: 978-1-7375863-4-0

Copyright © 2022 by James Farris
Printed by Charis Publishing
charispublishing.com
@charispublishing ⬛

Published May 2022

For my family,

for Kelsey,

for God

In the Year of Our Lord 1519
during the month of Gemini,
a sole Spanish ship roamed
somewhere,
someplace
in the Atlantic Ocean
searching for the famed,
the revered,
the mysterious
Spice Islands of the Far East . . .

ACT I

Captain Gaspar

Scene: Mad Overture

ᚼᚼᚼ

"**M**Y DUCHESS, MY mistress, my moon called Luna. Beautiful art thou dressed in thy night's gown of translucent glow. Sing me thy hymn. Play thy chord to guide me to the spice, to the stone, to the island of the ancients. Guide me. Steer me. Illuminate my path through the dark maze to the forsaken island. Aye, great lamp light, glow through my dark despair. Doubt me not, for the heavens I see awaiting the *Valencia* and me, there, across the sea."

I was inside my quarters, the captain's quarters, aboard my ship called *Valencia*. I stared out through my windows toward the dark sea and night sky—thinking, questioning, and wondering.

Thoughts crept into my mind like a daydream or nightmare, both the same to me. *What is my answer? Who am I? What is my dream, day and night? Where do I go?* Yes, yes, for I am Captain Gaspar of the ship called *Valencia*, a Spanish ship. Aye, the crew and I crossed the Atlantic for the strait, the strait to the Pacific, by the undiscovered western way, the western way from Spain through the New World to where the spices are grown and traded. We sail for the famed, the mysterious Spice Islands near Arabia, near India, near China. I could smell them now—ah, cloves, cinnamon, mace, and nutmeg.

I closed my eyes. *Yes, the perfume of ground nutmeg and sweet cinnamon. What a shame that Spain is behind Portugal in dominating the spice trade. Spain is late to the race because Vasco de Gama—that mean, ruthless Portuguese bastard—took the southern way, the way around Africa to get there, to the Spice Islands. The southern tip of Africa worked well for*

3

the Portuguese. I took that way myself years ago for I am Portuguese, sailed for the Portuguese, used to be Portuguese. Nay, now I sail for Spain, for King Charles V of Spain, not for Portugal, not for King Manuel of Portugal. I spit on Manuel and his whole empire for what they did to me. He shall regret it; regret it, he will. I hold the secret, the power, the knowledge of the undiscovered western way, the way to the island.

I turned to my long mirror next to the open window. I caught my reflection—my state, my mental state. What did I see? A broad-shouldered man with large brown eyes, bristled brown eyebrows and beard, a pronounced jaw line, a tall frame. I was not too old—*Was I forty years old? Or forty-one? Did I look presentable?*—and my dark brown eyes were sunken in, painted with purple circles of a sleepless mind, an obsessed mind. Sleep—a thought, an activity, both far from my sight—was whisked away by a strong sea wind. Aye, the sea, the wind was rough tonight.

The ship swayed back and forth as waves crashed against the bow of the ship. Lit candles hung above my wooden desk near the mirror, swinging from a small chandelier. Hot white wax melted down from the fire-tipped wick, falling to the wooden floor of the ship. *Drip, drip.* The sea air continued to rip through my quarters, lifting, scattering pages of my nautical charts and logs.

I took a deep breath as I felt the cool air whisper her secrets into my ear, brush against my arm; strong, stronger the wind blew. *Could this wild wind be a sign, a sign from the zodiac? Has my mistress, Luna, brought news from her brothers and sisters of the constellations, from the celestial heavens above?*

I turned my attention to my bronze armillary sphere. It was created, crafted by my friend Cosimo to my exact specifications. The sphere was adorned with colorful designs, painted by a Florentine painter. The instrument was composed of multiple intersecting layers of rings around a small terrestrial globe at the center.

As I adjusted the rings to measure my latitude, I spoke aloud. "Aye, Ursa Minor, Pole Star, but wait . . . The constellations are not . . . Let me check once more."

I readjusted the rings and recalculated the cosmos, the stars, and all other celestial beings in perspective. "Nay, this be not right, not right at all." I rubbed my forehead, agitated. "What are you telling me? Tell me the truth, my mistress. Hide nothing from me! Are my coordinates correct? Sonne, Mars, Jupiter—all wrong. Preposterous! Have you led us astray?"

I checked my calendar, scanning each entry and date. *Here. Yes, yes. This would mean we are near the passage, the strait into the Pacific. I have never seen this, measurements like these before, before, before . . . We are lost in the middle of sea, leagues away from the strait.*

Frustration and confusion coursed through my veins. I threw my nautical charts and calendars to the ground and cried out to my mistress for her horrible abandonment of me, of us, of the Valencia. I slumped to the ground, realizing our doomed fate foretold, revealed to me through the stars.

In that instant, the wind's ghostly wisp blew strong against the *Valencia* and through my windows, scattering my charts and papers further across the floor.

"Show me!" I cried out.

The wind's roar turned the rings on my armillary sphere quickly and violently. I looked to the sphere as it spun in an odd elliptical fashion. I pulled myself up, dried my tear-filled eyes, and checked my colorful sphere. Rotated—rotated, it did—to ways I never dreamed it could.

"There, there. I see! I see the answer!" I cried with a wild smile and laugh. "The passage, the island, has been revealed to me. Close, so close it is."

I picked up my nautical charts and calendar from the floor and began sketching, logging these new findings. I shrieked with hysterical laughter.

I opened a compartment in my desk and pulled out a small shard of a crystal, red in color. I rubbed it between my fingers, smiling. "The transformation, the knowledge, and the power shall be mine. No man, no king shall take it from me, not even . . . Nay, not even the shadow, the dark shadow, shall stop me."

I turned toward the opened windows, faced the dark blue abyss before me, and said, "Hear me! No man, beast, or spirit will stop Gaspar from reaching Adaman, Retjenu, the red gold!"

Thump. Thump. There was a sudden knock on the cabin door. Again, *thump, thump*, loud and abrupt. A voice came from the other side. "Captain, Captain . . . Is . . . is everything fine?"

I calmed down, controlled myself—my feelings, my thoughts—took a deep breath, and replied, "Aye, Jaipur. Was the hot candle wax, dripped down on my hand, burned me."

"Much fuss for a burn, Captain Gaspar," replied Jaipur, a touch of islander added to his formal Castilian Spanish, the language spoken on the *Valencia*. "May I come in, sir?"

"Step in, and tell me what you bring."

Jaipur opened the wooden door. Jaipur had a younger face, one of the youngest of the crew. His eyes looked islander; he was Far Eastern with tan skin and a fresh, youthful look.

As he looked around the room, Jaipur took in the empty bottles of wine. Then, his eyes lingered on me. My hair was a mess, my coat stunk of sweat, and my shirt was unbuttoned; I still maintained a crazed look in my eyes.

Jaipur closed the windows, and the sound of the heavy wind dissipated. I propped myself against the desk.

"Sir?" said Jaipur.

"I hear you," I replied. "What is it?"

"Edward Swift spotted land ahead. Cosimo believes it to be the strait to the Pacific."

"The strait? Could it be?"

"Come up. Look for yourself."

"The charts said it was near, or did they not?"

Jaipur looked to the charts and sphere on the ground. "Did they . . . say anything else?"

"To the deck, Jaipur. Destiny awaits us."

Jaipur

Scene: Appearance of the Slave

oⱿⱿⱿ

I FOLLOWED CAPTAIN Gaspar up the stairs to the deck, catching a view of his room before I closed the door. It was a disaster. The thought of what this mad captain was doing behind this bolted door terrified me to the point of hysteria. He had become worse, much worse, over this voyage.

His stubborn stupidity with his fantastical ideas and strange methods put my life at risk. How many times had I caught him crying, moaning to the moon, calling it "Luna"? He was in love with the moon. What sane person is in love with the moon?

He was a good-looking gentleman—many women liked him— yet he was obsessed with the moon, in love with a glow in the sky. He was mad, mad I tell you. I did not encourage his antics or his voyages. I wished he had left me in Spain; at least there I knew I was safe, secure, away from his mad antics. As a slave, as *his* slave, I did not have a choice of what I did or where I went.

Gaspar took me—yes, *took* me—bought me from a slave trader when I was only ten years old on an island near my home: Sumatra, part of the famed Spice Islands. All of this grief, this journey, this wretched journey was for spices. This glorious endeavor of exploration to find the western passage from the Atlantic to the Indian Ocean was not for discovery but for gold and status, typical of the Europeans. The western route through the New World had never been attempted until now.

Damn King Charles of Spain. Was he mad? Who would hire Gaspar? I would not, and I lived with him. He was a father figure to me. I was only twenty-one years old. I knew him better than anyone and, I hate to say it, loved the man to a certain degree.

Being told this journey was to spread Christianity, I could not help but laugh. Bring out the court jester to tell this joke! Aye, this was all for gold, status, and honor—for the spices—and as Gaspar's slave, those spices were worth more than my own weight in gold. Glad to know I was worth less than cloves and cardamom. I had to stop thinking about it. Worth . . . What was worth to a man? My life was worth less than spices, that's worth.

Lucky I was, Gaspar told me, that I was no ordinary slave. Nay, I was something far more valuable, for I was bilingual. Gaspar told me if I assisted him in this outrageous journey across the Atlantic, freedom he would give to me. Throughout my life, he had treated me right, always with respect, other than our past adventures across the sea where we almost died multiple times. This time was different. He had no common sense. None.

He was a Portuguese—*Portuguese*—captain sailing under a Spanish flag on a ship filled with Spanish sailors. The moment these Spaniards felt the wind of his madness, it would be off with his head or off the side of the ship. If this Spanish crew threw him overboard, then a slave I would stay for the rest of my life. A slave . . . for life! He needed to get his act together and stop yelling at that cursed moon! I worried for him.

I followed the captain up to the deck. Land was visible in the distance—faint, but there past the fog, revealed by the great lamp rising behind us. I stood close by Gaspar, servicing all his needs. Excitement filled the deck with hoots and hollers of *Land ho!* The crew was composed of about one hundred men, mostly low-class Spaniards, roughnecks. We spoke the Spanish tongue aboard.

"Where's Cosimo?" asked Captain Gaspar, rushed. "Cosimo!"

Cosimo was one of the naval pilots on our journey; he was a specialized cartographer, bookkeeper, scribe, and cosmographer. Cosimo was the most educated man aboard the *Valencia*. Gaspar found him in a monastery outside Florence. Sharp he was, though he had no tan and never saw the sun.

He was an invaluable member of the crew. He used to work under the papal state in Rome before Gaspar recruited him. I thought he was foolish, second behind Gaspar in common sense for joining this doomed endeavor. Few ever made it to the Spice Islands; fewer returned. The Spice Islands were a world away from Europeans, farther beyond Arabia.

"I see him now," I pointed out.

Cosimo pushed his way through the crowded deck. Refined and cultured, he was more charming than the rest of the men. He was from Florence and looked Italian by his features. Cosimo maintained a youthful touch in the eyes and few wrinkles above his black brow. He had long black hair, a slender frame, pale skin, long fingers and nose, and no beard. He wore gentlemen's clothes—a white linen shirt, brown pants, leather boots, and a red overcoat—as opposed to the other sailors, who wore shirts and pants and went barefoot.

"Captain!" exclaimed Cosimo, cheerful and excited. "Swift used his Jacob's staff and calculated our position off the Southern Cross constellation. We are only a few leagues from the strait."

"Did your map correspond with this?" asked Gaspar, holding on to Cosimo's shoulders.

"Indeed, it did!" replied Cosimo. "The strait! Oh, the sweet strait through the southern land! It's here before us after our long months at sea."

Captain Gaspar's face grew wild with enchantment as he rubbed his hands together in delight. He yelled, "The passage is ours, men!"

The crew replied with great cheers and hollers.

He continued, "Bring me Swift without a moment to lose."

I yelled up to the crow's nest, high above the deck of the ship. A minute later, a man cascaded down from the nest. He swung right in front us with his Jacob's staff slung around his back. I was not too knowledgeable about nautical instruments, but from what Cosimo told me, the Jacob's staff was a pole with length markings to determine a pilot's latitude using the stars as a reference.

"Ahoy, Captain," said Swift, smiling and still clinging to the line.

Edward Swift, an English fellow, was informal, vibrant, and uncontrollable. He had long blond hair tied into a ponytail, a rough face, defined cheekbones, and bright green eyes. He wore a long, baggy, white shirt and brown pants. Swift was another naval pilot of the *Valencia*, reporting to Cosimo and Gaspar. Swift, unlike Cosimo, was known for his informality. I liked him. Fearless he was. Funny, too.

"Did you see the strait up top?" asked Gaspar. "What does she look like?"

"No, sir," replied Swift. Using his hands to demonstrate the ship's path, he said, "But there, the southern continent bends. We follow around the bend to the Pacific. The passage west was never *through* a continent but around it, good sir."

"The Arabian charts said it was a bend, also," interjected Cosimo.

"Praise be to the heavens," remarked Gaspar. "Your eyes are sharp like a bird's."

"I do what I can, Captain," said Swift.

"Good," said Gaspar. "We follow the bend, find the zenith, and follow the sun westward. There, the trade winds shall guide us to the islands!"

"Aye, faster than the wings of Pegasus," remarked Swift.

"Captain," interjected Cosimo. "Quick!"

"What?" said Gaspar, agitated, as if Cosimo wanted to suck the magic from his excitement. Cosimo was very particular, straight in everything he did.

"Need not forget," said Cosimo, "we must to stock up on provisions before setting west. My catalog suggests we're short on such things. Best stock up now with land in sight."

"Unknown land is dangerous," replied Gaspar. "We know not the tides of the port. One bad move, we strike rock, and the *Valencia* goes under. We continue on."

"Captain, sir," interjected Swift.

"You, too?" barked Gaspar.

"Cosimo and I have consulted the tide volvelle," said Swift. "We've considered the current, the relief of the seabed, and the weight of our cargo from Cosimo's catalog."

"Your point?" asked Gaspar.

"I can dock the ship," replied Swift, "with ease."

Gaspar looked at Swift with apprehension, his crazed eyes both doubting and accepting Swift's capabilities. He rubbed his coarse chin.

"Jaipur," called Gaspar to me.

"Aye?" I replied.

"If we encounter any natives, could you speak their tongue?"

"Perhaps. Perhaps not."

"Hmm," remarked Gaspar, his voice slow and rough, like the tumultuous dark blue sea, as he looked to the land mass upon the fixed horizon. "What do you say, Cosimo?"

"We need provisions, Captain," replied Cosimo. "Natives or not, we will perish without more provisions."

A man in a full officer's regalia pushed his way into our circle. His name was Zaragoza, a Spanish agent placed aboard the *Valencia* by King Charles V to oversee the king's investment. The deal with King Charles V of Spain was rights to the western trade route and Gaspar's valuable nautical charts, along with two thirds of any spices with which we returned.

"Why was I not told of land?" demanded Zaragoza.

He was a tall, clean-shaven man with broad shoulders, a sharp face, piercing eyes, a pointed chin, and black hair with hints of gray.

"How should I know why not?" replied Gaspar.

"No plan may be exacted without the order of King Charles," insisted Zaragoza. "As ordered by the king, I'm his voice and rule of law. Remember that, Captain Gaspar."

"I wouldn't dream of testing you or the beloved crown," re-marked Gaspar. "I dream only of my mistress and the island."

"Keep your dirty thoughts to yourself," replied Zaragoza, disgusted. "There's land . . . Are we docking? I would welcome a stretch of the legs."

"Aye," remarked Gaspar. "Bring out Faustino, the coxswain. He'll arrange the boats. Swift, anchor the ship, and watch the tide. Jaipur, prepare some of the crew to go ashore."

"Will do, Captain," I replied.

Faustino

Scene: Appearance of the Tormented

⌇⌇

NOTHER DROP OF *wine will do. Let it pour down my throat. Ah, it tastes so sweet, refreshing, invigorating, my scarlet nectar.*

I sat in the hold of the ship, the place where all the men rest, eat, and gossip—an awful place to spend time. It offered little sunlight and smelled of old sweat and sea air, but it was all a sailor had besides the deck.

The ship continued to sway back and forth.

This is my favorite time. The time for my mediation, my prayer, my answer, this bottle of wine. What hour of the night has come? Is the moon still out? Does my end come soon?

I noticed a knife on the table, picked it up, and held it firmly in one hand, my bottle in the other. *Which one is more useful?*

No one was around at this time. Sleeping, they were. God had tormented my soul with that shadow. The shadow haunted the night, hid in the corner, roamed the deck.

Why did I join this expedition? Was it to escape the shadow? Nay, he followed me here. I will die on this ship. Nay, nay, I will die by the hand of a savage. Nay, by the hand of a Muslim. Nay, nay, by my own shadow. I will die by stupidity, yes, by signing up for this terrible expedition to find the Spice Islands.

I'm equally as mad as Gaspar. "Moon! Moon! I love the moon!" What a joke all of this is. The crew figured it, too. Strange though. A part of me likes Gaspar, but death and madness await all of me. Sounds like the perfect reason to drink. Those debts, such heavy debts …

"I needed the money," I said aloud. "I have no money. Same for all of you?"

I looked around for an answer. Funny. I was alone, or was I? Why search for a response when alone? Was I alone? Nay, yes, nay. I took a gulp. *Ah, refreshed.*

"Land ho!" yelled a crewman from the deck.

"Land ahead!" shouted another.

I looked around, anxious. I placed the knife down and took a deep breath. I ventured into my thoughts again. *Could land be here, in the middle of the Atlantic? Or were we in the Pacific? Oh, Gaspar will need me if there is land. I'm the coxswain. Yes, yes.*

I could not mess this up. There had better be gold on this island. I came for gold. If there was one thing that I loved more than wine, it was gold.

Loud footsteps, chatter, and banter filled the ship. The whole crew went up top—running, yelling, and hollering, excited at the sight of land. Sad, my eyes would not, could not, should not drift past the bottle before me. All of a sudden, I heard my name.

"Faustino! Faustino!" yelled the figure.

I turned around. Jaipur, Gaspar's slave. He was a young lad, a good boy. I had not a problem with him, unless a problem was made between us.

"Faustino," said Jaipur.

"Hmm?" I replied.

Jaipur looked at my condition, then at the table. He sniffed the foul air around me, then gave a face of disgust.

"Are you drunk?" interrogated Jaipur.

"Me? Nay, I don't drink."

"Is that so?"

"Is what so?" I replied, irritated.

"Your drinking problem."

"I have none."

Jaipur shook his head.

Why should I lie? I don't have a drinking problem. Never have, never will.

"Gaspar needs you to arrange the boats. We're going ashore," said Jaipur.

"Will do," I replied with a smile.

Swift

Scene: Appearance of the Wild Lover

ᏕᎥᎳᎧ

O UT AT SEA, the waves tossed our longboat above the rolling white tips. We rowed, rowed, up, down, clashed, splashed, rowed, and rowed. My wooden paddle pierced the water. *Splash!* Water sprinkled on my face. The sky was covered with gray clouds; the air felt cold and blew strong winds. My hands and fingers turned purple from the cold and wet.

"See the shoreline to the right," I pointed out. "We'll move with the tide, head for the cove."

"Keep your eyes on the brush, men," ordered Gaspar.

We had two longboats filled with sailors headed toward the shore. On my own boat were Captain Gaspar; Jaipur, his slave; Cosimo; and Faustino, the coxswain. The rest were roughneck sailors and myself, one of the pilots of the *Valencia*. Zaragoza maintained the other ship. He was a terrible Spaniard, only out for himself. Weren't we all though? I kept my mouth quiet.

Zaragoza stood pronounced, upright, like a Roman legionnaire, a conquistador. He dressed in full military regalia. I could guarantee he'd mutiny our ship in time. What could I expect? We were on a ship full of Spaniards, and the hierarchy was not Spanish. I was one of the pilots and English. Thanks be that I spoke Castilian Spanish better than the lower rungs of sailors aboard. I knew the sailors respected me.

Row, row, row. We dug into the sea and pushed the vessel toward the shoreline. It was frigid out there, our clothes sopped with water. These past months had been hard on me. I would never show it or complain about it, but hard they had been.

Oh, my love, I see you now in our small home. I see a beautiful day— you, us, nestled in our London townhouse. Rose loved to sing the sweetest tunes. She had long, thick beautiful brown hair with the most charming smile. I could see her, yes, in her elegant white dress as I entered our modest home. I could see her there, singing, cooking in a hot pot over the fire. She would look up, turn to me, smile.

"Look there. Look!" screamed one of the sailors. I left the thought of my love and returned to the dark sea.

"It's people—yes, people—coming from the tree line," insisted Cosimo.

"Natives," stated Gaspar. "Hold steady! Prepare your arms! Wait for them!"

I felt the grip of my cutlass between my hard hands and said, "Return to your warmth, I will, my love, my Rose."

"They are coming to us. See the boats!" shouted a sailor.

"Gaspar," yelled Zaragoza over the loud sea. "I shall shoot them if they come near, hear me?"

"No," replied Gaspar sternly, as he positioned his hand outward, signaling. "Hold steady. Wait for my mark."

The natives were massive, giants almost, covered in white paint, dressed only in simple scraps of cloth covering their genitalia. The natives rowed toward us in four slender longboats full of warriors. There appeared to be a king among them, dressed in furs and feathers, older than the other men. I noticed they were armed with bows and knives. The other sailors seemed hesitant, outright scared. I had dealt with action before: I had been in the Royal Navy my whole life prior to this. The natives drew closer. Tensions heightened.

"Jaipur," whispered Gaspar.

"Yes, Captain?" replied Jaipur, seated next to him toward the aft of the vessel.

I looked to Jaipur, listening closely. Jaipur had tan skin, Far Eastern islander eyes. The young lad was shorter than I. He was eager, vibrant, and curious. I'd never been to the Far East. My whole life, the Far East was a legend, a mystery, a place of great wealth. I needed great wealth, spices for my dear love. The whole crew, all of us, needed wealth. Was the risk worth this potential wealth? I say not. I say not, but what choice did we have? What job could pay my worth?

Perhaps Jaipur, because he was from the Far East, might be our chance for success, however slim that chance for success would be. Gaspar had assimilated Jaipur into European customs, language, and culture, and he now looked, dressed, and acted more like a European than anything else. Nevertheless, Jaipur was the only one who could speak the Far Eastern languages, though it had been many years since he had the chance. I hoped he still could.

"Jaipur," said Gaspar. "Tell them in your native tongue we come in peace."

Jaipur nodded, then spoke aloud to them in words I knew not, looking to the king for answers. A minute went by. Still no answer. I'd never seen natives like these before. Never had I navigated this far west before either. No European had.

Jaipur tried again, yelled out once more. Then, the king spoke in his strange tongue, similar though different. I could tell Jaipur understood him slightly.

"What did he say, Jaipur?" implored Gaspar, on edge as if his feet dangled over the side of a mountainous cliff with jagged rocks in the sea below. Jaipur said nothing, attempting to discern the king's vernacular. Gaspar whispered again. "Jaipur, what did you say?"

"I'll blow these savages now. Hell will welcome them," said Zaragoza, restrained. "I swear that to you, Gaspar."

The king of the natives waited for an answer. His eyes scanned our vessels. The other giants were brute, kept longbows out. Still, they remained silent.

"I . . . I think the king said . . . " said Jaipur. "Let my men aboard. Gifts they bring."

Gaspar looked to the king, to his men, to the rough sea, each enveloped in the ebb and flow. *Tricky situation*, I thought.

"Let them aboard, Cap," I suggested. "Show them the mirrors. Trade they will for provisions. Show them the mirrors."

"I say we blast them with cannons," said Zaragoza. "Scare them off. Find provisions ourselves. Savages are all they are."

"Diplomacy is what we are," stated Cosimo.

Cosimo had a heart, a good heart. He cared for each person's word; no matter slave or king, each was equal in his eyes. I was a little rougher around the edges—more brutal and realistic, I'd say. Cosimo was locked in a monastery for years. He knew nothing of the real world, and the real world knew nothing of him. If it were not for Gaspar's breaking him out of that monastery, he'd still be there, on his knees day and night.

"Diplomacy?" scoffed Zaragoza. "Not with savages. Only with God-fearing men."

I noticed near the king a woman in simple clothes, adorned in strange necklaces and wearing beads inside her nose. She held up a staff with a skull on it, chanting phrases, chanting words.

What was she chanting? She must be a witch.

"Jaipur," said Gaspar. "Tell the king a few of his warriors may board."

Cosimo

Scene: Appearance of the Curious

☙

THE FIRST INTERACTION with the natives was strange. What happened after was stranger. We returned to the ship, followed by three longboats filled with natives and provisions. The king returned to shore, allowing his representatives aboard. The males were painted white from head to toe. The warriors brought forth some provisions in woven baskets.

On deck, the crew was enthralled with the exoticness of these giants. Around ten or so warriors boarded the ship; some of them carried wonderful fruits, vegetables, and an animal that appeared like a goat but with a long neck. The native warriors walked around the ship, observing this massive floating vessel, paying close attention to our clothes, weapons, sails—anything that piqued their interest.

I paid close attention to their movements, the way they carried themselves, and how they spoke and interacted with each other. I had a keen eye for observation. I learned by watching and listening. I had read of natives before. The books were inaccurate, always claiming natives were cannibals, savages. I disagreed with that reasoning. They were misunderstood people like us—like Muslims, like me.

The natives carried large knives, teal in color, attached to their belts. By their aggressive movements, I grew hesitant of them. They seemed violent; maybe they *were* cannibals. The natives began to rummage through the sailors' things. I kept my distance and helped Gaspar to the best of my ability. In my mind, peace was first and foremost.

The warriors snooped around the ship, examined the hold, took a few kitchen utensils. Then, they came upon Gaspar's quarters. A few candles were lit at the time, giving off a fresh aroma behind the bolted door. The warriors were intrigued by the fragrance and wanted to view the room. Though he appeared restrained, Gaspar encouraged them. Gaspar wanted to be a good host, wanted the provisions, so he allowed four of the warriors inside his quarters while the rest of the natives returned to the deck.

Inside the captain's quarters were Gaspar, Swift, Zaragoza, Jaipur, and I, following behind the four giants. We kept a close eye on them. Gaspar showed the warriors a mirror, presented it to them with great delight.

"See reflection," suggested Gaspar, smiling.

The warriors each picked up the mirror, shocked and amazed to see such things. They looked at their reflection in delight, passing the mirror to one another.

"Yes, take, take," said Gaspar, gesturing with his hands.

"If they make one move on me," remarked Zaragoza with his back against the wall and one hand on his sword.

"Stay calm, Zaragoza," I replied.

The warriors started to pick up anything they saw and place it in a sack slung around their backs. Each one rummaged through Gaspar's wares and trinkets, more aggressively than before. Gaspar began to bite on his thumb, his leg fidgeting.

One warrior was fixated, dazed in a dream-like state, as he looked at Gaspar's armillary sphere. The warrior approached the sphere, touched it, played with the rings, tried to understand its spherical motion. From what I could see, he knew it was a measuring device. These warriors were not savages at all. I wondered what type of astronomical devices they may have used.

"Wait, wait!" cried Gaspar. "Tell them, Jaipur. This is not to touch."

Jaipur tried to communicate with them, but it was to no avail. I noticed the other warriors kept taking, taking, and taking any object that fancied their desire.

"What should we do?" asked Swift with eyes on the four giants.

"End this nonsense," suggested Zaragoza.

"No," I pleaded in a whisper. "They know not."

I studied the warriors and their fascination with Gaspar's instruments. Then with a quick flash, something caught a warrior's eyes over the sphere. On top of Gaspar's desk were a series of colorful drawings, charts, and maps. The warrior's head tilted, back bent down, eyes drawn to the desk. The others stared at him, hesitant, concerned; I was intrigued. What did the warrior see? I knew the look the warrior gave, a look of . . . understanding? Of what? What piqued his interest? What could Gaspar have that he knew of?

The warrior's eyes grew wider than the horizon. He pushed the charts and maps away, then picked up a drawing of strange symbols that not even I knew of or had seen before. I glanced at it, discerning what in this geocentric universe it could be. It bore some familiarity to me. From where? Where?

It was a drawing of what seemed to be Egyptian hieroglyphics . . . of a bird? a man? perhaps Anubis? Around the hieroglyphics was a map, encircled with coordinates, degrees, and measurements. I'd read of Alexandria, of Cairo, of Egypt before. I knew what hieroglyphics looked like though the drawing was sketched by a modern hand—not Gaspar's, but rather someone very skilled. I was from Florence. I knew art, skillful technique, precision; that drawing was done by no ordinary hand.

The warrior held it up, like a sacrifice during a ritual, then chanted unintelligible words. I stared at the drawing, squinting my eyes to catch a full look of it. His words were fierce and loud, alerting the other warriors in the room. I felt adrenaline pump through my arteries as the atmosphere of the room changed from that of a silent night to a hot day, bustling with activity.

"Jaipur," I murmured, but Jaipur was enveloped in listening, discerning the warriors' discussion. Swift, in his calm, cool demeanor, waited for the moment to grab his cutlass. I whispered again. "Jaipur, what are they saying?"

"The drawing," urged Swift. "Why *that* drawing?"

The three warriors were lost in Gaspar's strange drawings. I felt the tension in the room hit a boiling point. Gaspar could not keep still; he inched closer and closer to the warriors with a wild look of obsession in his eyes.

I could tell Gaspar would strike them at a moment's notice. *Why?*

Why this drawing? The more obsessed and crazed Gaspar became, the more I did, questioning this drawing myself. I felt my heated blood run through my face

"We'd better kill them now," said Zaragoza, "while they're occupied."

After a moment of deep analysis, the warriors took the paper and silently made way for the exit, knives drawn.

I gripped my sword. Gaspar drew his cutlass upon the warrior bearing the drawing. *Slash!* The warrior turned with no emotion—no pain but only astonishment as the scarlet blood dripped from the wound in his stomach. The other warriors engaged in a quick manner, yelling, hollering, and striking at each of us with their knives.

"Jaipur!" I yelled. "Tell the men up top! Quick!"

"Say kill them all!" yelled Zaragoza.

Jaipur flew out of the room faster than a crashing lightning strike without a moment to spare. Swift drew his blade and struck one of the warriors in the side—elegantly, quickly. *Step, flash, death.* Zaragoza grabbed the other warrior by the shoulders, holding him in place. Gaspar drove his blade into the stomach of the painted native. The native's body crumbled to the ground, lifeless. I froze, dropped my blade to the ground.

Gaspar, Swift, and Zaragoza quickly slew the four warriors in the room. Up top, chaos erupted as the crew began to fight with the remaining natives.

"I told you," said Zaragoza. "I told you savages have no souls. Never deal with a savage."

I was still frozen in place, breathing heavily.

Zaragoza picked up my blade on the ground. "This is no place for a monk."

I took the blade from him. "I am no monk."

Cannons were fired on the deck, followed by yelling, blades clashing, and loud movement.

Jaipur returned panting, exhilarated by the action. "The men . . . the natives jumped overboard."

"All this for a bloody drawing?" fumed Swift.

"Gaspar, let me see it." I held out my hand.

"No," replied Gaspar.

"No?"

"I said no," replied Gaspar.

A strange feeling crept down my spine, damaging my ego and trust of the captain. I was his loyal friend, perhaps one of the few on this ship. Why could I not see it?

"What now then, Captain Gaspar?" asked Zaragoza. "More savages?"

"Cosimo," said Gaspar. "Find out our longitude. Perhaps the astrolabe would do since the sun's out. Swift?"

"Aye," replied Swift.

"Set the course around the bend, westward."

"West? You can't be serious," interjected Zaragoza.

"Why say this?" asked Gaspar.

"Why?" said Zaragoza. "The Spice Islands could be an unimaginable number of leagues away from this point. The wise thing to do would be return to Spain while we still have the energy and manpower. We could return in the future. We know the bend is there. Our goal is accomplished; the western way exists. We can return at some other time."

"We can't turn back now," said Swift. "We found the bend to the Pacific. By my measurements, the Spice Islands are right around the corner."

"You're mad too," said Zaragoza. "We have not the provisions!"

"The natives brought us a few things," said Jaipur.

"A few won't get us too far," I said.

"Right," said Zaragoza. "So we turn back."

"No," replied Gaspar.

"No? *No?*" exploded Zaragoza. "May I state my case before you, Captain? With all due respect."

"Go on," said Gaspar.

"Did you estimate enough provisions into your timeframe?" asked Zaragoza.

"Aye, we'll find more," replied Gaspar.

"I speak the truth," said Zaragoza. "You'll get us all killed—killed, I say. We have not the provisions! Tell him, Cosimo."

"He already knows," I said. "We will run dry soon."

"I said we'll find more," said Gaspar.

"From Proctor John, eh?" laughed Zaragoza. "Three long months at sea have depleted us, inside and out. We might—*might*, I said—have enough provisions to return to Spain. If we venture further west, as great as the bend may be, I promise you death will occur from the blue depths below."

There was a sudden knock on the door. "Captain."

"Yes, who is it?" asked Gaspar.

"Faustino," said the voice beyond the door.

Swift opened the door to the Spanish coxswain, drenched in sweat.

"We've handled the natives with ease," said Faustino. "Most of them jumped overboard at the cry of havoc."

"What of the king?" I asked.

"They've all disappeared," he replied.

"Diplomacy at its finest," said Swift.

"Send down four men to clean up these bodies," stated Gaspar. "Give word we depart soon. That'll be all."

Faustino nodded with a smile and left for the deck. Gaspar walked over to his desk, checked his armillary sphere, nautical charts, and a few notes scattered on the desk. He seemed content in his decision and not at all hesitant.

"We continue westward," said Gaspar. "We'll reach the islands before our supplies run dry."

"That'll be your end, Gaspar," predicted Zaragoza. "Your end, my end, all of our ends." He stormed out of the room.

"Nay, only the beginning," suggested Gaspar with a smile. "We've found the passage to the Pacific."

"Rough," I claimed. "Rough, it shall be."

"I'll die." Jaipur shook his head, as if his death were signed with ink. "No, I won't die."

"I didn't come this far without finding cloves and cinnamon," said Swift. "I'm not returning without cloves and cinnamon."

I looked to Swift and sighed. "You may never return at all."

"I'll return," Swift nodded. "I'll return to my love."

Jaipur

Scene: Best Friends

⊙ЛЛ⊙

Т HIS IS NOT *good, not good at all. Gaspar, why would you do this to me? I could escape, perhaps take the ship with me. I bet Faustino would come with me. No, no, he's a drunk. I wouldn't make it far with him at all. What do I do? The crew will mutiny. I can feel it in my bones. But I can't save Gaspar from himself. I have a feeling they will loop me in with him, kill me also, throw us overboard. Oh, these thoughts terrify me! What can I do? Yes, I know what I shall do—talk to my good friend Toro. He's one the strongest crew mates on the* Valencia. *He's not Spanish, so he might speak the truth on what the crew is thinking. Yes, a genius idea!*

I went down to the hold, and seated upon the table was Toro, carving wood into what appeared to be a figurine of a bird. I sat across from him. "Ah, Toro, my best friend."

Toro was a large ebony-skinned man from Timbuktu. He had short black hair, broad shoulders, and stern face full of personality.

"What do you want?" asked Toro without looking up. Toro had a low, rough voice.

"Thou art a good friend. I wanted to say hello."

"And?" He continued to carve the figurine.

"Some fight yesterday, eh?" I gave him a smile, nudging him. "Those natives. Who would have thought?"

He looked up at me, sighed, and laid down his figurine on the table. "Tell me what you want."

"Fine." I paused, then leaned in toward Toro. "What do you . . . " I looked over my shoulder. "What does the crew think of Gaspar?"

25

"I like him."

"What of the others?"

"Can't speak for the others."

"You heard anything?"

"I hear lots of things."

"Right," I said, excited. "Tell me what you have heard."

"Hard biscuits for dinner again tonight. For the fourth time. I hate those biscuits."

"I meant what you heard of Gaspar."

"Should I have heard something?"

"Yes."

"Heard what?" asked Toro.

"That's what I'm asking you!"

"Stop your worrying," said Toro. "Allah shall take care of you, with or without provisions."

I sighed, slouched down, and shrugged my shoulders. "I guess you are right." I looked to the side, questioning, running scenarios through my mind. "Well, if you don't want your biscuits, can I have them?"

Toro rolled his eyes at me and left the table.

"What'd I say?" I remarked with my arms open.

Zaragoza

Scene: Appearance of the Blue Blood

〇ⱳⱳⱳ〇

M Y THOUGHTS RAN high after the native encounter.

They talked with savages. I told them not to talk with savages. Look what happened. Blood was spilled, spilled across the room and deck. I had no problem killing them. They were nothing more than a heap of flesh. The natives have no souls though I have a soul. I want to protect my soul. Therefore, I will not die by the hands of that Gaspar, that . . . that . . . that Portuguese filth.

What was King Charles thinking, allowing Gaspar to pilot this ship? Why not a Spaniard? Why not me? What edge does Gaspar have over me? I am Castilian royalty, the most prestigious pilot in the king's armada. Gaspar is a nobody from a small village in Portugal, from nowhere. A peasant.

Sure, Gaspar's been to the Spice Islands before—admirable, for I haven't . . . yet. Gaspar is the only man I know that has seen those islands because of Vasco de Gama. Vasco was a mean, unpleasant Portuguese man, smelled funny. Met him a few times on the international ports around Italy. He was no different than any other Portuguese rat. The Spanish, not the Portuguese, own the New World. They are beneath us, beneath the Spanish. They could never compete with us. I never liked the Portuguese and never will. Savages, I say, all of them. Gaspar is no better than any of the other Portuguese rats. No, I take that back. He's the worst of them all. He was turned down by his own King Manuel, turned away by his own people.

Why though? I say for the sole reason Gaspar has gone mad and chants at the moon. Still, yet still . . . I can't quite put my finger on Gaspar. Where did he get the idea to go west? He did find the western route to the Pacific.

Did King Charles see a chance in him, thought he was the best way to the Spice Islands, enchanted by his wild, mad ideas? Ugh, he found the western way. He'll take the credit. Think, a Portuguese rat found the western way. Gaspar should not have the glory. A Spaniard—like me, a true, blue-blooded Spaniard—should. He has gone against the king's orders at this point. We said, agreed . . . if we find the strait and have enough provisions, we will make a dash for the Spice Islands. This boat, these crewmen are expensive, quite expensive. I can't allow him to waste away the king's investment, the crew, and most importantly, my life!

Gaspar would not turn the ship around . . . Why? Was it because of provisions? Nay, it was because he knew I would return with his charts. I, not he, would claim the western spice route for Spain. Gaspar's name would vanish in the sands of time.

I'll give him this: I never expected a western route to exist, nor did I expect to make it this far. I joined this expedition only on orders from the king so that I could find favor in his court. Then, I would make my own trip east.

I will not die out here. Gaspar knows if he returns to Spain without a single spice, his career will end. He would be fish bait for the Portuguese. The Portuguese want his head. Gaspar turned on them, joined their most hated enemy, Spain. He's right though. King Charles of Spain would turn his back on him if we return without spices. Gaspar and I both know he cannot turn around. For Gaspar, it's either death or spices, one or the other. Not for me! My own dice have not been cast yet. I will not be a gravestone due to this madman's illogical ambition. Yes, I've made up my mind. I need to do something—yes, something—about this. Talked with savages . . . I told you not to talk with savages!

The sun was setting on the open waters, creating a magnificent orange hue in the sky. I walked down from the deck to the hold where a few men were eating, drinking, chatting with one another. I noticed on the other end of the table, Jaipur was there with Toro, that ebony-skinned brute. Jaipur annoyed me, pissed me off with his small, pointed eyes and face. Best not let him notice me. Ugh, the hold smelled like bad mold. It must be the men. You wouldn't believe how grotesque some of these men were. Rats, all of them. I sat down across from my good friend, a good, loyal Spaniard called Javier. He was drinking some ale.

"Javier," I said.

"Zaragoza? *Here* ? In the *hold*?" mocked Javier. "Has the moon been eclipsed?"

"You are funny, Javier," I remarked.

Javier had a brown, thin mustache and goatee, a scrappy frame, and a pointed nose and chin; he was very slender. He was one of the lead sailors aboard, more so the lead voice for common crewmen.

"I jester for the court in my spare time," said Javier.

"I bet ye do," I said. "I've come to talk."

"About?"

His breath was terrible, smelled like rotten fish.

"What is to be done," I said.

"What *is* to be done?" he asked, taking a swig of ale. He then burped loudly. I did my utmost to restrain a look of disgust.

"A power shift," I said.

"A power shift, eh?"

"Yes."

"Between?"

"We take the ship."

"Who?"

"The Spaniards. Us," I said, growing agitated at his insolence and slowness.

Javier chuckled. "You think the *Valencia* would be better off with you over Gaspar, eh?"

"Aye, verily. We are running out of food, water, and medicine to name a few. Soon, Javier will have no more ale."

Javier took another swig and paused.

More intensely, I murmured, "The *Valencia* may have a month or two left before she runs dry."

There was a moment of silence. Javier continued to stare downward.

I asked, "Did ye hear me?"

"I heard you, Zaragoza."

"We must do something."

"Doing something is dangerous."

"We have no choice."

"Gaspar said land was near."

"It's not. He's lying!"

"Are you sure?" asked Javier.

"I've seen the charts."

Javier rubbed his beard, thinking. "You want to mutiny, eh?"

"Not for me," I said. " For the king. Gaspar is Portuguese, Javier. He cares not for our king. He's gone against King Charles."

"How?"

"Gaspar told the king the Spice Islands were a few months away. It's been almost a year at sea with what spices to show?"

"None."

"We're on a wild goose chase for golden eggs. We need to turn around, head back for Spain with what few supplies we have left while we still have the energy."

"I see what you mean," said Javier, twiddling his beard. "We can't go against King Charles, side with the enemy. And the men . . . they tell me how tired they are."

"Yes. Yes, Javier!" I said, excited. "I have a plan."

"Say it."

"Help me kill Gaspar in his sleep—quick, easy."

"What of Swift?" questioned Javier.

"What of him?" I replied.

"He might be angered with such an act."

"Then, we'll kill him, too."

"Sounds well thought out," said Javier, sarcastically.

"And you have a better plan?" I asked.

Javier took another swig of ale. "Soon, I will. Soon."

I smiled. "Do you have the crew?"

"Most of them. They'll follow me when the time comes."

"That's all I wanted to hear, Javier."

Cosimo

Scene: Dance of the Shadow

⚭

THE HOUR WAS late, the moon was out, and the sea was calm as I studied my books. I brought many books on the *Valencia*—volumes on chemistry, astrology, geography, history. And the Bible. I kept the Bible hidden from my collection, kept it stowed away. I was sick of it, sick of it. I couldn't open it. Each time I gazed up at the Holy Word, a sickness grew in my stomach; it made me think of the monastery in Florence. My back ached at the thought of opening up the Bible, studying those hypocritical words. Hours, days, nights were spent reading those words. I blamed Him—yes, the Lord above—for my situation.

I was taken there, left there by my parents to be a monk. I never knew who my parents were or why they left me there. Perhaps I was the tithe, the payment for my parents to enter heaven. Oh, I hated that monastery, that terrible place with that terrible friar. I shuddered at the thought of Friar Marzano. I felt my back, lifted up my shirt, felt the lashes. *Whip, whip, whip.* I closed my eyes as a tear followed close behind. I had escaped and would never go back.

I told myself that I must not think of the past, that I must think of now. The *Valencia* was in a dire situation—yes, dire indeed. I opened the log that tracked our supplies and materials. Our supplies . . . Oh, how much time did we have left in the open sea? Yes, biscuits, ale, yes . . . a month, a month.

I rubbed my chin, trying to understand Gaspar's decision. We had only a month. One simple month until death. I shook my head. I looked to my Bible for the answer, for a prayer, an old habit of mine. I opened up a compartment in my desk, and there it was.

Would His Word help? *No, I can't. No.* I closed my desk compartment.

I sat there in silence as my mind drifted toward those natives. I felt bad, sad how they died, though those warriors should not have taken Gaspar's notes. That drawing . . . Wait, what was that drawing? Hieroglyphics. Yes, I had seen them before. I believed I had.

I checked my small library, scanning each title. Then, I picked up a large book with a light blue cover. It was a book on the ancient Egyptians—a hand-painted, handwritten, stunning collaborative work. I read through it until I found a similar hieroglyphic of Anubis to the one Gaspar maintained.

On the page was a colorful picture of Anubis wearing a large pschent, holding up a strange orange crystal. Yes, that was what I saw on Gaspar's page, this orange crystal. The description in my book said the crystal was called "Retjenu Gold," a powerful alloy stronger than gold.

Odd, I thought. *What does stronger than gold mean? As in density? Hardness? Where did this come from?* The book said nothing of the crystal's origin. But why did Gaspar have this particular drawing? I knew not why.

I decided to keep these questions in the back of my mind, but for now, our low supply situation was far more serious than colorful pictograms. I must tell Gaspar of our terrible situation or at least give the captain a timeframe of our dire predicament before it was too late to recover from an untimely demise. Our timeframe might wake him up, bring him back to reality.

Reality . . . Such a complex subject.

I looked out my window. The moon glowed in the celestial sphere. I forgot how late in the night it was. Gaspar never slept. He would be up. Yes, he would be up.

I closed the door to my cabin quietly so as to not make a sound. The *Valencia* swayed from the crash of waves. The whole ship was silent. Most of the sailors slept, tucked away in their wooden bunks. Only a few people took on the night shift to watch and care for the ship.

I carried a small lit candle to give me light in the dead of night. I walked past the sailors' quarters and heard snoring, coughing, and restless sleeping. I continued down the hallway until I reached the aft of the ship where the captain's quarters were. I knocked on the door—*thump, thump*—then waited. *He should be up. Gaspar was always up.* After a moment's pause, the large wooden door was unhinged, then creaked open.

"Captain?" I asked. "It's Cosimo. May I come in?"

"Aye," replied Gaspar. "Thought it was you. Cosimo, come, come."

The room was a mess: books, pages, and charts were scattered across the room. Gaspar looked rough with his sunken purple eyes, wild hair, and thunderous eyes. His back window was open wide to the fixed horizon and the bright moon above. The wind, strong and cold, cut through the room, shuffling the papers and rotating his armillary sphere. I helped construct that sphere with him. Why else would Gaspar have broken me out of the monastery? I was well learned and had access to key documents and information, important sources to find our way west.

As for the sphere, my own accumulated charts of the stars and world maps, combined with Gaspar's nautical portolan charts, helped create this incredible sphere.

"Did you check the sphere?" I asked.

"Always," he replied.

"And?"

"We are near. Verily, near."

Gaspar moved toward his shelf lined with glass containers filled with different colored liquids. He searched through each of them and began to put them into a brown bag.

"You cleaning up?" I asked as I watched him shift through his vials.

Gaspar ignored my question as he continued to examine his shelf.

He should not be like this. He used to be direct with me, used to be sharp and brilliant. What had this voyage done to him? This was nonsense. Those vials were useless. He was no chemist but rather a nautical pilot! Was Zaragoza right? Were we all doomed? I could not think that now.

"Gaspar," I said. "I've come to talk about our dire situation."

"You see this?" said Gaspar, holding up two vials. One vial was blood orange, the other silver white.

I sighed and shook my head. "Yes."

"You know what this is?"

"Uh . . . Liquids? Maybe metals?"

Gaspar smiled. "Aye, sulfur and mercury."

"Hard to come by."

"They are."

"May I ask why do you have sulfur and mercury?"

"These two materials are the basic components of matter."

"Yes, I know that."

"Ah, Cosimo, my mind is brighter than the great lamp." His wild eyes flashed. He placed those two bottles into a brown bag, then grabbed two more small bottles from the shelf. "What of salt of tartar and salt-petre?"

I stared at Gaspar for a moment, astonished and confused. "Salt fire. You want to make salt fire?"

What did any of this have to do with our situation or the Spice Islands? I knew Gaspar was into chemical mixtures of sorts, but salt fire? Why did he need an ancient mixture to bring forth a chemical fire? He had gone mad and had lost track of our duty, of our mission. We did not need metals; we needed supplies, provisions, and so much more other things yet unspoken. He had lost touch with reality.

Gaspar smiled at me, understanding what I was thinking. He placed the two vials in his brown bag. "Come. Look here, Cosimo." He gestured toward the armillary sphere and adjusted the rings. I analyzed the sphere. He brought forth an old map of the Far East. "Check for yourself."

I calculated our position, looked to his charts. *Wait a second* . . . "That can't be right, not right at all."

"Aye, but it is," returned Gaspar.

The coordinates, according to the alignment of the stars, suggested that during the past month we had crossed the Tropic of Capricorn weeks ago and were near the supposed Spice Islands! *Impossible, impossible. These charts must be wrong or* . . . *were his time projections correct?*

"How could we be moving so fast?" I questioned.

"By the Great Chord conducting the trade winds, as a maestro does, to our tune."

"I must check with my maps. This makes no sense. It's illogical, Gaspar."

"We are near, Cosimo. Near we are. The Moluccas were closer than we thought." Gaspar looked at me with confusion, bending his brow. "Cosimo, what's wrong with you?"

I paused; my eyes darted to the side. "I don't. I don't understand any of this."

"What's there to understand? After years of studying and chart-ing—years of pain, disrespect, and rejection—we've made it, Cosimo. Riches and glory are upon us. What's hard to comprehend?

"I–I thought," I stuttered. "I must see it to believe it."

"You still doubt?"

"I don't know."

"You didn't doubt me when I helped ye escape the monastery."

"No, I didn't."

"Or when I told you of the western way."

"No."

"Then why do you doubt me now?"

"I, uh . . ." I stumbled.

"Because you doubt yourself," remarked Gaspar. "Go get some sleep, Cosimo. You look tired."

"Yes, Captain," I replied and left his quarters.

I continued down the hallway, lost in my thoughts. I needed some air; the deck would give me that. Confused, I hurried to the deck, ques-tioning myself and Gaspar. I didn't know what to think, whom to believe, or whom to trust. He was right; I was confused.

I hurried to the deck. Up top, the wind was cool and crisp and blew strong in the night sky. It was nice here, quiet. I was alone. The moment the sea wind hit my face, I was relieved. My stress whisked away with the breeze. I closed my eyes, feeling the wind, and cleared my mind.

I took a deep breath and stared out across the sea. All was bet-ter now, then . . . I heard a sudden footstep behind me. It scared me, shocked me straight to my core. The footsteps were hurried. I turned around to see who might be up at this hour of night.

"Hello?" I asked, looking about. "Sailor?"

No one was right behind me. I scratched my head, wondering where that sound had come from. Perhaps it was the stress causing me to hear things. I heard it once again.

"Who goes there?!" I yelled.

There, on the deck, walking, was a dark figure. I couldn't quite make out his features. He looked like a tall sailor. He grabbed my attention. Why was he out on deck? The dark figure continued to walk without turning his head.

I was intrigued and walked closer to the figure. "Was it you, sailor?"

There was no reproach, no sound, and no turn of the head.

"Answer me, sailor."

Still, there was no response. He walked in a slow, stiff, unnatural manner.

The dark figure approached the rail of the ship and stood up on it. My heart began to pound. Was this man trying to kill himself? What could he be doing?

"Hey!" I yelled out. "Hey!" I hurried toward him. "Come down from there. Hey!"

At that instant, the dark figure jumped off the rail and into the sea.

"My Lord, no!" I yelled. I looked over the side of the ship into the crashing blue abyss and saw nothing—no splash, no cry, nothing. I couldn't breathe. I knew what I had seen. He was there. What was going on? Was I mad? Where was the splash? My hand began to shake uncontrollably. A deep shiver crept up my spine to the tiny hairs on my neck. I saw a man. I saw a man. Did my eyes mistake me?

I heard laughter from behind me. I turned. It was Faustino, sitting on the deck with an empty bottle next to his leg.

"The night," said Faustino, laughing. "The night spooked you, eh?"

"I saw a man," I said, breathing fast.

"Many men are on this ship if ye haven't noticed."

"No, no, I meant this man jumped over the rail, but I heard no splash, saw no face." I stared at the ground confused, worried.

Faustino stood up. "Let me see." He looked over the rail, examined the water. The sun was beginning to rise in the distance in the direction of where the dark figure jumped from the side of the rail.

"Were you there the whole time?" I asked.

"Aye, I was," said Faustino.

"Did you not see it too?"

Faustino took a sip of ale, stared at me with a blank look. "I always see the shadow, and the shadow always sees me."

"Shadow?" I questioned. "What do you mean?"

I was growing concerned, feeling like my world had been flipped upside down. It was as if I had abruptly woken up from a dream, believing a rat from my dream was in my bed, and the moment I awakened, I found the rat on my arm.

Faustino gave me no answer.

"Did you not hear me?" I said once more.

Faustino was fixated on the horizon, on the rising sun. Without turning his head, he said, "Land ahoy."

Land rose out of the fogged dark abyss, illuminated by orange and pink hues of the great lamp. The sun, with her golden locks, cut through the darkened mist, claiming her bright throne. She revealed a tropical paradise before me.

Swift

Scene: Enter the Island

༄࿐

T HAT MORNING, I said to myself, *Land, I can't believe it. We found land. One step, one day, one hour closer to my love, Rose.*

We were close to the Spice Islands. Could this island be one? Could this island harbor cinnamon and cloves? Spices were all I needed. I believed once I had my spices, all would be well. I was a little desperate after the incident with the natives. We were running a little low on supplies. I put on a front—a tough man's front, confident, strong—though I was worried, as worried of death as the others were. Of course, I was fearful. What man wouldn't be?

Much of the crew began to fall under a terrible spell, a sickness I had seen far too much at sea. Their gums bled, turned black they did. I helped with the bodies, so many bodies. Did Gaspar know of the bodies, of the sick men turned blue? I lived with the crew—well, in my private cabin—but I dined with the crew, knew the crew. They were dying, dying from the sailor's disease. The men talked, heard them. Gaspar would not last long as captain if more men met their fates by this terrible spell. I looked in the mirror and pulled down my lips. My gums, sensitive they were, scarlet red they were. I had the spell. Land, oh, land! Help me free my soul from this spell.

I left my cabin at dawn, ran up to the deck to see the land for mine own eyes. By the looks of the island, it appeared tropical. I thought we must be near Sumatra or Molucca—any and all of those well-known Spice Islands. Before this, we Europeans had no idea where the Spice Islands were. Spices were traded hand to hand, road by road, ship by ship before reaching us in Europe, the very end of the spice trade route. The way of Sinbad, the way through the Red Sea, was cut off to us, for the Muslims owned it and controlled it. Hence why we, the *Valencia*, circumnavigated the world to find a new way to the mystical Spice Islands.

All we needed was one single Spice Island to make a large trade for our wares. Once we had traded, we would continue eastward, then under India and around the southern tip of Africa, as Vasco de Gama had done prior.

Oh, land! This must be it. Gaspar did it. He was right! The world had no edge; it was spherical. I believed him when he told me, recruiting me back in Seville, and look at us now. Regardless if spices were on this mysterious island, there should be provisions. We must stock up on supplies, or the crew will mutiny. The crew was at their wit's end—fed up, tired they were. The crew wanted to return home. I wanted to go home, too, but I couldn't without those spices, for my love needed them. I thought about the last few months—or was it a year?—at sea. Life had been brutal, so brutal for us all. Yet, here was land! From hence forward, I prayed to see only clear skies, spices, and my love ahead.

Jaipur

Scene: Round Dance of the Sailors

⌀⎇

T HERE IT BE. Land! I could not make sense of it, not in the slightest sense. I had believed we were leagues away from the Spice Islands. Maybe this wasn't a Spice Island but a random island far out at sea. That was more realistic.

Wait a second. From what I remembered as a child when I lived on Sumatra, it looked like this—similar, if not the same island. The island was tropical, mountainous, filled with vegetation. I was on the deck, staring out across the sea, surrounded by a mass of sailors doing the same. As the sun's piercing rays cleared the fog, the island appeared far bigger than a lone island, extending far into the distance with no end in sight.

A sailor nudged me. "Look like home?"

"Not sure," I said. "Could be."

"Better be," said another sailor, roughly. "After all the pain Gaspar's put us through, better be. Aye, better be for his sake."

My heart was pumping. Heat filled my blood. I knew the sailors were on the verge of destruction, angered by Gaspar. From the looks on the sailors' faces, they were irritated, if not outraged. I decided Gaspar was on the outs. I kept quiet so as not to cause diversion from the glowing island. I debated whether the only thing keeping Gaspar afloat among the crew was this island. I knew this was going to happen! Didn't take an astrologer to predict this one.

"Aye, too bad for poor Pedro," said a sailor.

"Eh, what of Pedro?" asked a sailor.

"Died last night from the black gums."

"Another one dead!" yelled a sailor.

Faustino came out of the hold, looking rough, drunk I'd say. I kept behind the men, keeping my distance from the mob.

"Men!" yelled Faustino.

The crew shushed one another and quieted down, though some were reluctant to heed the order.

"What is it, Faustino?" asked a sailor.

"Captain said two ships go ashore," said Faustino, "handled by your favorite coxswain." He smiled.

"Can we all go?" asked one younger sailor.

"Can we all be rich and handsome?" asked Faustino.

"What?" questioned the sailor, confused.

"It means no," said Faustino.

"Why not?" asked another sailor, agitated.

"Gaspar wants to take measurements, chart, talk to the moon—I don't know," said Faustino. "Doesn't matter why! Orders are orders."

"You can't be serious!" yelled another sailor.

"For how long?" asked a sailor.

"You know him," said Faustino, growing agitated. "Could be days."

The crew sighed, kicking and talking among themselves

Faustino continued, "Hey, I don't make the orders. We go ashore in the next hour. That's all."

I shook my head. All of the crew around me muttered to themselves. It was not a good feeling. This was the tipping point. I felt it. Gaspar had no idea, no idea how the men felt. Where was he? What captain did not care for his crew?

I knew where he was: locked away in his room, as always, doing Lord knows what. Where was Swift or Cosimo to quell the situation? Hell, where was Zaragoza? Aye, they were putting makeup on, powdering their noses, in their exclusive cabins! I looked around the deck and noticed a small congregation around Javier, the most well-known Spanish sailor. What was he saying?

I couldn't save Gaspar or any of those other fools. I didn't care. I was done with it. Gaspar needed a trick up his sleeve—magic, genii, spices, something, anything—or we were dead men sailing.

Cosimo

Scene: Thought Variations I

❦

I WAS TERRIFIED, terrified of my own shadow. I saw it. There it was, there on the deck. I locked myself in my cabin, rubbing my head, confused, scared. *What was that thing, that entity that jumped overboard?* Not only did I see it, but Faustino, too. Could I say we saw it for sure?

Was it there? I was tired. Yes, tired. Did my eyes play a trick on me? What did it feel like, the presence? Nay, it was there. I knew it. I felt a dark, empty feeling in my soul. That smell of the shadow. Oh, it was terrible, smelled of rotten fish, death. That thing, that shadow had a smell. Only . . . only evil spirits had a smell.

A spirit? Are spirits even real? I saw that spirit The shadow looked real, felt real to me. What is real? Am I real? I thought for a moment, questioning my whole existence. I thought; therefore, I must be real, for I thought a thought. Yes, I was real, alive. I had a spirit and felt that dark spirit, the shadow. I had seen dark spirits before—yes, I remembered now—in the monastery, in that terrible, terrible monastery. One of the monks had a spirit, an evil spirit, inside of him. Wait, not one spirit, but many—a legion. The cry the spirits gave pierced my delicate eardrums. The horror

I shut my eyes, closing my mind to those thoughts. That same feeling, that same look—it was the same shadow from the monastery. I knew it.

I opened up the compartment inside my desk and pulled out my Bible, staring at it intensely. *Why torment me, Lord, with an evil shadow after all the pain I went through in that monastery?* Locked up behind stone walls for years I was, miserable and surrounded by mean old men. The worst part—aye, the worst pain—was the void of a woman's love. I read of love, dreamed of love, though never had love—only a dark shadow of where love could have been in my heart. I had had enough of it, so I escaped over the walls with Gaspar's help. The monsignor would have never allowed me to leave, never, for I was slave to them. Yet I was a slave no more!

I looked out the window toward the heavens and said aloud, "I know You are mad at me, Good Lord, for abandoning my house, jumping the walls. I had to leave, had to. My parents forced me there, left me there for life, abandoned me for life. I never knew my parents, though I wish I did. I choose my life, and my life is not behind stone walls but is free. What if I *am* mad at you? It was your fault I was locked away for so many years, *Your* fault! Did You ever think of what I wanted, what I dreamed of, what I loved? The shadow of my past has come to haunt me. Tell me, Lord. Tell me then what should I do!"

I listened closely to the winds, to my heart beating, to my breath. Yet there was no response. I let out a deep breath, followed by a single tear down my cheek.

"Are You silent? You have always been silent. Silent. If only You would send my golden rope to guide me through this maze of life, if only . . . but instead, silent."

Swift

Scene: Voyage

⁂

G ASPAR THOUGHT IT was best for only two groups of men, two longboats, to head ashore and scope out the terrain of the island. The rest of the crew stayed aboard the *Valencia*. I was desperate, almost dying, to step foot on land. A year at sea, tossing and turning, can do things to a man, change him. It had changed me.

Gaspar chose Cosimo, the monk; Jaipur, his slave; Javier, a lead sailor; Zaragoza, the king's emissary; Faustino, the coxswain; Toro, a strong sailor; and me to chart, coordinate, and search for supplies on the island. Gaspar also brought a few other sailors to watch over the longboats. I made sure to bring a bag stocked with some supplies, as Gaspar suggested, in case we were on the island for longer than a day or two. It was always wise to bring useful materials on an expedition, for anything could happen.

The waves were rough as we approached the island. The weather was warm, warmer than usual. The last time we saw land near the bend, frigid air it was, yet the polar opposite now. I could hear seagulls chirp as they flew above my head. I was excited, couldn't wait a second longer to step foot on solid soil. The water was crystal blue, clear enough to see life bursting below the ebb and flow. There were orange coral reefs, majestic fish, and dolphins all around us, all of which refreshed the morale of the men in the longboats.

The boats ran ashore. The sand was coarse and white. I picked up some of it, feeling in my hand and letting it fall between my fingers. I exhaled at the feeling of stability. Green palm trees and other colorful exotic plants surrounded the beach. The island was very mountainous, much larger than I anticipated, going on and on in the distance.

"Javier," said Gaspar.

"Aye, Captain?" he replied.

"Pick four sailors. Watch over the longboats."

Javier nodded.

"As for the rest of you, let's have a look around," said Gaspar. "I want you, Toro, with us."

"Yes, Captain," said Toro.

Toro was a large, muscular, broad-shouldered, ebony-skinned man from Timbuktu. Gaspar had personally recruited him for this journey west, for Toro was strong and practical and knew the trade customs of the Islamic world. Islam stretched all the way from western North Africa, to the far eastern recesses of the Spice Islands. From what I could remember, Toro was a cattle tradesman in the North African region, trading from Marrakech to Cairo by land and sea. Gaspar believed he would be a vital resource when it came time to barter with Islamic traders on the islands.

"Javier," said Gaspar. "Keep watch. Any sign of distress, alert the men aboard. We'll be back either today or tomorrow."

"Yes, Captain," said Javier.

"If you want, Captain," said Faustino, "I'll stay and watch the boats, too."

"You do best with us, Faustino," said Gaspar.

"If you think so," sighed Faustino.

"I do," stated Gaspar. "Cosimo."

"Yes?"

"Have you your mobile compass?"

"Aye, in the bag."

"Good," said Gaspar. "Come, all of you. Make sure to bring a bag of supplies." Each of us then took supplies from the longboats, packing provisions into our bags.

I noticed a strange, hard-shelled, brown rock at my feet. I picked it up, looked at it, and jiggled it against my ear. Liquid was inside of it.

"It's a coconut," said Jaipur.

"A what?" I asked.

"I read of them," interjected Cosimo. "It's a fruit of some sort."

"Watch," said Jaipur as he took the coconut from my hand and cut it in half. He took a sip of the liquid, then handed it to me. "It's good, like milk."

"Let's go," ordered Gaspar as he walked into the brush.

I took a sip of the coconut. It was pleasant, felt like a healing nectar. I couldn't get enough of it. It quenched my thirst as I sipped. I wondered what other things could be on this island.

Before I stepped into the brush, I noticed Zaragoza talking with Javier, exchanging words I knew not. I felt trouble brewing in the water, trouble indeed. I heard there was strife this morning among the crew on the deck. I didn't think much of it when I was told about it, probably nothing more than complaining.

Should I have taken more interest in it? Nay, we found the island, the answer to our prayers!

Zaragoza

Scene: Game of Mischief

⟨ɷⱳⱳↄ⟩

PERFECT, PERFECT, I said to myself as we made our way through the thick jungle shrub. *The stars have aligned for my plan to be carried out.*

The sailors wanted change. Tired they were, primed for a change of leadership. When King Charles asked me to join this expedition to find the Spice Islands through the Atlantic Ocean, I thought he was jesting with me. He was not. Startled, I had asked if I was to be the captain of this voyage, and I couldn't believe it: the king said a Portuguese man would be the captain. Over me? Our enemy, the Portuguese, over *me*, over a true, blue-blooded Spaniard? It was never going to work. What was the king thinking? It didn't matter now, for the king was a world away, and here I was, ready to take the helm, the *Valencia*.

I never imagined we would make it this far west, let alone past the Canary Islands. Who would have thought Gaspar knew somewhat of what he was doing? Here we were, near the Spice Islands. Maybe this island was a Spice Island. It had come out of nowhere. I knew not how. Still, this island changed nothing. I had been planning this mutiny for months, and now was the time for us real Spaniards to take control.

I couldn't let Gaspar take glory for this expedition, for finding the Spice Islands through the western way. He was Portuguese, for God's sake. Savages, all of them! A true Spaniard should take the glory, the victory of this discovery. Javier, a true Spaniard from Seville, was the perfect person to help me in the act. He was a people's man, the voice of the people. Javier was my perfect asset.

Javier and I planned for me to go into the forest with Gaspar and the others while Javier and three other Spanish sailors rigged Gaspar's longboat with explosive black powder. Once Gaspar and his small group boarded their longboat, I would light the powder and blow them to smithereens. Javier and the three other sailors would help me kill off the remaining survivors. Brilliant.

I believed Gaspar and the others would never expect a maneuver like this. I could see it now as I walked through this hot, humid jungle. I would become captain of the *Valencia*, retrieve the spices for myself, and return to Spain with all the glory I deserved.

"There! An open spot ahead," pointed out Gaspar. "Cosimo, hand me your astrolabe. I must find our latitude and time."

Cosimo was silent, inert, staring at an open shaft in the mountain. It looked like an entrance to a cave.

"What are you staring at?" asked Jaipur, catching his breath.

"Cosimo?" asked Gaspar.

"Eh, Cosimo!" yelled Swift.

What in the world was wrong with him? I didn't have time for this. Cosimo was one of the few sane ones of the group. Sad, it seemed madness got to him like everyone else on this damn expedition.

"What is wrong with you?" said Gaspar, holding out his hand. "Cosimo!"

"Oh, I . . . I'm sorry, Gaspar," said Cosimo. "I thought I saw something back there."

"Happens to me every time," said Faustino with a smile.

"What kind of something? Savages?" I interjected. "Damn savages."

"No," said Cosimo. "Nothing."

"Focus," said Gaspar. "The astrolabe, please."

Cosimo

Scene: Valse of the Astrolabe

꧁꧂

I TOOK THE golden astrolabe from my bag. It was a circular disc composed of the seven seas and landmasses, painted green, pink, white, and blue. At the center of the astrolabe was the fixed windrose surrounded by a smaller, circular rule, adjusted for time and latitude.

Gaspar made the measurements while I assisted him, logging our findings in my books. Gaspar looked troubled, recalculated the position three times over.

"This can't be," murmured Gaspar.

"What is it?" chimed in Swift.

"We must go up," said Gaspar as he picked up the astrolabe. "We must go higher."

"What of provisions?" I asked.

"The next group will do that," hurried Gaspar, a wild look in his eyes. "We need these measurements now. Higher! Up the mountain!"

"If you say so," grumbled Zaragoza.

We followed Gaspar up the ridge. I did my best to forget about the shadow. Still, my thoughts wandered.

"Watch out, Cosimo!" yelled Jaipur from behind me, pulling me from my thoughts.

I stopped in my tracks and looked up. Before me were large, sharp wooden spikes pointing out of the ground. On the tips of the spikes were bones of past victims, impaled to death. I caught my breath from the shock.

"A trap," said Toro.

"Means people were here," said Jaipur.

"Are here," pointed out Swift.

"Natives," interjected Zaragoza.

I looked up at the bones, at a skeletal face of a past life. It sent shivers up my spine.

"Watch out for more spikes," warned Toro.

"Or ye will end up like our friend here," quipped Swift.

"Don't want that," I said.

"Gaspar," cautioned Jaipur. "A tribe must be nearby. Best not test them."

"I agree," said Zaragoza.

"Me too," added Faustino.

A strong wind cut through the jungle, blowing the treetops back and forth. Above the terrestrial surface, dark clouds floated toward us.

"We won't be here long," said Gaspar sternly. "Forward!"

We continued upward through the thick jungle. I heard faint sounds of birds chirping and leaves swaying in the wind. After a while of hiking up a ridge, we came to the top of one of the peaks with an open flat ledge overlooking the island and ocean.

I felt the sweat drip from my face. My bag was heavy, filled to the brim with supplies and instruments.

"There," pointed out Gaspar. "That ledge shall do."

The wind blew stronger than ever. In the distance, a powerful black and blue storm was approaching us.

"Hurry! The astrolabe!" said Gaspar. "Before the great lamp goes dark."

I quickly took out the astrolabe. I helped Gaspar set it up, but the wind made it quite difficult. Swift hurried over and helped us keep the instrument still.

"Gaspar," called Swift over the loud, blowing wind. "The storm! We should return before the storm traps us here."

"We need the measurements," replied Gaspar. "I won't leave until I have the measurements."

The group had a collective look of trouble on their faces. The only person still maintaining a normal composure was Faustino. Zaragoza looked the most fretful as he tapped his right foot.

"We need to leave," said Zaragoza, "or we'll be stuck out here for who knows how long."

"Then you go back," said Gaspar, obsessed with the astrolabe.

Faustino laughed. "No one's making it back."

"There are savages here. I can't go alone." Zaragoza looked around at the group. "Anyone?"

There was a silent pause.

Zaragoza continued, "All of ye are mad, mad I say! All of us will die if we stay on this island."

"Quiet!" cried Gaspar as he calculated the celestial sphere.

Zaragoza shook his head, muttered unintelligible words under his breath, and turned toward the coast in a hurried manner.

"He won't make it far," said Faustino.

Gaspar continued to check the astrolabe. He calculated, recalculated, and checked his book of charts. His eyes flashed with a magnetic burst. The wind picked up with the clouds now blocking the great lamp's rays above.

"What, Gaspar?" I asked. "Where are we?"

The whole group huddled together around Gaspar, anxious and excited.

"This is it," said Gaspar.

"It?" asked Swift. "What's 'it'?"

"The Spice Islands?" asked Jaipur.

Gaspar nodded. "The island."

Swift

Scene: Dance of the Marooned

⟨✣⟩

W E HURRIED DOWN the ridge and through the thicket as the storm crashed in the distance, booming like an ignited cannon through the sky. Toro, Jaipur, Cosimo, Faustino, Gaspar, and I were left to contend with the storm. Zaragoza was not in sight.

Could this be one of Spice Islands? Had we, in fact, made it here? Could I be this near to my love? Oh, my dear Rose, the spices were near. I promised my return, and my promise I shall keep with spices to pay for all the expenses.

I was excited, thinking our journey had come to its climax. Storm or no storm, we had found the spices!

The wind continued to rage as we maneuvered through the winding jungle. Odd, I didn't remember coming this way.

"Gaspar," I called over the wind. "Are you sure this is the right way?"

"Aye, Toro was leading the way back," said Gaspar.

Toro stopped, abruptly. "I made a mark on that tree." On a tree was a large X, marked with a blade. "Do not let the jungle fool you, or lost you shall be."

"I grew up in a jungle like this and still know not where to go," said Jaipur.

"See there, the low ground to the right of the tree," said Toro.

"Aye," I replied.

Toro picked up a stone and threw it to the right tree. The moment the stone hit the ground, a large spike sprung up—another trap.

"That would hurt," said Jaipur.

"Being eaten would be worse," remarked Faustino.

"Let's not find out. Move quickly," ordered Gaspar.

We made it past the tree line, following the marked trees, until we reached the beach. I felt small drizzles of rainwater hit my face. The storm was about to unleash its power upon us. I looked around for our longboats. We yelled to one another, confused, as the rainfall picked up. The boats had disappeared, but I didn't want to panic.

"The boats—" said Cosimo.

"—are gone," finished Jaipur.

"Those bastards," said Gaspar intensely. "Mutiny! Mutiny!"

My heart sank to the ground. My love, my hope. I felt that I could throw up in that moment. That eerie feeling of hopelessness destroyed my euphoria. I told myself I wouldn't panic.

"They could have moved them down the shore," suggested Cosimo.

"They were moved," said Faustino. "Moved to leave us here."

"I saw it coming!" yelled Jaipur. "Saw it coming, I did."

"The crew," sighed Cosimo. "How could they?"

"How?" asked Jaipur. "Just like that!"

"Focus, all of you," said Gaspar. "Not the time to fight."

"We need shelter," said Toro.

"I can't believe it," I remarked, stupefied. "I can't believe it. We were left."

Only strong black clouds, white-tipped waves, and open ocean filled our horizon.

"Hey!" yelled a familiar voice. Then once more, "Hey!"

It was Zaragoza coming from behind the brush with a look of desperation and panic.

I ground my teeth at the first sight of Zaragoza. I had had it with him. I would not have been shocked if he were part of this whole thing, this mutiny. "I bet he was a part of this," I said, sword drawn.

"I saw him talking to Javier earlier," said Jaipur, drawing his sword, too.

"What do you mean?" asked Gaspar.

"I saw Zaragoza talking, conspiring with Javier on the deck this morning," said Jaipur.

"Wait, no! No, not I!" pleaded Zaragoza, drawing his sword. "I did,

I did talk to Javier about the island, but I had no idea about this . . . this mutiny. Why would I be here if not?"

"He has a point," stated Cosimo.

"I speak the truth," said Zaragoza.

"He's lying," said Jaipur. "Let me at him."

"Wait, Jaipur," said Gaspar.

"There's more," said Zaragoza. "Come look. Look!"

We kept our swords drawn and followed him, keeping our distance. Zaragoza hurried to the brush, and there behind a tree were the bodies of two sailors, cut, tattered, and dead.

"Look at what the mutineers did. Killed them," said Zaragoza.

"What a shame," remarked Faustino.

"It was planned," said Cosimo.

"They've been planning," said Jaipur.

"Quiet!" insisted Toro, startling me.

I said, "What? What?"

Toro pointed to the brush and whispered, "There, in the brush. Lit torches. The tribe."

"They must have heard us," said Jaipur.

"So many torches," said Cosimo. "Hundreds of them."

"What if they want new friends?" I spoke.

"I'm not waiting to find out," said Faustino.

"We run up," said Toro.

"But the *Valencia*?" said Cosimo. "What if they come back for us after the storm?"

"What if they don't?" I added.

"The *Valencia* is gone," said Gaspar sternly. "We're on our own now."

Zaragoza

Scene: Thought Variations I

❧

J AVIER! CURSE YE, *Javier! Curse ye. You left me to die, took my plan, betrayed me, sentenced me to die like a savage! You left me to die on this island, to be eaten by savages!*

My thoughts spiraled with questions. How did he do it? How? The crew must have been behind him this whole time. The crew—full of little minds, peasants—listened to him.

When I returned to the shoreline, the longboats were gone, disappeared, with the exception of one surviving sailor—a French one, the only French sailor on the *Valencia*. I forgot his name, but it did not matter. The French sailor was lying on the beach, cut up, bleeding out, moaning. I rolled him over and asked him what had happened. The moment the sailor saw my face, he cussed, said Javier had told him of the plan: the plan to kill Gaspar, Jaipur, Toro, Cosimo, and Swift, then take over the ship. The sailor refused Javier—hence, his imminent death.

With this strong storm, the crew couldn't dock. They wouldn't, or didn't care to, investigate. The crew will be forced to accept Javier's conclusion that we died by those savages!

Gaspar was right: the *Valencia* will not be coming back for us. Why would they? The crew had been wanting to dispose of Gaspar and his loyal foreign pack. It took only my own initiative to stage a coup on the *Valencia*. What was I thinking? The crew wouldn't question Javier about our whereabouts. Nay, he did them all a favor, he did. The crew was starving, hated Gaspar. But why did they hate me? I knew why: they were simple-minded peasants.

They won't come back. No, they won't. Accept it. Accept it. If I make it out of here—oh, if I make it back to Spain—I'll kill that no-good Javier, one way or another.

Jaipur

Scene: Thought Variations II

⌘

I KNEW THIS was going to happen. I knew it! I had heard them on the dock. I blamed Gaspar, blamed him and the others. I told Gaspar it was only a matter of time until they turned on us, and look what happened. If I had to pinpoint it on one thing, one thing alone, Gaspar was mad and oblivious. Swift and Cosimo were oblivious to the workings of the crew, of the Spaniards. How did Gaspar not see this coming after multiple warnings?

It was as if Gaspar wanted this to happened, wanted to rid himself of the crew. He received his wish. I was so angry and frustrated; I gritted my teeth. We had lost the way home.

Wait a second. My true home, Sumatra, was nearby. What if I could learn the language of this tribe? I could use them to my advantage. I could be done with Gaspar once and for all. What if this was my chance for freedom?

Yes, yes, this was my perfect chance! On the other hand, Gaspar and the others needed me, never treated me wrong. Friends they were to me. Should I run away, run to the tribe? Or should I stay with my hard-headed friends and by some slim chance finish our search with bags filled with spices? My friends could use me—they needed me, in fact— yet my freedom was right in front of me.

Oh, if I stay with Gaspar, he'll get me killed, but he is my friend, my mad friend. What do I do?

Faustino

Scene: Thought Variations III

A FTER THOSE EVENTS, I thought to myself of our situation; it was unfortunate, oh so unfortunate, about the *Valencia*. Worst of all, what would I do without ale? These natives chasing us might have ale, pom juice, or another other weird alcohol concoction. I'd like a pom juice, coconut, and alcohol concoction while I lay under a palm tree, feet stretched out in the white sand and sun on my body. I'd like that a lot. Those native women weren't too bad looking either. I liked their dark skin and those seductive simple cloth tops and bottoms. Oh, I liked them indeed. Pom juice and simple cloth tops and bottoms under a palm didn't sound so bad. It had been a while since I had had cordial relations with a woman. Being captured by the natives might not be so bad after all . . . Well, it might be bad if those natives ate me. Aye, they might eat me indeed. Fine, fine. Best to keep running.

Cosimo

Scene: Thought Variations IV

꩜

MY THOUGHTS TRANSFORMED into a circus of panic, concern, and confusion.

What are we going to do? The crew abandoned us, left us here to die. I don't want to be trapped here. No, no, not at all. What if we are captured by these natives, these cannibals? Would they eat us, kill us? What would they do to us? I don't want to find out. No, we'll outrun them. Don't panic. Stay calm. I'll get through this. It's pointless now to think of the Valencia. *Pointless. I must focus on my survival.*

That shadow, that dark shadow, that bad omen. It was a warning. I am scared, terrified, but . . . something inside of my soul, I feel it, is telling me to be strong. I'll be strong, have to be.

If You do exist God, help me. Help us home.

Gaspar

Scene: Thought Variations V

ଓଙ୍କାର

M Y LUNA, MY mistress, show us the way to our transformation . . . the island, island, island.

Toro

Scene: Appearance of the Firm

◌◌◌◌◌

I KEPT MY movements quick, watching each step, praying a silent prayer to Allah, as I rounded trees and bushes on an upward slope.

My mind wandered. By the looks of the island and the tribe behind us, this must be one of the Spice Islands. The island looked and sounded similar to the stories I heard back on the dock in Cairo.

I was fulfilling my shipment of cattle. I struck up a conversation with a trader, asked him about his cargo of spices. What was his name again? Ah, his name was Ali, a Far Eastern spice trader. Ali's dhow was filled with spices and exotic wares of the Far East—of India, China, and the crown jewel, the Spice Islands. Wild stories he told me of the islands filled with bloodlust cannibal tribes, monstrous monsoons. Could this storm be a monsoon? Could be. Yes, could be.

Ali also spoke of adorned sultans and boundless spices. I was most shocked to hear of sultans. They didn't know Islam spread so far east. Ali said our faith was brought by my brothers, other Muslim traders. By the way Ali spoke of the land, of the trees, the humid air, and native tribes, I'd say this was a Spice Island with a great civilization nearby, wherever nearby was. I put my faith in Allah.

Jaipur

Scene: Native Dance

ᖇᴡᴡᕲ

I KEPT BEHIND Toro, Swift behind me, as the storm crashed around us. Behind us, hundreds of lit torches followed right behind us, inching closer by the minute.

What if that was my old tribe? Could my family be with them? My mother, oh my mother, what if she's there?

A tear trickled down my cheek.

How do I know this is Sumatra? I could yield to them, speak my tongue; the tribe could take me in, and free I would be. What was freedom? Have I forgotten true freedom? Do I turn, flee, run to my people? Do I stay with Gaspar and my friends?

I stopped for a moment, conflicted, running my whole life before my eyes. Rain poured through the jungle, carried by strong sea winds. I stood, inert like a mountain.

"What are you doing?" said Swift. "We can't stop, Jaipur. They'll kill us if we stop."

I looked to Swift. "I was native once, savage as you say."

"What do you mean?"

"I am one of them, those savages. I was born a savage, purchased as a savage, called a savage, am a savage."

"You are no savage. You are a man, a smart man, a friend."

"Zaragoza told me differently."

"Nay, he was wrong and still is. What makes a person a savage is not his appearance, where he came from, or what people think of him."

"Then what makes me not a savage? I am a slave, a slave to Gaspar."

"You have a soul that no man can put a ball and chain upon. You are no savage, Jaipur. You are my friend, and when this is all said and done, you shall be a free man with untold riches, inside and out. We need you now. I need you. Don't run away. Don't."

Through the hailing rain, I stared at the blazing torches ascending up the mountain toward us. I was thinking, debating, and wondering. I exhaled and closed my eyes as a tear fell from my lash. I shook my head, turned upward, opened my eyes, and continued up the slope.

We climbed the slope, reaching an area covered with brown, wet mud. I clung to the rock face, watching each step I took. That instant, there was a shriek. Cosimo had slipped. I grabbed onto his arm, holding him tight, with half of his body over the side of the cliff. I held on to him, gasping with pain from the pressure on my arm.

"Help him!" yelled Gaspar, running to my aid.

The others pulled on my shoulders, pulling Cosimo back up.

"You . . . you . . . " stuttered Cosimo. "You saved my life."

"No time to chat," said Toro. "The tribe heard us. Up, up."

Toro moved fast, not even once turning around to see if we were behind him. The lit torches were gaining on us, much too close for comfort. We reached the lookout point where we were earlier in the day. The sun had reached the horizon, extinguishing her light and bringing forth the dark night. We needed to hide.

"What do we do?" asked Cosimo.

Toro looked around for another path, anything to escape the tribe.

"We fight!" said Swift as he drew his sword.

"I'm not being eaten alive by those things," said Zaragoza.

"Do you have a choice?" Faustino chimed in.

"Hold," said Gaspar as he scanned the lay of the land.

"Here!" yelled Toro. "A cave."

"I have a torch," I said, "but no light."

"Can't go in a cave with no light," said Faustino.

"We don't have time to light a torch," said Swift.

Gaspar dug into his brown bag, pulled out a wooden torch, a small vial, and a carbon striker. He doused the torch with the liquid, struck the carbon striker, and the flame erupted, bright and hot, in a second.

"That's impressive," said Swift.

"Get in the cave. Quick," urged Gaspar.

We dashed for the small opening in the mountain, illuminated by Gaspar's torch. The opening was tight enough to fit one person at a time. The opening led to a large rock cavern, descending downward. We maneuvered our way down, using Gaspar's torch to see where to go.

"Ouch!" cried Zaragoza. "My leg. Ah, cut from the rock."

"Put the light out!" said Toro. "Hide, all of you. Hide!"

Gaspar and Swift put the torch out, and each of us hid.

I heard chatter near the opening of the rock. It was a few of the natives. Light then filled the cave, lit by their torches. The native spoke again. I listened closely and understood what he said: "Check here."

A single native climbed down into the cavern. He seemed to be a male by his voice. He maneuvered down the rocks, inching closer and closer to us. After a second, the native was right on us, searching the cavern with his torch. I noticed Faustino and Cosimo, trying to squeeze deeper into the rock without being seen. The native walked barefoot, no more than four feet away from me. I could see only his feet. I covered my mouth to hold the sounds of my breath. I noticed Swift grip his sword. I shook my head at him.

Another native yelled from up top in their native language: "Stop! We found another trail. We shall not let them venture to the evil deep. Come."

The native turned around and left the cave. We held there, motionless for two more minutes, until it was silent. A second later, light again filled the cavern. Gaspar held up his torch.

"I thought he saw me," said Cosimo.

"You pushed up against my arm on the rock," said Faustino. "It was going numb."

"Had to," exclaimed Cosimo. "He almost found us."

"Good job, Toro," said Gaspar.

Toro nodded.

"Damn savages caused my leg to bleed," added Zaragoza as he assessed the cut on his leg.

"What now?" askedSwift.

"Listen," said Gaspar as he looked around the cavern. "Do you hear that?"

There were subtle sounds of trickling water in the cavern.

"Water," said Toro.

"Might be a stream," said Swift.

"Aye, we follow it out," said Gaspar.

"I don't like caves, and caves don't like me," said Zaragoza.

"Then go back up," I replied.

"We go down," said Gaspar. "Does each of you have a torch?

The group checked their bags to see what they had inside. Everyone except Zaragoza pulled out a torch.

"I don't have one," said Zaragoza.

"Interesting," said Swift. "Why would you not pack a torch, eh?"

"Didn't think I would need one," remarked Zaragoza.

"I have an extra one," said Cosimo. "Here."

Zaragoza took the torch from Cosimo. "These torches might last us only a few hours."

"Not with this," said Gaspar as he held up the clear vial.

"I thought it was fire salt," said Cosimo.

"You and those colorful mixtures," I said.

"Aye, this will give us light for a few more hours," said Gaspar.

"Let's get to it then," said Faustino. "I'm getting hungry."

Swift

Scene: Waltz of Lovers

৩৩৩৩

T HE CAVERN WAS tight and jagged, with winding paths. We continued on the path. I kept a close watch, noting the cavern ceiling protruding downward and checking the balance of my feet on this uneven subterranean surface. The rock walls felt of slime, smelled like rotten eggs. Cosimo looked at me as I sniffed the air.

"Sulphur, I think," said Cosimo.

"Good to know," I replied.

It was hot in the cavern; sweat dripped down my back and forehead. I was miserable. Everyone was miserable. It was a hard walk, a hard walk indeed. A deep tiredness consumed me. We had been walking all day, all night, on the move with no breaks. If this was bad, what about that ancient Greek marathon runner who brought the news of the Greek victory over Persia? How far did he run again? What I am doing is more, must be more than he did. No wonder he died at the end of his journey. My feet were blistered through, my shoulders ached, my neck was stiff, and my calves were burning.

My head drifted toward the only thing in life that I knew was good: my dear love, Rose. I couldn't think of the *Valencia*, of the crew. I would die if I thought of that, of the *Valencia*. What kept me alive? My Rose. Her image, her fragrance, and her touch keep me alive.

I pondered her, pondered the moment I met my love.

It was a beautiful blue day in London three years before this excursion. I was working for the Royal Navy, up and coming as a pilot. I was dressed in my uniform, royal blue with golden buttons, my hair well kept. I was young, alive, and in my prime. I had finished my duty at sea, fighting with the French and Venetians all across the Italian Peninsula. I was attending a party, a celebration for what again? I'd wager for the hard-fought war.

It was a ball—masquerade ball, in fact—on a beautiful fall night in London. The leaves were changing from green to yellow to red to brown, and wind brushed through the tight streets, causing each leaf to elegantly fall to the ground. I could still hear that sweet music as I walked up the stairs to the magnificent orchestral building.

"Nice to see you finally show up, ole chap," said my friend Charles. He was a bachelor of sorts and had a curved mustache. He was a slender, sleek, black-haired fellow, far too concerned with staying fashionable. He was the epitome of London society, uptight, illustrious, and rotten. The men and women of this society appeared like a young, crisp, firm, ruby red apple; once bitten, they revealed a rotten, bitter, and wrinkled interior.

"How did you see me through this mask?" I asked Charles. I wore a black masquerade mask with golden lines throughout it.

"Edward," replied Charles with a sly smile. "No mask could hide the people here. I see right through each and every one of them." The orchestral music continued around us.

"Is that so?" I asked sarcastically.

"More so, been so, and still will be so," he replied. "Come, let us grab some wine. Tell me all about your adventures at sea."

We walked across the ballroom floor toward the wine bowl. I told Charles only the most exciting of my stories, from sword fighting around the Italian Peninsula to jumping ships off the coast of Normandy. Charles was delighted to hear each. I'd say he was more delighted to be seen with me at the ball. We stopped each moment to engage with a few other aristocrats, talking of useless things.

Until one moment struck.

"Ah, hello, cousin," said Charles, grasping the hand of the most beautiful woman in the room. "Beauty is your weapon, my dearest cousin, Rose." Charles twirled her in a circle. I was mesmerized, lost in her delicate movements, her graceful bow, her charming smile.

"Oh, stop it, Charles," said Rose, blushing. "He always makes a show of me."

She wore a red mask and an elegant white dress. She had long, voluminous brown hair, a button nose, and a sweet smile. The white dress accented her defined curves and arched back. I caught her attention, and our eyes locked. Powerful, it was. Her eyes twinkled, and then she looked away.

I felt the pull in my heart where words venture not with the same force that pulled the moon, stars, earth, and sun toward each other. Love between two souls intertwined—by the stars, by the zodiac, by the Lord in the heavens above all celestial spheres—was the strongest force in the universe. I could not breathe, for the air had escaped my lungs. Did I say love? I didn't believe in love. Love did not exist, until . . . until the force in my heart felt a pull never heard, smelled, or experienced before—the fragrance, the magnetic attraction of newfound scarlet love.

"Rose, my dear," said Charles, placing his hand upon her shoulder. "Meet my dearest friend, Royal Pilot Edward Swift."

Her eyes flashed up at me with her puckered lips tasting the scarlet nectar of the heavens. She said nothing. I said nothing back, for words had nothing to say. Elementary words have no place in love. Charles stared at the both of us, perplexed, with a hushed laugh under his breath, as the breadth of the love between Rose and me grew beyond any league or measurement.

"Rose?" asked Charles.

She snapped out of her daze and looked at me. "Yes, it's a pleasure to meet you, Sir Swift." She bowed.

"The pleasure is mine," I replied and bowed to her presence. The orchestral music continued around us.

"I must get going," fumbled Rose.

"Nonsense," interjected Charles. "Have a drink. Talk to Swift. Listen to his adventures abroad, cousin."

"I wish I could," remarked Rose, gentle and proper. "Something has come over me."

"Are you sick?" questioned Charles.

She nodded. "Sick? Yes, sick. Please excuse me, gentlemen." She left like a fallen petal taken by the wind.

"How interesting," stated Charles.

"Aye," I replied, shocked.

"Better go see. Best be swift, or she'll slip away." Charles smiled and sipped his red wine.

"Right, right," I remarked, and off I went.

She moved through the crowd like a shooting star through the night until she stopped on the outskirts of the floor. Rose was about to remove her bloodred mask until she looked up, and there I was without a word to say. Our eyes caught once more, interlocked like the earth and moon.

"You forgot something," I said behind my mask.

"I rarely forget anything, let alone something," said Rose.

"Then tonight you forgot the only something not to forget."

"Tell me. What have I forgotten which should not be forgotten?"

"A kiss from my lips."

I saw her throat tighten, elegant, adorned in a necklace of diamonds, jewels, and more. She looked down, then back into my eyes in the most serious of ways.

"I know you not," said Rose.

"I know you well," I replied.

"How?"

I took off my mask and then moved ever so close to her, closing the breadth between us. I placed my hand upon her neck, which felt like a bouquet of pink lilies, soft like a white feather.

"By a kiss," I replied.

Cosimo

Scene: Journey through the Cavern

꙰

"Aye, let's stop for a break," said Gaspar. "Rest for a moment."

"Thanks be to the good Lord," expressed Zaragoza as he threw his things down.

"How's the leg?" I asked.

"Terrible," said Zaragoza, stretching out his leg.

I noticed Gaspar examining the cave, focused on the contour of the cavern. Gaspar dragged his fingertips along the surface, listening, figuring out where the water might be. Toro walked over to him, conversing and giving Gaspar his opinion of the cavern.

I couldn't help but wonder as I stared at Gaspar. *What was he after? Why was he so calm, indifferent to the* Valencia?

"Hey," said Swift, pulling me from my wondering. "How are you holding up?"

"Been better," I replied.

"What do you think of all of this?"

"Still trying to figure out how we ended up here."

"Close call with the natives, eh?"

"That's an understatement."

Swift laughed, then hit me on my shoulder. "That native was inches from you and Faustino. You both looked terrified." Swift made an expression of fear, opening his mouth wide, imitating my expressions. Jaipur and Zaragoza laughed.

"You saw him!" interjected Faustino. "Thought he would take a bite out of me. Scary thing to meet face to face."

Swift continued in his laughable act. "Faustino, big as he is, squeezed into the tiniest crack in the rock. His big ole butt wasn't going to fit in there!"

"Aye, my buttocks fit just fine in the crack," said Faustino.

"You could say that again," added Jaipur, jesting.

"If he made one move on me," insisted Zaragoza, acting like his right hand was a sword, "that head of his would have been off. Cut, flop."

"At least it's over. That's all that matters," I said.

"You hope it's over," said Faustino. "Though when is it ever over?"

"When she catches a first look at your face, Faustino," said Swift, cracking up.

The whole group erupted in laughter.

"Aye, my face may be ugly, but it's the best one out of this group," said Faustino proudly, "which isn't saying much."

Jaipur booed Faustino, waving him off.

Swift was a good guy. I had known him since the beginning of this expedition because he was one of Gaspar's original members. I felt that I could trust him. I couldn't say the same for Faustino or Zaragoza. I had mixed feelings for Jaipur. Regardless, we seven were in this together. We had to rely on each other, differences aside. I hoped all of us would make it home.

My mind began to wonder. Where were we? I couldn't consult my maps, though I had a few rolled up in my sack. Needed a table to unroll my maps. I could use my mobile compass; that could show at least how distant we were from the prime meridian.

I reached into my sack, pulled out my mobile compass, and watched the iron needle move on the wind rose. I tried to make sense of the needle's movement. My eyes widened. I was gripped with confusion as I attempted to make sense of my bizarre compass. The needle moved in a continuous circular fashion, never stopping.

At that moment, I heard a crack, as if a stone had fallen near me. I looked up fast. In the distance, between two small cracks in the rock, I saw glowing yellow eyes, staring right at me.

I jolted, gasped aloud as the sight before me.

Yellow eyes, yellow eyes . . . what were those yellow eyes that looked upon me?

I drew my sword, then looked back toward the crack, though nothing was there. Was I going mad? First a shadow. Now yellow eyes. What was this?

"Cosimo!" yelled Swift.

"Are you okay, Cosimo?" asked Gaspar.

"I . . ." I stuttered. "I . . . thought I saw something in the dark."

"He's going mad too," interjected Zaragoza.

"What was it?" asked Jaipur.

"I don't know," I replied. "I don't know."

"The cave plays tricks," interjected Toro. "Darkness plays tricks."

"Ale does the trick," said Faustino with a wink.

"Best we get a move on," said Gaspar. "Toro found a small stream down here. Must be the way out."

We picked up our things and set out. I felt a slight uneasy feeling as we walked on. Our group continued down a steep slope, accompanied by unsettled stone pebbles rolling downward with each step. Our voices began to echo more loudly than before. We must have entered a large open area in the cavern. The sounds of rushing water grew more pronounced the farther down we went. A few minutes later, I heard splashing. Then Toro yelled, "Water! Here! Here!"

"Water!" yelled Zaragoza.

"What a relief," I exclaimed.

We were all relieved, revitalized by the discovery.

All I needed to feel whole again was daylight and some sleep. Yes, sleep. I was tired and stressed. What if that caused the visions? I bet so. How long had it been since I slept? Too long, too long.

I needed water. I dipped my head into the cool water. The ice water soothed my head and heart, calming my soul. I exhaled, letting out all of the impurities in my lungs.

Toro accompanied me, dipped his head into the water, and took a sip of the crystal blue. "It's fresh water with slight salt."

"It's wonderful," I said.

"What do you think of the stream?" asked Gaspar.

"Eh," gestured Toro as he rubbed his bristled chin, thinking, calculating the stream. "I say the river leads out. Could have strong rapids by the flow and rocks over there."

"Hey!" yelled Swift. "Look over here. Rubble!"

Jaipur shined his light next to Swift, and before us was a mixture of old pieces of wood scattered on the bank. It looked like pieces from old Islamic dhow ships. It appeared to be a ship graveyard brought here by the current. I picked up a piece of wood and turned it over; faintly inscribed on the back of the wood was Arabic text.

"Islamic ships," I announced.

"Odd place for them to be," added Faustino as he picked up one of the boards.

"The stream must have brought them in," said Toro. "The river must bend here, changing directions, bringing debris ashore."

"Ahh!" yelled Jaipur.

Startled, we all looked at him and asked what was wrong.

"Please stop with the yelling," insisted Zaragoza, clenching his heart. "You will kill me from a heart attack."

"Speak up, Jaipur," said Gaspar.

"Bones," said Jaipur. "Bones. All kinds of bones. There. Look there!"

I shined my torch in the direction pointed out. It was unsettling. There was a collection of carcasses of all different mammals and reptiles littering the shoreline. I picked up one of the bones. I thought it was part of a vertebrae by the shape of it. The bone looked to be from some sort of massive fish embedded with large gashes and teeth marks.

"It was eaten by something," I said. "Something big."

"Aye, there are human bones here, too," said Swift as he held up an intact human cranium.

"Fantastic," said Zaragoza. "Who would have thought?"

"What beast could eat humans like this?" asked Jaipur, worried.

"Let's not find out," said Gaspar. "We could use the debris to build a raft, get down the stream, and lead ourselves out. What do all of ye think?"

"No other choice," said Toro.

"It's an idea," I added.

"Best one we have," said Swift.

"Could be fun," said Jaipur.

"Until you fall out," said Faustino.

"I won't," replied Jaipur.

"I'm indifferent," chimed in Zaragoza.

"Quiet," ordered Gaspar. The chorus went silent. "We build two rafts to go downriver. Gather rubble, wood, and rope; any and all will do. Let's be quick while we still have the light."

Toro

Scene: Thought Variations VI

෬෴ඉ

T HE RIVER WAS crystal clear and ice cold. I was ready to face the river, face the rapids downstream. We constructed the rafts from the rubble, rope, and wood of past ships. I had seen this wood, this type of board, this style of craftsmanship. This was the standard material of Islamic trading vessels; I had used them more than a few times to trade my cattle from Timbuktu to Cairo by desert and by sea.

I told them I was from Timbuktu though I grew up in a small village near the city along a vast river. I used to take a boat downriver to Timbuktu, carrying my father's cattle. I would trade it there myself. I built good wealth from this. Trading in the city exposed me to the world abroad—to languages, customs, and beliefs I had never seen, heard, or learned before. It was there on those trading docks along the river that I learned of Islam and submitted to the faith. The river was a paradise for me, like that of the river Nile to the Egyptians. I loved that river. It reminded me of my family, of home.

Rubble found in this cave reminded me of my past, of the ships, of the docks, of the river, of my home. Aye, River, don't let your cool flowing waters fool me. Nay, they are tricksters, like a magician. Rivers flow fast, steady, until you come upon rushing rapids, terrible rushing rapids, able to destroy any ship or any man.

This river, pray to Allah that this river is not like the rapids from home.

Swift

Scene: The River

⟨∞⟩

A s I STARED at the makeshift rafts. I was not so sure. They looked rushed. I had worked hard tying these boards together, so these rafts better work. Hmm, the rafts might be strong, might be weak . . . Weak, aye, weak.

The rafts were composed of pieces of wood stacked upon each other, wrapped in ropes tied by hand—not much of a looker, but they would do, or so I hoped. I disagreed with Toro as he suggested rapids were downriver. I begged to differ. The river looked calm and easygoing from where I was standing. The river was in a cave. How could there be rapids in a cave?

"What do you think, coxswain, master of the longboats?" I asked Faustino.

Faustino shrugged his shoulders. "Looks sturdy, but I've been wrong before."

"Wrong about what?" I asked.

"Been wrong my whole life," he remarked.

"That's reassuring."

"I think the rafts look like rubbish," interjected Zaragoza.

"No one asked you."

"I asked myself and replied," said Zaragoza.

Jaipur asked, "Did you find the answer you were looking for?"

"Look at them. The rafts speak for themselves," said Zaragoza.

"Gather round, all of you," announced Gaspar, gesturing with his hands. "We have two rafts, two groups. First raft, Faustino, Cosimo, Jaipur, and myself. The rest of you are on the second raft. Is everyone fine with that?"

"For now," said Zaragoza.

Gaspar's eyes flashed. "What is that supposed to mean?"

"Nothing," remarked Zaragoza slyly.

"Better be," said Gaspar. "Let's get to it. Rafts out. Godspeed to all of you."

I dreaded the thought of being tied to Zaragoza. If he made any move, anything that caught my eye, I would shove him off my raft in less than a second. Toro was strong and quick to end foolishness.

On my raft were Toro, Zaragoza, and I. To steer ourselves in the water, we constructed wooden paddles from the rubble. I wasn't expecting much action along the river, which appeared to be moving at a snail's pace.

We boarded the raft, set out from the bank, and began our journey down the flowing river into the dark unknown. Zaragoza held on to his torch sprinkled with salt fire. Don't ask me what salt fire was; I had no idea. We added three more lit torches to the raft and tied them on the corners of the raft to give us light. Toro and I kept pace with the other group as we paddled and maneuvered through the winding stream.

Paddling was hard, as I worked my arms and back to exhaustion. It had been a while since I'd rowed like this. I was panting, losing my breath with each stroke. I should have stretched before this. Then I looked at Toro; he was a beast, breaking through the water with his paddle. He was a one-man team. I couldn't believe his strength and endurance. I couldn't compete on his level.

"What do you think, Toro?" I asked.

"Of what?" replied Toro.

"The bloody river," interjected Zaragoza.

"If rapids come, follow my directions. Keep paddling no matter what. Understand?" remarked Toro.

"You think rapids are coming?" I asked.

"Might be," replied Toro.

"Why so fearful?" asked Zaragoza.

"I'm always fearful," said Toro sternly and calmly.

"You never show it," said Zaragoza.

"No need to show it," remarked Toro.

The river began to pick up speed, accelerating the raft. The sound of water grew louder. *Whish, whish. Splash, splash.* It flowed faster. I started to worry; I didn't think a river could go this fast.

I had never been on rapids in my life. This was becoming worrisome.

What if I fall out? No one can stop and help me. Where do these rapids come from? Listen to Toro. Paddle, paddle. Yes, paddle.

The other raft was next to ours with some breadth between us. Faster, faster. The river picked up.

"This is no stream," I said. "No stream at all!"

"Paddle," said Toro. "Paddle!"

We entered rapids, tumultuous rapids. In front of us were openfaced, jagged rocks, boulders edging out of the water, illuminated by the dim light of our torches. I couldn't tell how tall the cavern ceiling was. Our raft brushed against a rock.

"Help me, Allah," cried Toro. "Help me!"

"Brace for impact!" yelled Gaspar. "May my Great Work transform each of you!"

"What does that even mean?" asked Zaragoza as he clung to the raft for dear life.

I thought of my love, my love, in my sweet home. *I shall return to you by the Lord in the celestial heavens. He shall bring me back, Rose.*

"Bring me back," I said aloud. "Bring me to Rose."

"Only dead men fear death!" said Faustino with a wild laugh.

Zaragoza bent down, held firm to the raft, and began to pray the act of contrition under his breath, still holding on to the torch. "O my God, I am sorry for having offended You."

We delved deeper into the roar of the rapids, clashing, splashing, fighting as the river god, Scamander, fought Achilles at Troy.

Swish, swish. Our raft moved side to side. *Clash, swish, crack!* Our raft rammed into a jagged rock protruding above the water. If not for Toro's grabbing my arm and pulling me back, I would have flown off the side. Our poor makeshift raft broke into pieces, though it still held together, part mangled, above the water.

"Paddle!" yelled Toro.

"You hear him?" cried Zaragoza. "Paddle for God's sake, Swift. Paddle!" Zaragoza still clung to the raft, inert with fear.

I dug my paddle with immense force deep into the water, putting my whole being into each stroke. I pushed, pushed, and pushed the water.

The other raft veered out of control, crossing in front of our raft in chaotic fashion, spinning wildly. Jaipur was gripped with fear and without a paddle or a clue of what to do but hang on for his life. Cosimo continued to paddle, focused on his rowing. Faustino held onto Jaipur's shoulder as he gripped the bottom of the raft. Gaspar kept firm and upright as he steered that forsaken raft.

Clash! Their raft struck a rock. Jaipur flew off, followed by Faustino. *Bam!* Their raft struck ours, broadside up. We held firm. Our rafts were one behind the other.

The rafts then spiraled out of control. *Swish, crack, splash, up, side, down, right, left, left, right, left, twirl.* Toro, that damned Toro, steered our raft better than any man could.

I rowed with a solid grip on my wooden paddle as our own raft entered into chaotic motion. *Swish, right, back, left, and twirl.* Then, yes, thanks be, the river began to slow down, slower, slower. Out of the darkness, in the far distance, I saw light at the end of the cave. Sunlight!

We all yelled, "Light!"

The river calmed as we drifted through the narrow cave until it emptied into another open section of the cave into a lagoon or, rather, a hidden pool of crystal blue-green water. The walls of the cave still surrounded us, extending upward in a curved dome formation, leaving a circular hole at the very top of the dome and allowing a beam of sunlight inside the cave. The curved rock walls were covered with green vines and yellow, white, pink, and blue flowers, all fighting for the light above.

Both of the rafts flowed to a soft drift as we all gazed at the rock dome, at the flowers, and at the light—such comforting light. Nothing was more comforting than sunlight; nothing in this world gave me, gave *us*, more hope in that moment than the great lamp's life-giving light.

"Toro," I said, fixated on the light. "Damn good job."

"I . . . I . . . second that," said Zaragoza with wide, astonished eyes.

He bowed. "Not possible without you two."

Cosimo

Scene: The Gate

⌒⬮⬮⬮⌒

WHAT A RIDE *it was. What a ride it will be.*
Gaspar yelled out to Jaipur and Faustino, scanned the
water for any sign of life. From below the surface, Faustino
sprang up, holding on to Jaipur.

"Aye, good, good," said Gaspar, concerned as he helped them into
the raft. Jaipur looked worn down and seemed he was on the verge of
drowning. Jaipur coughed and coughed, ridding himself of the swal-
lowed water.

"Wild ride, eh?" said Faustino, catching his breath.

Jaipur nodded, laboring for air, coming back to life.

I was happy to see the both of them. Looked like everyone made
it at least somewhat intact. My attention shifted, and there before me
was, to my wonder, two massive Egyptian colossi painted into the rock
face. The figures were at least twelve meters high, appearing to be Egyptian gods, perhaps Horus and Anubis, carved and painted with exquisite
detail. The colossi both carried a single red stone in their hands.

Between the two colossi were two full-length portraits of an Egyptian pharaoh from Memphis from roughly the twentieth dynasty. My
monastery in Florence had an immense library, and I had an immense
amount of time to read in that library.

The pharaohs seemed to be performing a devotion to the
hawk-headed god, Phre. The figure maintained a powerful physiognomy,
composed of pronounced lips, a curved nose, reddish skin. His right
hand was up, and his left hand was at his side. The figure was dressed in

full Egyptian royal regalia, wearing a teal and gold pschent, a white and light brown silk robe, and a golden belt lined with colored jewels. There was an exact replica facing the opposite direction on the other side of the wall. Between the two painted pharaohs were lines, words, phrases painted in hieroglyphics.

I couldn't fathom how this was there. Why . . . *How* would Egyptians be this far east, thousands of leagues away from Memphis? They wouldn't have the skills or technology to make it this far by sea. It would have been impossible for them to travel here across the Atlantic or Pacific. Why were the Egyptians here in the middle of this cave painting, of all places? This was the discovery of a lifetime, a hidden, forgotten secret if verily the ancient civilizations made it to the Spice Islands. Who could explain these phenomena?

Perhaps Gaspar . . . But the drawings . . .

But I could not think about this now.

"My Gates to the Work," said Gaspar, lost in a dream-like state.

"What in the name of all things?" questioned Swift. "Did I hit my head, or are we in Egypt?"

"Why?" said Jaipur. "Is that from Egypt? Can't be. Egypt is on the other side of the world. Wait, are we on the other side of the world?"

"No," said Faustino. "You are in the Pacific. Checked my own head to make sure."

"Not Pacific," I said. "The Indian Ocean."

"Same thing," said Faustino.

"You can't say Indian Ocean for sure," added Swift.

Swift was right. I was not sure where I was. My mind was blown from its foundation.

"This painting thing is out there, way out there," exclaimed Faustino. "Is this normal for the Spice Islands? Do all these islands have stuff like this?"

"Nay," said Jaipur, stupefied. "I don't know what normal is anymore."

"There. Aye, Horos—god of the sky with a head of a falcon, son of Isis—watches over his slaves, the people working and crafting the golden Retjenu below," said Gaspar.

On the center stone between the pharaohs and below the falcon-headed god above was a scene of four red-skinned Egyptian slaves in short white garments carrying on their shoulders baskets full of glistening, golden-orange precious stones. They moved toward a large teardrop furnace, dumping the stones into it. By the looks of the painting, the slaves had an extensive knowledge of metallurgy.

Below that panel was another scene, surrounded by light blue hieroglyphics, of a slave laboring over the teardrop furnace, mixing, sprinkling other materials into the furnace. Chaotic lightning swirled around the teardrop in the colors of red dragon's blood, lemon yellow, white chalk, indigo, Egyptian blue, and bright green malachite.

"Did he say gold?" asked Faustino. "That looks like gold, golden lightning!"

"Eh, it's orange," said Swift. "Never seen orange gold."

"You have never seen gold at all," chimed in Zaragoza.

"As a matter of fact, I have," said Swift.

"Not I," added Jaipur.

"Gold is worth more to me than endless wine," said Faustino. "Gold is worth more than life itself."

What did Gaspar mean by golden Retjenu? Was golden Retjenu this golden orange stone? Retjenu sounded familiar to me. Where did I read that? Wasn't golden Retjenu some type of secret mixture?

I think it was. I remembered reading about it somewhere in some book, but what did it say?

Gaspar examined the stone slab adorned with intricate hieroglyphics and paintings, rubbing his chin deep in thought.

"I do not think this was done by the ancient Egyptians," interjected Zaragoza. "Done by an Islamic imposter. Worthless. I know these things, yes."

"That's a far-fetched answer," stated Swift.

"Not at all. I can tell it was done by an amateur's hand," said Zaragoza. "I know things of this sort, things a sailor would like ye would never know."

"Quite the connoisseur then, eh?" remarked Swift.

"Been told that once or twice," said Zaragoza as he looked at his nails.

I rubbed the stone wall with my hands, feeling it and rubbing it between my fingers. "It's limestone."

"Cosimo, my bag," said Gaspar, gesturing toward me without taking his eyes off of the limestone wall.

Each of us kept our bags roped to the raft. Luck was on our side that day: none of the bags had fallen off. I untied Gaspar's bag. It was heavy, and I felt the weight as I handed it to him.

Gaspar picked through the bag. I could hear the jingle of the glass vials inside. He pulled out a bronze tablet, etched with hieroglyphics and a series of phrases underneath each in a language I knew not.

Gaspar, Gaspar. How . . . What do you knew of this?

I looked at the others; by their facial expressions, I could tell we were all thinking the same thing.

"Are those translations?" I asked.

Gaspar ignored my question as he followed the symbols upon the wall, pointing at them, then looking at the tablet. A dark blue sky with golden stars was painted above the hieroglyphics.

"The stars," said Swift, "the stars, arranged like true constellations. See? Look!"

I looked for myself, calculating and analyzing the painted blue night sky. "O, you are right. You are right."

Gaspar stood back and roared, *"Ja win ni pa tow bow ti bi an na fir se e nu!"*

Silence followed. We looked around, waiting for something to happen.

"That wasn't Spanish," said Faustino.

"You are mad," said Zaragoza.

"Where's the boom?" asked Swift.

An immense shockwave vibrated through the water, tossing our rafts backward.

"There it is," joked Swift.

"Gaspar," I said. "Tell me, what is going on?"

"Watch," said Gaspar.

Another second went by. Then, the mountain rumbled and shook like an earthquake; waves formed in the pool of water. Rocks fell from the ceiling around us—*splash, splash, splash*—missing our rafts by less than an inch.

"Earthquake!" cried Toro.

"A trap! A trap!" yelled Jaipur.

The stone slab adorned with hieroglyphics began to rise up, slowly and steadily.

"The wall . . . It's rising!" said Swift.

"It must be a door, a gateway perhaps," I stated.

A strong current of water, displaced by the rising stone gateway, pulled us closer to the wall. The current felt like a riptide or a whirlpool deep at sea. The mountain still shook around us.

"You hear that?" asked Faustino.

"Hear what?" said Zaragoza.

"Sounds like . . ." said Jaipur. "Water. Lots of water. Oh, no."

We all turned around and looked at the mouth of the cave, the way from which we came. The sound of water roaring toward us grew louder and more intense.

"That can't be good," said Swift.

"It's not," said Toro.

"Hang on, all of you," said Gaspar.

I gripped the raft, holding firm to the wood and ropes. I took a few deep breaths, waiting, waiting, anticipating, looking at the cave. The stone slab continued to rise as water pulled us under it.

"Come on, you!" yelled Swift.

"I'm not paid enough for this," sighed Faustino.

Water projected out of the cave at an unbelievable velocity, filling the domed cavern, roaring toward us as a massive wave. The force almost threw me off when the wave collided with us, but I held firm. In less than a second, the wave pushed us through the gateway into a narrow, dark cave that flowed downward. Our speed was amplified from the rush of water, moving faster than a skipping rock on a lake. Wind blew all around us, blowing my hair back. I wanted to paddle, to try to steer the raft, but it was long gone. Our raft maintained speed, kept upright, and flowed on a downward sloped path.

"We know not where this brings us!" yelled Swift.

"Aye, to the other side," remarked Gaspar.

"Keep paddling," exclaimed Toro.

"I don't have a paddle," I said.

"No one does," said Jaipur.

Swift, Toro, and Zaragoza's raft was behind us as we moved with the flow of the rushing water and heavy wind. The river returned to a level plain though still moving fast. There, at the far end of the narrow cave, light was bursting through the darkness. The ferocious river was leading us toward the light; it must have been a way out.

The raft then bolted through the light into another open chamber. We were still locked in the fast current, unable to break from it. My eyes had to adjust to the sudden change of aperture. The bright light dimmed, revealing not the sunlight but rather blazing volcanic rock.

"My God, is that—" screamed Zaragoza.

"Magma!" I yelled over the rush of the water. The river that carried us curved around a lake of magma, refulgent and bubbling, while illuminating an enormous, hot, and sprawling cavern, able to fit a whole mountain inside of it.

The narrow river bent around the lake of magma, encircling it like a snake. The current continued to carry us at an incredible speed around the lake.

I clung to the raft with all the power and might of my soul. We all did. The current carried us around the lake, through the open cavern, and then into another narrow cave, illuminated by magma and our remaining lit torches.

"Look up," yelled Faustino. "Be gems above."

"Crystals," said Gaspar.

On the ceiling of the cave were large clusters of crystals of all different sizes, colored ultramarine, malachite green, lead-tin yellow, white gypsum, and carbon black. The crystals lined the ceiling and cavern walls, engulfing us in a sparkling dream of the heavens. I could see my reflection in the clear crystals as their smooth surfaces refracted light. Embedded in the rock near the crystals were scores of sparkling diamonds, glistening from the magma light and lit torches. Beautiful, it was. Following the crystals, I noticed embedded in the rock large fragments of what appeared to be plants—rather an outline of plants, ancient plants I'd never seen before.

"What be that?" asked Jaipur. "Plants? Here?"

"A skeleton of a plant," I said. "Buried in the rock."

After the plants, we saw bones and carcasses of large animals or reptiles trapped in the rock, buried like the plants—connected, intact, and preserved by the rock. Nay, these were no ordinary mammal bones; these were bones of massive beasts with huge jaws larger than a bear's—sharp teeth, long necks, and spikes protruding from their backs.

"Never seen bones this size," said Zaragoza.

"Or creatures like this," said Swift.

"Monsters!" yelled Faustino. "Monsters exist! I knew it, knew it all along."

"The monsters are stuck in the rock," said Jaipur. "How'd a skeleton cram itself in a rock?"

"Buried over time, if I had to guess," I added.

The cavern widened and felt blazing hot, though the water and high speeds of the river provided enough airflow to keep us alive and cool.

Our rafts, adjoined to the current, flowed into another section of the cavern, still moving at a fast velocity. On my right and left were large arches of jagged rock at least ten stories high, scattered across the vast, open cavern and illuminated by distant magma, intermixed with pointed crystals of the same height, though much larger than the crystals we witnessed earlier. The stone arches and multicolored crystals towered over us like a curved bridge above our heads. Beyond the arches and crystals in the vast abyss were roaring geysers—*Pssh!*—emitting hot vapor to the surface of this subterranean chamber. I felt the vapor trickle down my face like a mist as we raced down the river.

We then entered another narrow cavern where the river leveled itself out. At the end of this narrow tunnel was a piercing light, so bright I could not gaze upon it. Could this be our way out? This light was different, more vibrant than the magma light.

"Sunlight," I said.

"Our way out!" yelled Jaipur.

"We're moving fast," said Toro. "Too fast."

"Hear that?" said Swift. "Sounds like a waterfall ahead."

"Hold steady!" ordered Gaspar.

I could hear water roaring ahead. I clung to the raft, bracing for whatever life threw at me. *If this is my end, end by a waterfall,* I said to the Lord above, the Lord I neglected, *forgive me. Aye, forgive me, Lord.* That was all I could say to Him. The water picked up faster, and the rapids crashed louder. I gripped the makeshift raft harder as we approached the light at the end of the tunnel.

"Death, oh, give me freedom before you take my soul!" cried Jaipur. "Let me die a free man in my mother's arms."

"I can't die like this," screamed Zaragoza, "like a savage!"

"My family awaits me," said Toro. "Nay, not today. Nay!"

"I didn't mean to Lord," pleaded Faustino. "She started it. She made me do it! Oh, I'm innocent, Lord!"

"You won't take my soul, river," yelled Swift, "for my love awaits me!"

"Luna, my mistress," said Gaspar. "Luna, my transformation."

Into the light we went.

Am I dead? Am I alive?

I opened my eyes, and standing over me was an angel, aye, an angel with the appearance of a woman. She had gorgeous, long, black hair, long eyelashes, bright eyes, and a curious smile. I must have died and gone to heaven.

Princess Nur-al-Arij

Scene: Appearance of the Prisoner

◠〰〰〰〰◡

I T WAS A bright blue day, a perfect day. I had to leave the palace walls. I had been locked far too long, far too long for a pretty day. I took a sack full of my finest books, books that told the greatest stories of adventure, love, history, geography, and science. My books were my only way to see above the walls, to gaze at the world abroad. The palace walls were large though my world was small, smaller than a fly. I was locked away behind palace walls.

Where could I go to escape? A place few knew of, where a river flowed through a miraculous forest outside the city gates. The only way there for me was through a crack in the high palace walls. The place, my secret place, was deep in the forest where a waterfall emptied its mouth into a pool below that flowed into the river. The sun shone bright on an open spot, clear from trees, where I could feel the mist of the water spray my skin as I sunned myself on green grass next to the river—reading, thinking, dreaming, and praying to Allah. Here I was free, free from my father, the sultan, free of responsibilities, free of my clothes. Free.

On this particular day, I was reading a splendid book about gems from around the world, how they are found, where they are produced— any and all things in regard to mineralogy. As I lay on the smooth green grass, on my floral red tapestry, without any silk or cloth to cover my body, I heard the strangest of noises, loud men screaming at the top of their lungs. I stood up, put on my robe, and scratched my head. Where was this sound coming from? Then, a collection of men tumbled down the waterfall.

What has the will of Allah Almighty brought to me?

I counted seven or so men, plunging downward into the river.

What should I do?

I should run, run back to safety, back to the palace walls. As my father had warned me, strange men could harm me.

I picked up all my belongings and started to sprint away until I noticed I left my book near the river.

I was conflicted. *Should I turn back?* I loved that book, couldn't leave my book. My books were my world.

I must turn back. Yes, turn back, grab the book, then keep going.

I turned around with haste, bent down, and picked up my book along the riverbank. As I was bending down, I noticed a white man, seemingly European, floating above the water, unconscious. I couldn't leave him there, leave him to die.

What would Allah want me to do? The man may be white, a Christian perhaps, but he was my neighbor. But he could be dangerous.

The man was dying, needed to be brought ashore.

Do I leave him there to die or bring him ashore, risking my own life in an attempt to save another?

The palace walls were safe, comforting; I knew them well, and yet this man, this situation felt different.

Did I want different? Have I not been praying to Allah for this long, asking the Almighty for . . . for different?

I sighed, looked up to the bright blue sky. "You better protect me."

I placed my materials on the ground, jumped into my water, and pulled the unconscious man to the banks of the river. The man had a bristled brown beard, long black hair, a pointed nose, long eyelashes, and a chiseled face. He was different and handsome—very handsome. I was intrigued by this European.

I pumped on his chest so that he might regurgitate the superfluous water. I learned this method from one of my medical books. After a few pushes on his chest, he regained consciousness, coughing while water poured out his mouth. I was caught off guard, thinking my attempts were futile. I backed up, slow and hesitant, as the mysterious white man opened his eyes. Fear gripped me, so I ran into the forest to hide.

Cosimo

Scene i: Journey through the Jungle

◌⟨ΤΤΤΤ⟩◌

MY ANGEL, MY angel, where didst you go?" I said, disoriented as I opened my eyes.

Where was I? Oh, oh, I survived. The Lord answered my prayer for the first time in my life. He sent an angel to help me.

Why didn't You send an angel to take me from the monastery? It matters not now, for I breathe. Thank You. Thank You.

I propped myself up and noticed I was on the banks of a flowing river surrounded by an enchanted forest of tall trees and chirping birds. Mist from the roaring waterfall fell upon my face, cooling my face and soul. Where did the angel go? Was this heaven?

I felt my chest, real and solid, felt my clothes, wet and heavy. I rubbed my chin, coarse like sandpaper from my small, prickled hairs. Aye, I was alive.

"We made it!" yelled Jaipur.

I looked to the river and noticed everyone above the water, swimming to me.

"I thought that would be my end," said Faustino. "We need wine. *I* need wine."

"Told you," laughed Swift as he swam toward the bank. "Told you the water couldn't kill Swift."

"Too much for me," expressed Zaragoza. "Too much for me."

"Hey, Cosimo!" yelled Swift. "How are you on the banks?"

"An angel saved me," I said.

"Allah saved me," said Toro.

"Glad to see you, Cosimo," said Gaspar.

"You too, Captain," I nodded. The others started to come ashore.

"Are we missing anyone?" asked Gaspar.

"No, we're all here," I replied.

"That was some ride," said Swift, smiling and placing his arm on my shoulder. "How about that magma lake, eh? Oh, I almost forgot. I grabbed your bag in the water, Cosimo."

"Good stuff, Swift!" I exclaimed. "Good stuff. I'll be needing this."

"Aye, if we had one of those crystals, one of those big ones," said Jaipur. "Rich men, all of us, rich men we would be!"

"Don't remind me," sighed Faustino. "Gold . . . So close, so close to my fingertips."

"Yet so far," added Zaragoza, irritated. "Where are we?"

"I saw something. There!" pointed Jaipur. "Look, look! In the brush."

"Better not be one of those cannibals," said Zaragoza.

The crew drew their swords, ready to strike at a moment's notice. I stepped in front of them with my hands up. "Wait, wait! Let me check, please."

Gaspar nodded.

I walked to the brush, watching each step, hands still raised. I glanced at the dark green, thick brush. I heard a twig snap, noticing a pair of brown eyes peeking through the brush. Another twig snapped; leaves rustled. The figure was turning its heel away in a great haste.

I called out gently, "Wait! Wait!"

I continued forward into the brush, stared into the bush. Then, a sharpened dagger touched the tip of my throat.

"A knife!" yelled Jaipur.

"Kill the savage now," said Zaragoza.

"No one move!" I ordered.

I started into the bush, feeling the sharp blade tickle my throat. I could see through the shadowed leaves beautiful brown eyes, vibrant eyes, angel eyes.

"Come, please. Put the blade down," I said, softly.

The blade trembled upon my neck.

I continued, "It's okay. It's okay." I reached for the tip, steadily and slowly. I grabbed the tip of the blade. The blade resisted, pierced harder. I stopped for a moment, then reached again for the tip and pulled the blade away. I took a deep exhale and opened the bush.

Before me was the most gorgeous women I had ever seen before. She walked backward, hesitant, knife still up. The woman looked no more than twenty-five years old with light brown skin, luscious black eyes, dark brows, jet black hair, long eyelashes, defined cheekbones, and a face like that of a bunny. She was slender and had perfect posture and curves. She wore a dark blue dress of Islamic fashion. I noticed a red book or scroll clenched in her right hand.

"It's all right. Please, come," I said gently, gesturing to her to come hither.

The others crept behind me, breaking through the brush. Her eyes flashed at them.

"A native," said Zaragoza, disgusted.

"The silk tapestry in her hand," said Toro.

"Aye?" said Gaspar.

"By the cut and design of the silk. Only Islamic royalty has thus," said Toro.

"Royalty?" questioned Swift.

"Great," sighed Jaipur. "More kings."

"Bet she has gold," said Faustino. "We could offer her up as ransom. Gold for us all!"

"We shall do nothing of the sort," I demanded.

"Think you could stop me?" laughed Faustino.

"Yes," I remarked sternly. I moved between the group and her with my sword drawn.

"I'd ransom her," said Zaragoza.

"We came for diplomacy, not ransom," said Gaspar. "Put your swords away."

"Today diplomacy," sighed Faustino, sheathing his sword. "Tomorrow ransom."

Toro spoke out to her in Arabic. Her eyes glimmered. Toro spoke another phrase in words I knew not. She responded to him, and they conversed for a minute or two. Her voice sounded light like a flower petal, and her words were sweet as honey. Toro shrugged at her, gesturing toward us.

"What say she, Toro?" asked Gaspar.

"I can speak for myself," replied the majestic woman in Spanish.

We all gasped, amazed how she was able to speak Castilian Spanish so fluently.

"You know Spanish?" I asked.

"She might speak Spanish better than you, Cosimo," said Swift with a laugh. "Better than me, too."

"Yes," she replied.

"How?" I spoke.

"Learned it," she answered.

"My roots, my heritage must be from Arabia," stated Jaipur. "Heard of nearby islands full of Arabians. They have eyes not unlike my islander ones."

"Are Spaniards here? Any Europeans?" interrupted Gaspar.

"No Spaniards," she replied.

"What place is this?" asked Zaragoza.

"Boubazar," she replied.

"Can it be?" said Gaspar, astonished.

"You know Boubazar?" I asked.

"Only from stories. Sailor stories," said Gaspar. "Old stories which spoke of the great city of Boubazar in the far east."

"Did the stories speak of gold?" interjected Faustino.

"Or spices?" added Swift. "Better be spices here."

"Gold, spices, and more," remarked Gaspar. "Much, much more."

As the men continued to converse with one another, I asked, "What is your name, my lady?"

"Nur-al-Arij," she said.

I repeated her name—like a the most beautiful poem, Nur-al-Arij—under my tongue. "May I call you Arij?"

"If you so desire," replied Arij with a soft smile.

I blushed, and my heart leaped. "Pleasure to make your acquaintance, Arij. I am Cosimo."

"Cosi?" said Arij, struggling to say my name.

"No, Coz-ee-moe," I said.

"Oh, Cosimo," she repeated with a slight smile.

"Yes, yes," I said, excited.

Faustino yelled from the bank of the flowing river. "I see a boat down there—single mast, good boat, docked on the shore."

"Is that your boat, Arij?" I asked.

"Yes," replied Arij, hesitant.

"We could take the boat. Go downriver," said Swift.

"Nay, leave it for now," said Gaspar. Then, he turned to Arij. "Can ye take us to Boubazar?"

"If ye want," said Arij.

"Yes, we want," remarked Zaragoza with a hint of annoyance. "I am in a dire need of new clothes and a wash."

"I say we take the boat," said Faustino.

"We have no supplies," I said.

"We'll raid a village on the river," said Faustino.

"I'm too tired for a raid," sighed Jaipur. "I need food, for I feel weak and might pass out."

"Do what you want, Faustino, but I'm going to Boubazar," said Gaspar, and the group conceded, though in protest Faustino muttered a few sly remarks under his tongue.

"Wait a second," said Swift. "How do we know she's not leading us wrong, leading us to our deaths?"

"Fair point," said Jaipur.

"We have no other choice," said Toro.

"I'll cut her if—" said Faustino.

"No, you won't," I demanded.

"Watch yourself, Cosimo," exclaimed Faustino. "No stone walls here to protect a monk."

"I'm no monk," I remarked.

"Quiet, both of you," ordered Gaspar. He then turned to Arij and asked, "Will you bring us, Your Grace?"

Arij looked at each of us carefully. By the glimmer in eyes, I could tell she was sharp, quick minded. "Follow me."

We set out from the river, following Arij through the dense, wooded, mountainous landscape.

I looked at the way she moved, the way she walked, and the way she carried herself with such grace and strength. I did not want to come off as obsessive or weird, so I kept back the floodgates of my love. *Who was she, her true self?* We were different, so different, from one another but I liked that, loved that about her.

We walked silently for an hour until we broke through the tree line and came upon a chalk-white road. I thought it was limestone; the road seemed expensive, well crafted, and placed with perfection. Not even Florence had roads this exquisite—perhaps in the Medici residence but not for us mere mortals to walk upon. I then heard a faint gallop in the distance, a clopping on the stone road. I squinted my eyes down the path and saw four men wearing black armor from head to toe, galloping toward us on Arabian steeds. Tension filled the air as we crossed eyes with one another, deciding if we should draw swords, run, or remain quiet.

"Horseman," said Gaspar. "Four of them."

"Looks like the sultan's personal guard," said Toro. "His best troops."

"We could fight," suggested Swift, "and take the horses."

"Not these ones," said Toro.

"I say we run," said Jaipur.

"Let's use the girl as a hostage," said Faustino.

"I concur," remarked Zaragoza.

"I said no to hurting the girl!" demanded Gaspar.

"What do we do, Arij?" I asked.

"Sheath your blades!" said Arij.

"Are you mad?" asked Zaragoza intensely. "This is her moment to get us all killed or make us slaves! I'll die before I become a savage slave."

"No more slave traders," said Jaipur, sword drawn. "I can't. No more slave traders!"

"Let's listen to her," I demanded. "Gaspar, listen to her. Please."

The horsemen were closing in on us. *Clop, clack, clop, clack, clop.*

Gaspar was conflicted.

The horses continued. *Clop, clop, clop.*

Sweat poured down from Gaspar's forehead as he thought of the right decision to make.

"What do you say, Gaspar?" asked Swift, sword up and ready to fight. "What do you say?"

"Let's kill them," said Zaragoza. "Kill the savages now while there are only four of them."

"We must not fight them," said Toro.

"Decide Gaspar, or I'm killing them," said Faustino.

"No more slave traders. No more!" said Jaipur.

Clop, clack, clack.

"Put down your sword, or they will kill you!" said Arij.

Clop, clop, clop, clack, clop.

"Trust her, Gaspar," I said. "Trust her."

Clop, clop, clack.

Gaspar sheathed his sword. "Put your swords away. Put them away."

Zaragoza shook his head, then sheathed his sword as he let out a sigh of anger.

"Oh, be right," said Jaipur on the verge of tears.

"I see who you side with, Gaspar," said Faustino.

"Gaspar sides with reason," said Swift. "I hope he sides with reason. I hope."

"There are no sides," I said.

We all sheathed our swords, and the four horsemen approached us. The horsemen encircled us, carrying long spears.

"Say nothing," ordered Gaspar.

Arij yelled out to the horsemen. The horsemen conversed with one another in a tense tone. One of the horsemen stepped down from his horse, took off his helmet, and spoke to Arij, face to face. They seemed to know another.

The guard then came to us, squared up each one of us. Arij continued to speak to him as he looked us over. The guard looked right into Gaspar's eyes, unflinching, unbreaking, though Gaspar stood firm and didn't blinked. The guard then made an order and walked back to his horse. I exhaled, feeling the anxiousness leave my body.

Arij approached me. "Thou art safe."

"I give you my gratitude, my lady," I replied with a bow.

She nodded her head at me with a smile, then turned to the others. "All of you are safe now. Allah has found favor in you, Spaniards."

"I owe you my life, Princess," said Toro.

"As do I," said Gaspar.

"Oh, praise God. Praise Allah," said Jaipur.

"Princess?" I repeated, coming to terms with her position.

"These men are my father's guard. They will escort us to the palace."

"Who is your father?" I asked.

"Sultan Muzaffar Shah, Sultan of the Indies, Commander of the Faithful," she said.

Cosimo

Scene ii: Entrance of the Guests

◈

W E WERE LED by Arij and the four horsemen through the dense, mountainous forest. We encountered a few villages along the way. I was shocked to see the architecture and style of Arabia here in these villages. The houses were made of cream-colored stone with domed roofs built into the mountainside. The forest transitioned from trees into more arid land, similar to the Greek isles.

In the distance upon steep cliffs was the city of Boubazar overlooking the magical ocean below. The city was surrounded by large stone walls many stories high. I looked below the cliffs to my right and noticed hundreds of ships docked, sailing, or wading in the ocean. The port city of Boubazar was the center of the Islamic Far Eastern trading apparatus, gaining its wealth and prestige as the gateway between the Islamic world and the Far Eastern islands.

As I stared at the crystal blue water, I couldn't help but think of the history and of the people that had come here before to trade their goods—their blood, their sweat, for riches, for opportunity, for who knows what else. They were once here, and now we Europeans were here to do the same.

We walked up to the city gates, constructed with enormous turquoise and gold arches and adorned with countless jewels of all cuts, sizes, and colors. People were moving in all directions, yelling, chattering, shoving. My first impression of the city was that this was a chaotic, booming metropolis with far more energy than Florence. The streets were made of tile and cream stone with large boulevards and super tight alleyways, like that of Venezia. The streets sloped upward since the city was on a steep cliff. We were amazed and intimidated by this exotic city and felt insignificant, smaller than ants.

We continued through the winding streets, following behind the princess and the four horsemen. Everything was moving so fast.

We arrived at another stone gate, two stories in height. This was the gateway to the grand palace. We had to give up our weapons in order to see the sultan. Beyond the wall was the grand palace with gorgeous fountains and gardens.

The palace was framed with white marble and red sandstone. The palace had four onion-shaped domes and four large towers called minarets surrounding the center of the palace. Inside the gardens in front of the palace were multiple small pools of water with pink and white flowers floating on the surface. The exterior palace walls were engraved with the most magnificent gems, carved like mosaics. The gems were carved into the white marble in a floral design. The flowers were cut in that of bas-relief, in which the flowers protrude outward from the marble.

From the gardens, we entered the palace, walking into a large throne room. The throne room contained the most expensive wooden furniture. I doubted the Medicis could afford furniture this costly. The chalk-white walls of the throne room were lined with the most detailed carvings of flowers and landscapes, depicting deserts, mountains, and tropical islands in different panels. Amazing to think of the time and effort to construct this one room and bring these carvings on the walls to life.

Seated upon his throne at the center of the room was King Muzafar Shah, sultan of the extended Indies. He was dressed in long white robes with floral turquoise patterns and wore on his head a pure white, cylindrical turban.

Arij bowed before her father, embraced him, and then spoke to him in Arabic. The sultan was an older man; he was slender with tan skin, a gray beard, and a stern and piercing gaze. We waited for Arij to introduce us.

"I've heard of these kinds of kings" whispered Swift. "The kind of king who would cut your head off on a whim."

"Whose head?" whispered Faustino. "My head?"

"He's going to cut off Faustino's head?" said Zaragoza, concerned.

"What's wrong with Faustino's head?" I asked. "Other than the lack of a brain."

"I'll take your head clean off, Cosimo," said Faustino.

"I need my head," cried Jaipur. "Don't let him take my head."

Toro sighed and rolled his eyes. "He will not cut off anyone's head . . . for now."

"Quiet, all of you," demanded Gaspar.

The sultan turned to us after listening to his daughter. Arij looked at me and nodded her head. I hoped that was a good sign. The sultan stepped down from his elevated golden throne and opened his arms toward us. Toro bowed, and then we followed suit.

"Good day to all of you," said the sultan in fluent Spanish. "Please, lift your heads. You are my guests, and I welcome all of you as such. I see all of you have met my daughter, Princess Nur-al-Arij. Thank you for returning her to me. She seems to always be getting into trouble these days."

"Our pleasure, Your Grace," said Gaspar.

The sultan nodded with a smile. "Are you the captain?"

"Yes," replied Gaspar. "I am Captain Gaspar of the *Valencia*, sailing under the Spanish crown of King Charles V, and this is the remnant of my crew."

"Spain. That's a new one," said the sultan. "Tell me, Captain Gaspar of the *Valencia*, how did you get here?"

Gaspar told our story from the beginning in Seville, then explained our journey westward from Spain on behalf of King Charles of Spain. Gaspar further described the perils along our journey and how we were abandoned on the tip of this island due to a mutiny.

The sultan remained calm and quiet. Gaspar continued to explain our passage here through a river inside a cavern.

I couldn't keep my eyes open as I stood there listening to Gaspar. All of us looked terrible, struggling with exhaustion. After hearing about our long journey from Europe, the sultan remained quiet, resting his chin on his right hand.

The sultan then asked, "King Charles of Spain, correct?"

"Aye," replied Gaspar.

"I've been to Spain before. Seville and Andalusia."

"Long way from here."

"Indeed, it is," replied the sultan. "I traveled there with my friend Ibn Battuta when we were young men. Have you heard of Ibn Battuta before?"

"No, Your Majesty."

"Understandable. He was from Morocco."

"Beautiful land."

"Yes, it is. I pray the Christians will keep their wars in Spain and not in Morocco. Would you agree, Captain Gaspar?"

"Aye, peace is always preferable, no matter your religion."

"Wise man."

"Are you from here, as in Boubazar?"

"Me? No, I am from Cairo, placed here on orders by the Baghdad Caliphate."

"I see. We do what we must."

"We do. You and your men must be tired, especially that one on the ground."

We all turned around, and there, passed out on the floor, was Jaipur. Swift was trying to wake him.

"He . . . he's tired," said Swift.

"I'm sorry, Your Grace," said Gaspar. "It's been a long journey."

"True, true," said the sultan. "It's not every day one runs away from cannibals, right, Captain?"

"Only on Tuesdays, Your Majesty."

The sultan smiled and called his servants. By the grace of the Lord above, the sultan gave us a house outside of the palace to rest our heavy, tired eyes.

ACT II

Jaipur

Scene: A Stroll through Boubazar

ಀ

I OPENED MY eyes, feeling like I had drunk a tub of ale the night before. *Where was I? How did I get here? Did I drink something last tonight?*

I could hear the noises of the bustling city and the birds singing outside of my window. I rubbed the crust out of my eyes and propped myself up. I must have slept for at least a day.

"Took you a while to wake," said Toro, lying in the other bed and reading a scroll of some sort.

"What . . . How?" I spoke.

"You passed out in the throne room yesterday. Slept for a whole day, I'd say."

"That's right! The sultan! Did he . . . "

"We're fine."

"Toro, we almost died back there. *Died*," I said.

"Thou art alive," said Toro.

"Where should I begin?"

"Begin what?"

"What?!" I spoke.

"What?"

"What, as in the mutiny, cannibals, magma, Egyptian gates, fairies by the pool!"

Toro shook his head. "You need fresh air."

"I need to talk about it."

"Talk then."

"I can't talk to you when you have an attitude like that," I said.

"'Talk then.' Well, you never talk, so you wouldn't know what talking was, is, or should be."

Toro sighed, then forced a slight smile. "Better?"

"Aye, thank you."

"So, what's bothering you?"

"Toro, I thought Gaspar lost it, lost his mind. Then . . . where did that Egyptian hubbub come from? What about this island, this place?"

"Gaspar must have some connection to this island."

"That's what I thought . . . but how?"

"Why do the stars twinkle in the night sky?"

"That's irrelevant to our conversation, Toro," I stated.

"I mean, how would either you or I know why?"

"Right, we don't, so we need to find out why. And . . . and what of this sultan, this island?"

"You need fresh air," repeated Toro.

"Aye, fresh air might do me good."

"I want cheesecake," said Toro. "Let's go to the bazaar and find some."

"You have coins for such things?"

"The sultan granted us a modest sum of coins."

"Don't jest. I'm not in the mood."

"I don't joke."

"Where are the coins?"

Toro lifted up a brown bag and jingled it. "Here."

I cheered. "The sultan is not so bad after all."

"Told you not to fret," said Toro. "Let's go."

Toro and I made our way out of the two-story house while the rest of the crew was still fast asleep. It was morning, and dew collected on the grass gardens in front of the palace. It was a pleasant blue day.

The streets were alive with energy as shops opened their doors, horses clopped, and all sorts of people moved in all directions. I hadn't seen this many people since Seville. Was that a year ago? Could have been longer. Aye, longer.

I thought of my original home on Sumatra. It was night and day compared to this place, to this city. I didn't remember Islam having such an imprint on my village. Oh yes, I remembered now. Islam was spreading south to all of our islands.

I refused their religion—*refused* it—so they chained me and shipped me off. It was a Muslim trader, a slave trader, who sold me to Gaspar. In all honesty, I did not know Islam, Christianity, Judaism, or Hinduism at the time. I was just a rebellious boy caught in the wrong place at the wrong time. I did not want to think of such memories. Nay, not with a beautiful day out.

Toro and I continued down the main boulevard, admiring the change of scenery. The buildings were multiple stories high with arches, flat roofs, and colorful tents extending into the pathway. Toro could speak Arabic, which helped us maneuver with ease around the city.

"Is this what your own city, Timbuktu, looked like?" I asked Toro.

"No," replied Toro. "This is a magical city."

"What do ye mean by 'magical'?"

"What?"

"I said what do ye mean by 'magical'?"

"Can't be said in words. I *feel* it."

I thought for a moment. What did Toro mean by "magical"? For some reason, I loved this place. Perhaps that was the magic.

"Timbuktu must have had some magic, too," I said.

"It used to," said Toro. "Back then, it used to."

"Why? Did the magicians pack up and leave one day?" I joked.

"Enough questions about that," replied Toro sternly.

I left that topic there, not wanting to anger Toro.

We made it to the Grand Bazaar, which dazzled with colors and activity. We walked under large arches held up by chalk-white columns, draped in red cloth. I grew excited for this magical bazaar. On all corners of the market, brokers reached out to Toro and me, calling out aggressively, wanting us to buy their wares. It was a competitive marketplace to say the least.

As we passed by the colored stalls, one broker speaking to me in Arabic tried to sell me a long, ivory spyglass.

"What's he saying, Toro?" I asked.

"He said the spyglass could see anyone at any time if you look through it," said Toro. "Nonsense. Keep walking."

Another broker approached me, saluted me, and spoke in Arabic to me. The broker had a big belly and large beard and carried a pink, teal, and cream carpet.

"I don't need a carpet, as beautiful as it may be," I said.

The broker continued to talk into Toro's ear.

Then, Toro said, "The man claims the carpet can fly." Aggravated, he then barked to the broker in Arabic.

"Fly!" I repeated.

Toro shook his head. "Another scam. Pay him no mind."

We then approached a third stall filled with colorful silks, clothes, robes, and hats.

"You need new clothes," I said.

"What's wrong with the ones I have on?" inquired Toro. He was wearing brown, simple rags, full of dirt and old sweat. It smelled bad and looked like a blood stain was on the shoulder, too. I smelled my own clothes Oh, they smelled very bad. We *both* needed new clothes.

"What isn't wrong with those?" I replied, holding up a red turban. "Try this on."

The persistent broker chimed in. "Oh, yes. The finest silk in all of Arabia. Please, try on." He was a short, stout man with a large belly and a beard. After a moment, I realized the broker spoke Portuguese.

"You speak Portuguese?" I asked.

"And Spanish," replied the broker. "I've traveled to many lands in order to sell my wares."

"Incredible," I replied. "Try this on, Toro."

"I'm not wearing a turban," said Toro.

"Give it a feel. You might like it," I replied with a smile as I offered him the red turban.

Toro sighed, took the turban from my hand, and wrapped it around his head. "How do I look?"

The shopkeeper and I both stared at Toro, judging his appearance with delicate taste and discretion.

"You look like the sultan!" jeered the broker.

A slight smile grew on Toro's face. Feeling confident and prestigious, he felt the turban upon his head. "Do I look like the sultan?"

I nodded with a concentrated stare. Then, I shook my head. "It looks terrible, *terrible*. Take it off before someone sees you with it on."

Toro rolled his eyes, grunted, and took off the turban. "I want my cheesecake."

We continued to try on a few clothes until we each found our perfect full attire.

"How much for both of us?" I asked.

"Five silverlings," replied the broker.

"Five silverlings for this?" exclaimed Toro.

"My good man, two silverlings is reasonable," I replied.

"Four silverlings," said the broker.

"Not for four," said Toro. "You are mad for four."

"Two and half dinars," I said.

"This is the finest silk in the land!" said the broker.

"I don't care if the sultan himself wore it. It's not worth four silverlings," said Toro.

"Look how good you look though," said the broker.

"Not for four silverlings," said Toro.

"Fine, fine. Three and a half silverlings," said the broker.

"Three!" I exclaimed.

"Ah, deal," said the broker.

Toro and I replaced our rags with new outfits—pants, belts, shirts, bags, and everything in between. After our bargain and more roaming, we found a cheesecake stall.

Toro was delighted. His eyes flickered like a child at the smell of the sweet treat.

The cheesecake was yellow with red swirls on top of it. Toro was in heaven as we both took a bite.

"Such good cheesecake," said Toro with a smile.

Swift

Scene: Waltz of the Grand Bazaar

⟨∞⟩

O UTSIDE MY WINDOW, I could hear horses clopping on the stone pavement and chatter among the residents. I sat in a nice wooden chair, feeling the wind brush through the balcony of my room. It was a bright day in the late afternoon. I took a deep breath, closed my eyes, stretched my arms, and exhaled. Cosimo and I shared the room. I wanted to be quiet, for he was still asleep.

"Shadow!" yelled Cosimo from his dream.

A jolt ran through my body. Horrified by the sudden scream, I yelled, "What in the name!"

Cosimo was pulled from the dream, eyes wide open, breathing heavy.

"Caused me to have a heart attack," I said.

"I did?" said Cosimo.

"Yes, yes, you did, screaming about some shadow. What's so scary about a shadow?"

"I am not sure."

"Got the blood pumping, that's for sure," I said. "We must have slept for a whole day."

"I needed it."

"I need some food. What if we get some food?"

"We need to talk."

"About where to get food?" I replied.

"No, no, about where we are, what's going on—everything and anything in between."

"'Everything' is a large topic."

"First off, the *Valencia*."

"Aye?"

"We have no ship, nothing to trade with, and not a way home."

"We'll find a way back to Europe," I said, nonchalant. My eyes caught sight of a bright red apple on a table. I picked it up and took a bite. "I'm not worried."

Cosimo laughed. "I'm glad you're not worried."

"You worry too much."

"How did the sultan know Spanish, eh?"

"These people are smart, world traveled, well read."

"Thou art missing the point. If they know Spanish, I bet the sultan knows Portuguese."

"Oh, and you think if he, the sultan, knows Portuguese, then he's come in contact with the Portuguese, and the Portuguese have been here?"

"Not 'have been,' but are currently. Now!"

"The sultan knew Spanish, as well," I said, matter of fact.

"True. Something inside of me worries, worries that we weren't the first Europeans here on this island. And if the Portuguese were or are here…"

"Why does that matter if the Portuguese have been here?"

"Matter? The Portuguese are hunting us, hunting the *Valencia*, hunting Gaspar, a traitor to their people. Don't forget, Gaspar is Portuguese sailing under a Spanish flag for Spain, not Portugal. On top of that, the Portuguese had been to the Spice Islands far before Spain. Who's to say the Portuguese are not here now? The trip around Africa is quicker than across the Atlantic, you know."

I looked at Cosimo, puzzled. "Hmm, that's another good point. What can we do then?"

"I thought about it."

"And?"

"I think we should ask the sultan to loan us a ship filled with spices and men. We can promise he will be repaid in full by King Charles V of Spain."

"Good idea," I stated, thinking for a moment while taking a bite of my apple. "The princess, aye, the princess could help us with the sultan."

"The . . . the princess? I don't know. Wait, why are you giving me that look?"

"Not my look, but the look you gave the princess yesterday and the look she gave to you," I replied, excited. "I remember that now, yes."

Cosimo started to blush and turned his head away. "I have no idea what you are talking about."

"Of course you do. I saw it. She saw it. We all saw it. As obvious as the light from the great lamp in the sky."

"What look did she look?"

"The look of love."

"No, I mean, you saw her look at me?"

I nodded. "With her majestic bright eyes, flaunting those brows at you the whole time. If what you said was true about the Portuguese, Arij could help us, Cosimo. She could help you."

"You really think she was looking at me?" asked Cosimo.

"I don't think. I *know*."

A huge smile grew on Cosimo's face, for Cupid had struck the bottom of his bosom.

"She was beautiful, the most beautiful," said Cosimo.

"Her eyes were brighter than the Pole Star," I remarked.

"I may never want to leave if . . . if . . ." said Cosimo.

"Let's not get ahead of ourselves," I added.

"Right, right," said Cosimo. "We'll take things slow then."

"Good, but don't be too slow. Then, she'll slip through your fingers."

"Can't let that happen. Nay, I must hurry."

"No, no, no. Have you ever done this before?"

"Done what?"

"Date."

"I don't know the date of today."

I shook my head. "No, date. As in a date with a woman."

"Oh, no. I always wanted to, but the monastery—that friar, evil man he was—wouldn't let me."

"Sounds terrible."

"It was. I had to travel across the world to escape it."

"You here now, and in order to be seen by a princess, you must look like royalty."

"My family was royalty in Tuscany, or so I was told."

"Then why were you in a monastery?"

"Family put me there."

"Why?"

"I don't know. I was left there at a young age. It doesn't matter why. Gaspar helped me escape . . . Gaspar . . . "

"You are thinking about Gaspar and that Egyptian wall, eh?"

"That and other things. Gaspar knows something, something deeper. I need to find out more about this island."

"True, but I think it is more important to make a good impression on Arij and the sultan. I can't rely on Gaspar to bring me home back to my love. You know this. We ourselves need to broker a deal with the sultan. It's our only way home."

"I see," said Cosimo. "How do you suppose I impress Arij?"

"You need to look like royalty," I replied. "We need new clothes, a shave, the works."

"I would like that, yet we don't have any money."

I laughed. "The sultan left us a few silverlings, enough to splurge."

"Good man!" said Cosimo. "By God, I might have a chance to impress her. You think it would? You believe this could work?"

"Worth a shot. What do we have to lose?"

"Our heads," said Cosimo.

"They do say love is a bitter fight," I added.

"Who's 'they'?"

"Me. Got the scars to prove it," I stated. "Come, let's get to the bazaar."

"Wait, wait. But Gaspar?"

"How about this: you focus on Arij, and let me handle Gaspar."

"What are you going to do?"

"I'll follow him later today. See what I can find."

"Okay, Swift," said Cosimo.

At that moment, it seemed a huge weight was lifted off of Cosimo's shoulders. Did the thought of his leaving without giving Arij the age-old sailor's try worry him? He was stressed. I was stressed. I could sympathize with him, with a man in love. Was he in love with Arij? Cosimo looked like a man in love. I knew the look quite well. Why were there always obstacles with love, obstacles like the mysterious Gaspar, the Portuguese, the sultan, religion, race, distance, and sickness? Yet, in my heart I believed that true, honest love destroyed all barriers.

We left our room and went on our way. None of the crewmen were around the house. Everyone wanted to venture into the city.

The streets were bursting with energy and life. We wandered through winding alleyways, passing people of all shapes, colors, and sizes. We encountered an incredible mosque with four towers made of red sandstone with floral carvings painted throughout it, and the roof was a white, onion-shaped dome. The design was different, exotic in a sense, though it was beautiful, unlike anything I had ever encountered. I could hear chanting and singing from inside the mosque.

We continued to wander aimlessly through the streets for at least an hour or two until we stumbled upon the bathhouse. It was a large, gray stone building with a circular dome at the top, nestled deep in the heart of the city.

Cosimo and I paid the man at the front door and walked into this heaven of heat and steam. We took our time inside the large circular pool. I melted into the hot water, feeling its warm healing effects on my muscles. I felt the tension throughout my body dissipate.

While we were in the bath, a few of the locals tried to exchange words with Cosimo and me, but our language barrier blocked us from really communicating past a simple smile and head nod.

Next to the bathhouse was a quaint barber shop. We entered, and both of us got a nice haircut and a beard trim. The barber did a good job. He tried to communicate with us, but once again, we did not speak Arabic.

At one point the barber, as he was cutting Cosimo's hair, pulled out a scroll with the zodiac calendar. The barber pointed at the calendar in a worried manner though we could not understand him. Cosimo and I thought he was a wild figure. The barber could not communicate his point to us, so he gave Cosimo a piece of rope.

"Rope?" questioned Cosimo.

The barber nodded, and I shrugged. He was a strange fellow. We took the piece of rope, paid him, and went on our way.

Cosimo looked much better after a haircut. Before, his face and features were hidden by his long black hair, but now I could see his well-defined face more clearly. We both looked more presentable, clean, and proper.

"She will fall fast for you," I replied.

"I can only hope," replied Cosimo.

We strolled along the boulevard, and we came upon a huge festival at the center of the city. All sorts of people were circumambulating a wooden scaffolding at least twelve stories high, supported by an array of columns painted with buzzing insects, vibrant flowers, and winged birds. In front of the scaffolding, men and women dressed in red robes juggled lit torches and blew fire from their mouths.

Next to the jugglers were six or so mimes, mimicking sounds and expressions and cracking silent jokes. The laughing crowd loved it all, dazzled by the festival.

To the right of the scaffolding was a massive tent, larger than any tent I had ever seen. The tent was painted in a striped pattern of turquoise blue and golden brown. We followed the crowd to the tent, and inside was a large, circular stage made of sand, surrounded by wooden seats, like the Flavian Colosseum. Cosimo and I took our seats and waited in awe. The show commenced with the sounds of exotic Far Eastern music played from a collection of stringed instruments by men and women in red robes.

Then, a lion appeared before us, tamed by a man in a sparkling purple robe. I had never seen a lion before but had only heard of them from sailors, who heard of them from other sailors, and so forth. The beast roared with great might. The crowd loved it. I loved it.

Next in the act, a rope was extended from two distant platforms high above the sand stage. Two women in bright red robes climbed up a ladder toward the platforms. My palms began to sweat as I watched the two women climb up, then balance themselves on the slender rope without caution. This was an incredible feat of balance. The two women did numerous tricks, jumping on the rope and holding on to it by one hand. The show ended with two large monkeys playing tricks on one another, throwing food, and swinging above our heads. The monkeys were hilarious in the act, such a wonderful show. Rose would have loved it. She loved entertainment. I wondered what she was doing at that moment. She must have been cooking or walking. She loved to walk around London. The sickness, that terrible sickness, made it hard for her to walk. With this new money, I could pay for the treatment to cure her.

I will be back soon, Rose.

Cosimo and I left the festival and walked through the streets, talking and reminiscing on the show, until we stumbled upon an extravagant gate with an arch painted red and white. Here it was, the Grand Bazaar.

The bazaar was a long hallway inside a curved stone building, filled with wares of every kind. The moment I entered the bazaar, I could smell the exotic spices, foods, and sweet fragrances of the Far East. The floor of the exchange was chaotic, fast, and loud as hundreds of trades occurred by the minute. Cosimo and I browsed the stalls. Brokers from all angles aggressively approached and yelled at us, demanding our business.

One broker approached Cosimo and me, smiling widely and showing his teeth molded with purple gems. I thought they were sapphires for a moment, but never had I seen a gem of that color or as vibrant. The broker wore a long purple robe filled with golden trinkets. The broker started to rattle off words in different languages at us but then astonished us as he spoke Spanish. He saw by our facial expressions that we understood Spanish. The broker then said, "Good men, good men from faraway lands, gaze at my trinkets and ask for your souls' desires."

Cosimo and I stared at one another with apprehension. Then, I said, "What do you sell?"

"Anything and everything under the sun and stars," said the broker with a wide smile. "What might interest you? Perhaps a gift for a loved one back home or for one ye seek to love here?"

"Arij! I could give a gift to Arij for saving us," said Cosimo.

"Not a bad idea," I said, "though I say we wait on that."

"Why?" asked Cosimo. "Best show her my good intentions."

"Arij seems like the kind of woman who's tired of receiving gifts from newly introduced men. Best be different, unique. Let her get to know you before the gift and not the gift before you."

"Nonsense! Women adore gold, praise gold, love gold," said the broker. "Trust me. Women choose the man with the most gold, not the most love."

"I have heard that before" said Cosimo. "How much for—"

"Stop, stop," I interjected. "We are not after women who put gold before love, nor do we encourage that gesture. I assure you, Arij has enough gold and wants no more of it."

"You have a point, Swift," said Cosimo.

The broker laughed. "Women do not like to sacrifice. On the contrary, women want splendor and luxury. I have this necklace here. It was once worn by a queen, a priceless piece. But I could give it to you for a good price."

"This does look luxurious and beautiful," said Cosimo.

"Your wares are fine, fine indeed, but we do not need gold, at least not now. Come. Let's go, Cosimo," I said.

"Wait, wait!" said the broker. "What about this special serum?" He held up a vial full of a black liquid.

"That's a peculiar thing. What does it do?" asked Cosimo.

"Ugh, Cosimo," I remarked, frustrated.

"The power to make any woman fall in love with you," said the broker. "All one must do is mix your own blood into the black liquid, then drop it on her tongue."

"You speak of a potion," said Cosimo.

"Nay, this is a chemical solution," he said.

"But it's not our solution," I remarked.

"Well, I'm not into potions or solutions, but it's an interesting liquid nonetheless," said Cosimo. "Good day, sir."

"I see. Yes, not a problem," said the broker, smiling, as he closed his robe. "Maybe in the future."

We nodded at the broker and continued down the crowded path.

"What you need is not gold," I said.

"Then what do I need?" asked Cosimo.

"To look presentable."

"I am put together, inside and out."

"Not with those old, gross rags, you aren't."

After a few minutes of walking, I saw big Toro and young Jaipur eating a treat next to one of the stalls. It seemed they also wanted to check out the sights and sounds of the city.

"Look," I pointed out. "Jaipur and Toro."

"Ah, looks like cheesecake. I love cheesecake," said Cosimo.

We moved through the crowd and surprised our two friends. They were looking rather extravagant in their new clothes. We all greeted one another with a hearty hello.

"New clothes, eh?" I spoke. "I like your shirt, Toro."

"I liked my old one better," growled Toro.

"You will grow to like that one more," stated Jaipur.

"Could you show us where you got them?" I spoke.

"Down there lies the stall. We'll come with you if you want," replied Jaipur.

"Please do," said Cosimo. "I need someone there with style like Toro."

"I bet you do," remarked Toro. "I bet you do."

We walked over to the stall and outfitted ourselves with the finest silks and leather the broker offered. I bought two or three outfits. Nothing too fancy. The broker tried to upcharge me, but I bargained him down to a reasonable price. Cosimo was still trying on clothes. I had to make sure his look was spot-on in case the princess might want a piece of him. We patiently waited for Cosimo outside the dressing room.

"What's taking him so long?" asked Toro, agitated.

"Have to make sure his look is spot on," I stated.

"Who cares?" said Toro.

"The princess cares," I remarked.

"The princess?" questioned Jaipur. "Wait, Cosimo wants the princess? The sultan's daughter, the princess?"

"Everyone wants a princess these days," said Toro.

"You better hope he gets her, too. Might be our way home," I said.

"Relying on love is worse than relying on Gaspar," said Toro.

"I beg to differ," I said.

"Oh, so Cosimo and the princess. This is our plan to leave the island if Gaspar doesn't work out?" said Jaipur.

"You have a better one?" I spoke.

"No, he does not," said Toro.

"I do, thank you very much," said Jaipur.

"Do tell," I said, eagerly.

"We could . . . uh . . . " said Jaipur, eyes darting to Toro and me.

"We could, we could ... "

Cosimo came out of the fitting room dressed in an orange and teal robe.

"How do I look?" asked Cosimo as he turned around.

"You better hope your head doesn't roll," said Toro.

"What?" asked Cosimo, confused.

"You look splendid, like royalty," I said. "What do you think, Jaipur?"

"My head?" said Jaipur. "My head is here on my neck. You speak nonsense, Toro."

"Best hope I do," said Toro.

"Jaipur," I said, aggravated.

"Aye?" he replied.

"Look there at Cosimo. Doesn't he look splendid?"

"Oh, yes, Cosimo. I'm sorry," said Jaipur.

"Do I look like a prince?" asked Cosimo.

"You look, you look ... " stuttered Jaipur.

"Yes?" said Cosimo.

"You look ... I need another opinion, a veteran, one with seasoned taste," said Jaipur.

"The shopkeeper?" I spoke.

"No," replied Jaipur. "Toro."

We all looked to Toro, who was standing with his usual stoic expression.

"Me?" Toro pointed to himself.

"What do you think, Toro?" asked Cosimo. "Is it too much?"

"For what?" said Toro.

"For the princess," said Cosimo.

"For the princess?" repeated Toro, confused looking to each of us for an answer.

"Aye, the princess," I added.

"You can't be serious," said Toro.

"Love is serious, Toro," said Jaipur. "You should know this being old and ... old and all."

Toro grunted and rolled his eyes. "You are telling *me* about love? What do you know of love?"

"It's not about me," replied Jaipur. "We're talking about Cosimo."

"He met her yesterday!" said Toro.

"Time does not exist in the world of love," said Jaipur.

"I second that," I remarked, confidently.

"So, how do I look? Like a prince?" asked Cosimo, tapping his foot.

Toro shook his head, then glanced at Cosimo with a serious glance and shrugged. "You three will get me killed, but . . . you look like a prince from what I see."

"Sold!" I jeered.

With that one word known across the world, a word of trade, a word known in every language—*sold!*—the exchange was done. We gathered our things and walked toward the exit.

As we were walking out, we encountered one of the biggest stalls near the exit. Out on display in front of the stall were multiple straw baskets filled to the brim with spices of all kinds. No emotion could describe the feeling as we saw and smelled cloves, cinnamon, nutmeg, and mace. Spices once a world away were now in our grasp. We picked up some of the cloves, smelled them, and touched them, thinking that after so many months of hardship, here they were. Here were the spices, the keys to our wealth and our freedom.

I could have cried. These spices were the reason I had traveled across the world, the way to pay for my love, to save my love. Gaspar may be crazy, but he kept true to his promise: he brought us to the spices, to the Spice Islands. All that was left for us to do was bring them back to Europe.

"The spices are here. They are here!" yelled Jaipur. "We must buy in bulk!"

"Not here," said Toro.

"It's here before us. What do ye mean?" said Jaipur.

"Toro is right," I said. "We go to the sultan for a deal. We need a ship and a loan. How else would we return with the spices?"

"Fair point," said Jaipur.

We agreed that a deal with the sultan was our best shot at returning home with plentiful spices. We ended our time at the bazaar on that note.

Outside of the bazaar, the streets were packed with people flocking to the city center for the festival.

"Where is the crowd going?" asked Jaipur.

"It's a festival," said Cosimo. "There are tons of things to see up the street."

"Did we ever figure out what the festival is for?" I spoke.

"Nay, never did," said Cosimo.

"I love festivals and parties," said Jaipur.

"Toro," I said.

"Aye?" replied Toro.

"Could you ask someone what the festival is for?" I spoke.

Toro nodded, then spoke to a woman next to us, exchanging a few words in Arabic. The woman pointed to the palace in the distance. Toro thanked her.

"And?" inquired Jaipur.

"It's the princess's birthday tomorrow," said Toro.

"The princess Arij?" asked Cosimo.

"Yes," said Toro.

"Arij should have told us about her birthday," said Jaipur. "I hope we are invited to her party if she has one. Could be a good time to talk to the sultan. A good time for a deal, eh?"

Cosimo and I looked at one another, thinking the same thought: this might shake things up a bit. A large applause and hollering started behind us. We turned around to see the excitement. It was a strong man dressed in a marvelous white robe. He rode a black steed and was waving at the people while leading a parade of slaves and armed men. He looked like Islamic royalty.

"Who's that guy?" asked Jaipur.

"A prince," stated Toro.

"Must be here for the princess," said Jaipur.

"I would say so," said Cosimo.

"Say so," I sighed. "You still got a shot. Aye, you got a shot."

Princess Nur-al-Arij

Scene: The Sultan's Surprise

᠙᠊᠊᠊᠊᠊᠙

ALLAH DROPPED SEVEN Western men right in front of me. What were the odds of that happening? The celestial spheres work in such strange ways. As much as I had read, I would still never be able to comprehend Allah's ways. I had the choice to run away or save him. Why did I save Cosimo?

I walked around my room inside the palace, pacing back and forth on the cold stone floor. Why . . . why . . . that feeling in my heart . . . the flutter of a butterfly. To me, he had glowed on that bank. I had felt it, felt the flutter. I couldn't stop thinking about him, about his walk, his cute eyes, his humble smile. What was that feeling? Was it love? Was that what love felt like, or did my feelings trick me? How could I love a man after only a day? Love, love . . . You are more mysterious to me than Allah.

I could never love a man who was not a Muslim. Allah would forbid it. Yes . . . no . . . *Would* he forbid it? Allah had placed him before me. I prayed to him, asked him for my love to come. I could see Cosimo's side, learn his beliefs. I could love him for those differences. Different . . . I am tired of the same, bored of the same. What if I wanted—*needed*—different. I was different.

No, he was not royalty. My father would never allow it. He never allowed me to do anything other than stay behind the palace walls. My father was by the book; tradition was king. I was tired of tradition, tired of "by the book." I was tired of what he wanted for me. Nay, I wanted what I wanted, not what he wanted. I was tired of these walls both around the palace and my heart. Why couldn't I love a Western man, live beyond the walls, live in freedom? Allah put Cosimo here for a reason, for my soul told me thus. I needed to listen and trust my heart, wherever it took me.

There was a knock on my chamber door.

"Princess," said the servant. "Your father would like to see you. Come along."

"What for?" I asked.

"He did not say."

"Very well. Thank you."

What could my father want? Why does he call on me?

I hurried along the corridor, down a flight of stairs, and into the throne room where my father sat upon his golden throne.

"Yes, Father?" I asked, approaching him.

"Princess, my daughter, so beautiful art thou," replied the sultan, with a smile.

"Thank you, Father."

"Of course, do you know what tomorrow is?"

I laughed a little to myself. "My birthday."

"Yes, your birthday. Twenty-six years old. Do you know what a birthday needs?"

"What?"

"Presents and a party. A grand party."

I was unsure about a party. I hated when much attention was on me.

My father frowned. "What is the matter, my dear? I thought you would love a party."

"I do love parties. It's just . . . not when the attention is on me."

"My perfect daughter, the whole kingdom of Boubazar wants to see you, see your beauty. If only your mother could see you now, see how beautiful you are."

"But my mother is not here."

"Arij, I promise your party will be everything you want and more."

"Would you invite the Spaniards?"

"It's your birthday. You may choose whomever, but why?"

"I would like something different there."

"I have invited someone special for you."

"Who?"

"Prince Sikander, that's who."

"Oh, Father. I don't like him. He's pompous, prideful, and kind of mean. He's not my type."

"His father is the vizier of our neighboring kingdom. It would be best if you did like him. I believe over time he would grow on you."

I sighed. "If you think so."

"It's important we establish strong bonds with other kingdoms, Arij."

"Not at the expense of my love."

"We all have our duty, granted by the almighty Allah."

"What if Allah chooses another love for me, not Sikander?"

"Allah guides me, grants me wisdom, as he did with King Solomon, Arij. I know what's best for you, for our kingdom, to keep you safe."

"I feel like what's best for me is outside these palace walls."

"Nonsense. Your duty is here, not abroad. This is the real world, Arij, not one of those fantasy worlds you read about all day. It's time to grow up, assume your duty."

"I like those fantasy worlds."

"Yet you live in this world. That will be all for today."

"Yes, Father."

Gaspar

Scene: Mysterious Pas de Deux

⟨⟨⟨⟩⟩⟩

"**T**HE SERPENT IS the spirit of the universal world. The lapis is the spirit of the heavens, prepped by fire salt, drunk from the morning's dew teardrop. I prepare my transformation. Here before me, chiseled on this wooden door, are two serpents devouring one another from head to tail, tail to head. In order to achieve the lapis, follow the tail, ignite the flame, circulate, distill, and condense. King of the heavens, bring thy Great Work forth. Transform me. Give me the lapis from the hands of Gabriel."

I approached an isolated house, tucked away in the far recesses of the city. Chiseled upon the door to the house was a symbol of two snakes eating one another, a symbol of material transformation.

I knocked on the door, and on the third knock, the door opened itself to a dark room with no one to be found. The wooden floors creaked as I walked in. The room was constructed in the shape of a square surrounded with a long wooden countertop and shelves. Laid out on a table next to the countertop was an aligned skeleton of a snake with a string connecting its bones from the vertebrae to the head.

The shelves were lined with numerous bottles and jars filled with a wide variety of questionable things preserved in a green liquid—exotic flowers, plants, insects, butterflies, centipedes, and other strange insects I had never seen before.

Each of the bottles was marked in both Arabic and Latin. Next to the bottles of natural science were smaller containers filled with different liquid properties of all different colors. I picked one up and noticed dust from the bottle on my fingers. I blew it off, opened the bottle, and sniffed it. "Sulphur."

A woman came from the shadows, an attractive, tan, slender woman who was no more than forty years old. She was dressed in a purple robe that also covered her face though I could still see her eyes. She spoke to me in Arabic first, but I replied in Latin after seeing some of the bottles marked in that language.

"Do you speak my tongue?" I asked.

"Yes," she replied, resting her arm on the counter. "Latin, I do. What brings you here, European?"

"I'm looking for something."

"Travel far you do for something so vague."

"I need properties."

She smiled, pulled herself up, and sat on the front counter. "What are you making?" Her brown eyes glistened.

"A mixture."

"My properties are rare and expensive. Very expensive."

I took out a brown bag tied in a knot at the top, jingled it, and placed it on the counter.

"Gold. More than enough."

Her eyes widened when she felt the weight of the purse. "What properties do you need?"

"Tartar, sulphide, sal ammonia, salt-petre, alum, and vitriol."

She raised her brow, "Lapis philosophorum?"

"Perhaps. Perhaps not."

Her jaw muscle flexed, debating my order. "What is your name?"

"Gaspar."

"Gaspar," she repeated to herself.

"What is your name, mistress?" I asked.

"Peri," she replied.

"Will you help me, Peri?" I asked.

"Dangerous ye are, Gaspar."

"The world is a dangerous place."

She lifted up her dress, exposing her toned thighs. "Seems you want to know where to go, where to find the gate."

"Yes, that would help."

Peri looked into my eyes, raising her long black brows at me. She took off the cloth around her face, revealing her defined cheekbones and sumptuous lips. She then grabbed my neck, curled her hand around it, and stared into my soul. "The stars want you."

"I followed them here," I said.

"You hold a secret, a dark secret. The lapis, the shadow follows you."

"We all have secrets."

"One can make the lapis only if chosen by the celestial spheres."

"I could make the lapis with the properties I requested."

She laughed, pulling her hand from my neck, and walked over to the shelves filled with concoctions and materials.

"Do you know where the teardrop lies?" asked Peri as she fiddled with one of the containers.

"I have an idea where," I said.

"I know where the gate lies."

"Show me."

Smiling, she continued to play with the bottle in her hand. "For what in return?"

"Gold."

"I don't want your gold for this."

"What do you want?"

"You know what I want."

"Do I?"

"A drop from the eternal gold."

"To show me the way?"

"Yes."

"Deal."

"Give me time to prepare."

"I don't have much time."

"You have enough time for this," she said as she wrapped her leg around my own, placing her slender, arched back into my hand. She whispered into my ear, "Come back tomorrow, and I'll show you the way."

"Good," I said.

"Be warned, Gaspar. Few ever return from the transformation."

"I'll keep that in mind."

"I hope so," she replied with a smile.

Zaragoza

Scene: Dialogue of Zaragoza and Faustino

⟨∞⟩

F AUSTINO AND I shared a room in the house. Faustino was the last and only true Spaniard out of the bunch. I was troubled and had no idea what I was going to do without a ship and nothing to trade. I had to leave this place as fast as I could. I was out of my element. It was only a matter of time until the others—Swift, Gaspar, Cosimo, Toro, and Jaipur—turned on me. I could feel it, sense it in the air.

What if they offer me up to the sultan? What if they say I am mutinous or hate Muslims. Oh, the endless possibilities. Wait, wait, I could supersede them, go the sultan myself before they—those damn savages—turn on me, or I could run away. Where could I run to? I have no money and cannot speak the language. I must see the sultan; he's my only chance. I'll tell the sultan that Gaspar went mad and the crew disposed of him. What of me though? How did I end up with them? I could say I was caught in the wrong place at the wrong time. We were running low on provisions, and the crew was forced to dispose of Gaspar and his loyalists. Yes, that might just work. What evidence do I have of my claims? None. Zero evidence. The sultan wouldn't listen to me, but to whom could I go? I need someone powerful enough to trust me, to take my word as truth, and convince the sultan to behead these miscreants before they do the same to me. Perhaps I could use Faustino to assist me.

We sat in our white room. Faustino was looking around the room, opening the cabinets and checking the shelves for any type of alcohol. It was early in the morning.

"The sultan," I said. "If not today, he will one day cut my head off. Rest assured."

"Why you say that?" asked Faustino as he looked through a cabinet.

"Let me ask you this," I said.

"Aye?"

"Can we trust the others?"

"Who?"

"You know, the others. Swift, Gaspar, Toro, Jaipur, and Cosimo."

"Cosimo." Faustino groaned. "If he says one more thing to me, one more thing . . . "

"That's how I feel about all of them."

Faustino laughed. "Not hard to see that."

"We need to do something, Faustino, or you will never return home."

"I am doing something. I am about to daydrink."

"What if we did a little more than drink, eh?"

"Say we did."

"If we did, we could broker a deal with one of these Muslims, get a ship, fill it with spices, and head east back to Seville, only you and I."

"Gaspar might not like that idea."

"Don't say his name. He's the reason we're stranded here. We could leave them, Faustino, and go on our own. I could talk to the sultan, explain our situation, tell him the truth. See what I am saying?"

"I am indifferent to the matter."

"Indifferent? What do you mean indifferent?"

"I've thought about it. About Gaspar."

"And?"

"I believe Gaspar's cooking something up, something gold related."

"What does that mean? Gaspar doesn't cook."

"Not physically cook."

"One can only physically cook."

"No, no. I meant Gaspar has plans, secret plans. For the Lord's sake, he read an Egyptian stone wall covered with paintings of gold."

"Means nothing."

"Maybe. Maybe not. All I know is that I want to be there when he finds this gold—wherever or whatever gold it may be."

"Gold? What gold? We came here for spices, for exploration, to spread Christianity to the savages, for the good of Spain."

Faustino laughed under his breath. "You and I came here for the sole reason to exploit. Your lies work not on me. Please do not try."

"Lies? I have never lied to you."

Faustino smiled. "Neither have I lied to you or myself."

I bit my tongue as I thought to myself. I was insulted, insulted by this low-class rat. Who did he think he was, telling me I was a liar? I did not lie. I did what was best for the king, even if it required me to make immoral decisions. The Lord above understands my position. Court politics, war, and love were outside morality. Nay, I was not a liar. I only did my job, and I was great at what I did. I must find a court player in Boubazar, one who understands, one who wants to move ahead in life, one who could help me. Faustino was useless, a low-class peasant.

I calmed myself down, letting out a deep exhale. Then, I said with a smile, "Do what you think is best."

"Plan on it," said Faustino.

"I'll be back," I said.

"Where are you going?"

"Look around a bit, cook something up," I said and turned on my heel out of the room.

Gaspar

Scene: Dialogue of Gaspar and the Sultan

෮ᨪᨩ෮

T HE SULTAN ASKED me to enjoy some fruit juice in one of his guest houses next to the palace. We sat in an open-air room with a balcony overlooking all of Boubazar. It was a chalk-white room filled with expensive furniture and majestic silk carpets. The walls and balcony were draped with orange and teal cloths. We lounged on a plump red couch.

"Ever seen a view like this?" asked the sultan as he rested his elbow on the arm of the couch, staring across Boubazar.

I took a sip of the fruit juice. The liquid was hot, hotter than I expected. It burnt my tongue. The juice smelled of pine and had a piquant flavor, layered with a spice of ginger.

"I've never tasted a drink like this," I stated with a smile.

"That taste, the taste of exotic spices, is why you came here, is it not?"

"Indeed, it is."

The sultan smelled the hot liquid, breathed it in through his nose, closed his eyes, and drank it. "Cardamon, ginger, mace, cloves, and cinnamon—spices the world desires. How does it feel to be near them, smell them, taste them?"

"I feel nothing until I have them."

The sultan stared at the drink. "What drives a man across the world for this simple ingredient, for a spice?"

"Power."

"Ah, good answer. Power. This . . . this thing . . . this flavor provides power, stability, status, but it also brings forth war, destruction, and enemies."

"Yes."

"Yes, it does. My island, my people know this far too well."

"I do not want to bring war, Your Majesty."

"What do you want to bring, Captain?"

"Prosperity."

The sultan laughed under his breath as if he'd heard that answer before far too many times. "Prosperity. Let me ask you this: what would you do if I gave you and your king prosperity?"

"Is my majesty asking what I would do with great wealth?"

"Yes."

"I would buy my own freedom and my family's freedom."

"Are you not a free man, Captain?"

"No man is truly free until he obtains financial freedom, free of any king, tax, or debtors."

"Would my spices accomplish this? Give you your freedom?"

"Won't know until I return to Spain with a ship filled with spices."

"A reasonable answer. So what would you give me in return for a ship filled with spices?"

"A trade agreement with King Charles V of Spain."

The sultan laughed aloud. "Why would I need that?"

"Why *wouldn't* you need it?"

"I have better offers elsewhere."

"What offer is better than a newly discovered western route through the New World, charted by my own hand. Only I know the way."

"Ah, good point."

"I've proven the western route exists. With it, Spain will become one of the strongest powers in the world—richer than Portugal, Venezia, France, or England."

"Do you still have the charts?"

"I do."

The sultan paused for a moment, quiet. A light glimmered in his eyes. I took another sip of the fruit juice.

"I want to trust you, Captain Gaspar," said the sultan. "I want to, though I am having a hard time doing so."

"I understand your precautions, Your Grace," I replied.

"Are you hiding something from me, Captain?"

"No."

"If you are, I will punish you and your crew in the worst possible way. I will not let harm come to my people."

"Harm shall not come to them."

The sultan stared into my eyes. "Today, I cannot align with you or your king, for a mystery, a shadow sits behind your eyes. I need time."

"I see."

"What I will do is send my own emissary to your king in Spain. You and your crew will lead my emissary through the New World back to Spain. If your charts are true and your words are honest, then a deal will be struck with King Charles upon arrival."

"A fine deal. Would we return to Spain with spices?"

"If my emissary returns to me with good news, then I shall henceforth give King Charles all the spices he needs."

"But, sire," I said. "That voyage would take years, many years. Worse, my crew and I would never see those spices or profit from them. Our troubles would have been for nothing if we return empty handed."

"Nay, your troubles would have been for the prosperity of Spain, as you said."

"For Spain."

"Yes, for Spain, for your king. You are here for Spain, for King Charles V, correct?"

"I am. Long live King Charles V."

"Good, and with that decided, I want you and your men to join me downstairs for some afternoon wine as a token of my good faith in our prosperous future with King Charles V of Spain. My servant has told your crew already. I shall be there soon. Thank you, Captain Gaspar, for understanding my position."

"Of course, Your Majesty," I said with a bow.

Swift

Scene: Arrival of Royalty

ᏫᲛᲛᲚᎧ

O UR GROUP WAS invited by the sultan to drink in one of his prominent guesthouses next to the palace. It was a wonderful gesture for all of us to be invited for afternoon cordials. The ordeal was causal, and the sultan supplied us with bountiful wine inside an open hall with arches on each side, granting us a view of the gardens around us.

It was evening then, and the great lamp was dimming her light, granting us a rosy red sky to look upon. Our small group from the marketplace was seated in the hall, enjoying the wine and *hors d'oeuvres* to the fullest. I knew not where Faustino, Gaspar, and Zaragoza were, nor did I care. I was enjoying myself, more so than I had in the past months. I was tipsy from the red wine, drunker with each sip. We all were.

"Tell us," exclaimed Jaipur. "Tell us, Toro."

"Tell us what?" replied Toro.

"What was Timbuktu like?" asked Jaipur.

"I would like to know, too," said Cosimo.

"Were there elephants, tigers, snakes, deserts, and those things alike?" I asked.

"If each of you insists on knowing, I'll say," remarked Toro as he took a sip of wine. "The city is surrounded by great sand dunes. It is arid, hot—typical of a desert."

"How did Timbuktu flourish, gain its wealth?" asked Cosimo.

"How does any city flourish?" asked Toro.

I chimed in. "Trade."

Toro nodded. "I traded salt slabs across Northern Africa, from Timbuktu, Cairo, and even southern Spain. Salt was king in Timbuktu."

"Slabs are hard to transport if I'm not mistaken," said Cosimo.

"Are ye mad? I did not do it alone," said Toro. "I owned 1,001 camels and took my cavern to the salt mines north of Timbuktu. Then, I brought my caravan to the seaports where I could trade it. That's how I met Gaspar; he wanted my salt."

"Incredible," said Cosimo.

"But why leave that all behind?" asked Jaipur.

Toro took another sip of wine. "Cavern was attacked by Bedouin raiders. I lost it all."

"I'm . . . I'm sorry I asked, Toro," said Jaipur.

"Don't be. It's all part of Allah's plan. Let Allah's will be done," said Toro.

"I've struggled with Allah's plan," said Cosimo, beginning to slur his words.

"Weren't you a monk?" asked Jaipur.

"Aye," said Cosimo. "Used to be."

"Why did you leave?" asked Jaipur.

"Never wanted to be there. Never," said Cosimo.

"Where is 'there'?" asked Toro.

"The monastery," said Cosimo. "It was outside of Florence. I grew up there under a terrible friar named Marzano, Friar Marzano. He was a cruel man, treated me like a slave in that stone cold monastery."

"What did he do?" I asked.

"Friar Marzano?" said Cosimo.

"Aye," I replied.

"Whipped me, told me I was good for nothing, made me wear the most uncomfortable robes, sleep in cold cells—terrible, terrible things," explained Cosimo. "All I did was read, study, chart, read, study, and chart—my only escape."

"I thought my situation was bad with Gaspar," said Jaipur. "That sounds much worse."

"Gaspar. Yes, didn't he help you escape?" I asked.

"Aye, he did," said Cosimo.

"From what I remember, didn't you make maps?" said Jaipur.

"I did. Best maps in Europe," said Cosimo. "From my collected works and readings, I constructed the most up-to-date maps and nautical instruments in my spare time. You see, those maps were my dreams, my only hope to leave that monastery and see the world. I hoped and prayed to the Lord above that if I worked on these maps, then maybe, just maybe, someone would discover me and take me with him across the world."

"Gaspar found you," I said.

"Yes, he did, and he broke me out of that horrible place," said Cosimo. "I shall never return to that place, to the monastery. Never."

"I remember Gaspar talking of you years ago," said Jaipur.

A jingle rang throughout the hall. A servant came forward to announce that the Royal Commander of the Faithful, the sultan, would be joining our presence in a few minutes. I was a little nervous and didn't want to make a bad impression. Everyone was a little nervous.

Gaspar arrived from around the corner. He was well dressed in a navy blue shirt, his dark brown, coarse beard was tamed and looked presentable. His eyes still carried that sharp, piercing, and wild look.

"The captain cleaned up," said Jaipur.

"Aye, he did," I added.

"All of you doing well?" asked Gaspar as he took a glass of wine from the wooden table.

"The sultan is coming," I said.

"I know," replied Gaspar, taking a very large sip from his glass.

"Whoa. You must be ready to party, Captain," I said.

"Me too," said Jaipur, also taking a large sip of wine.

"Where are the others?" growled Gaspar.

"Haven't seen them," said Jaipur.

"Is something wrong, Captain?" asked Cosimo.

"No," said Gaspar.

I looked at Cosimo, feeling something off in the air. What was wrong with Gaspar? He seemed tense—well, more intense than usual.

There was another ring of the bell, and down the hall was the sultan's personal guard, walking toward us in formation. At the center of the formation was the sultan dressed in an elegant white robe. The sultan's stature and leonine stride appeared powerful. The servant alerted us of his presence, and we all bowed as he approached us.

In the corner of my eye, I saw Cosimo staring at something near the sultan. I followed his glance, and there before us was Nur-al-Arij, dressed in a beautiful turquoise dress with her face covered. I could tell it was the princess by her slender frame and large eyes.

"I hope each of you enjoyed the refreshments," said the sultan.

"We're quite thankful for your hospitality," said Gaspar. "It's an honor to be asked and visited by your grace."

"An honor, indeed," said the sultan. "It's the least I could do for my guests after such a long journey here. Further, I would like to introduce all of you to Al-Rashid, the vizier of our neighboring city." The sultan then spoke to him in Arabic, introducing us.

A shorter man stepped forward. He seemed like a nice older man with white hair, a long white beard, and a pronounced wrinkle on his forehead. The vizier bowed to us, silent.

"He does not speak your tongue," explained the sultan, "and this is his son, Prince Sikander."

"Nice to see faces from afar," said Prince Sikander in Castilian Spanish with a smile. Prince Sikander was tall and broad shouldered with a built stature, clean face, and dark black, curly hair. He wore a blue and white robe.

I had seen him before: he was the prince arriving in the city. I had known then that we would meet.

The sultan continued, "And of course, the angel of my eye, my daughter, Princess Nur-al-Arij."

"I am most honored, Father," said Arij.

She was beautiful, and her father adored her. As I stared at her, I caught Prince Sikander gazing at her and watching her every move. It was obvious why Prince Sikander was here in Boubazar. I turned to Cosimo, who seemed distraught.

"It is an honor to meet you, Vizier Al-Rashid and Prince Sikander," said Gaspar. "I am Captain Gaspar, and this is my crew."

"Where do all of you come from in Spain?" asked Prince Sikander.

"I am not from Spain," replied Gaspar.

Prince Sikander's right eyebrow rose. "I thought your accent sounded familiar."

"Familiar to what, Your Highness?" asked Gaspar.

"To the Portuguese," said Prince Sikander. "Is that where you come from? From Portugal?"

"Yes, I do come from Portugal though I am a citizen of Spain, a citizen under King Charles V, who extends his good graces to each of you," said Gaspar.

"I did not know you were Portuguese, Captain," said the sultan.

"You never asked, Your Majesty," said Gaspar.

"Yes, I did not," said the sultan.

"Well, we extend our own good graces to King Charles V of Spain," said Prince Sikander as he bowed with his hand over his heart. "Where are the rest of you from, Captain?"

"From London to Timbuktu," he answered.

"Astounding," said Prince Sikander.

"I am sorry to inform you that we cannot stay for refreshments this afternoon though I wanted to invite you and your crew to my daughter's birthday celebration tonight. We will honor her with refreshments and games, wonderful athletic games open to the public," said the sultan. "Would you and your crew be interested?"

"I like games," said Jaipur.

"Will there be food?" I chimed in.

"What?" asked the sultan.

Gaspar gave me a terrible look to be quiet. Then, he turned to the sultan. "He wanted to know if there would be food."

"Oh yes, tons. Enough to feed an elephant," said the sultan. "Does that answer your question?"

"Yes," I said.

"We would love to come," said Gaspar.

"Splendid. Make sure to tell the others," said the sultan. "It begins in a few hours. Please, stay and continue to enjoy my gift to you. I am a friend of King Charles V. I hope to see all of you soon."

Cosimo

Scene 1: Festive Preparations

⟨∞⟩

T HE MOMENT I returned to my room, I closed the door and stared out my window, thinking, planning, watching the sun leave her golden throne. I could not get Arij out of my mind. She looked stunning in that blue dress.

Wait, a party? A party tonight?

My heart rumbled in my chest, fluttering like a butterfly's wings. I felt sick, nervous sick.

I need to throw up. No, no. Hold it in. What if she catches me throwing up? No, no. Hold it in. I can sit still. Yes, sit still. What's wrong with my hand? Why is it jittering?

I grabbed my hand, trying to hold it still, control these nervous jitters. The princess was the woman of my dreams, so beautiful, so majestic. The thought of her excited me, brought me back to life, made me sing to the moon, to the mountain, to the air filled with her fragrance. No wonder Gaspar sang to the moon, to Luna. I could do the same.

Tonight is my chance, a chance to see her. I can see her, be near her. So close, so far. Her love. My medicine, my sickness, my desire, my obsession, my excitement. Her love. I must refrain, control my thoughts, control my desires.

I pondered about Prince Sikander. He would be there, of course. He came for her. I could tell by the glimmer in his eye. I didn't have a chance. No chance at all. He was strong, handsome. A prince! I was no prince. I was a nobody, a nobody from Florence.

No, no. I am somebody, born of royalty. Born, given away. Oh, why would she want me if my own parents did not want me? No one ever wanted me. I will not fall in that trap again, that swamp mud of doubt. How did I escape that mud, that imprisoning mud, that mud of the monastery, that mud of myself?

Nay, I escaped the mud, escaped the monastery. For I am strong. I believe in my worth. I don't care what Friar Marzano said to me or how he hurt me. I am somebody, somebody worth loving. I am royalty, but could she love a Christian? Would I convert to Islam for her? What if we don't have to? What if we could live in harmony with those differences and learn from our differences? Does religion matter if we both love the one God of Abraham? Why am I thinking this about this? I am crazy. Crazy! How do I even know she loves me? I am here for spices, for opportunity, for a new life.

Gaspar . . . Gaspar . . . I am forgetting about him, his secrets, this expedition.

What am I doing? Have I forgotten my intentions? What are my intentions?

The only intention for any man is to love and be loved. Spices or not, love has no price, no barrier, and no judgment. Love is love for love's sake. Nothing more, nothing less. I wanted nothing less than true love wherever her flower bloomed.

The door opened. It was Swift. "Thought it was you in here."

"You thought right," I replied.

"Troubled, eh?"

"Confused," I sighed.

"Arij, eh?"

"Yes."

"What's confusing about Arij?"

"Religion, Prince Sikander, Gaspar, spices, this group. What doesn't confuse me?"

"A bottle of wine."

"Thou art always joking, Swift. Joking, joking. Too much joking!"

"Hey, only trying to cheer you up! I'm sorry."

I sighed. "Nay, I'm sorry. I overreacted a bit. I shouldn't take my anger out on you."

"It's fine. I understand."

"I wish I could understand."

"You still thinking of Arij?"

"Do birds tweet?"

"I take that as a yes."

"What should I do? How will I be able to outdo a prince, a prince like Sikander?"

"Tough competition."

"Any ideas?"

"A few."

"Do tell."

"Arij doesn't love Sikander."

"You think so?"

"I know so."

"How so?"

"She would have been with him by now if she loved him."

"Arij could be playing hard to get."

"Nay, she doesn't seem like that type of girl."

"What kind of girl do you see her as?"

"I'm not in love with her. You are in love with her. Ask yourself that question."

I paused, ponder the question for a moment. "Arij is honest, open."

"Give me not the basic answer. Give me a real answer, an answer Prince Sikander has not. Why do you love her? If you can't answer that then—"

"I know her. I know her by her essence, by her soul. When our eyes locked by the river, I saw a piece of myself in her, a piece dormant in my soul. Our souls spoke to one another, like the whisper of God in the wind."

Swift smiled at me. "What did your soul say?"

"Inside her brilliant eyes, I found myself a prisoner and her the same. I felt how love's lost time hardened my heart like a shield. I was scared to be, scared to live, scared to love. Her gaze brought down my wall, my prison, and replaced it with love of fire to be, to live, and to believe."

A tear dripped from Swift's eye.

"Swift?" I spoke.

"Oh, Rose," he said. "Cosimo, if you feel that love for Arij, then nothing stands between you and her."

"I feel that, too."

"I'll handle Sikander tonight. I'll entertain him. It'll give you time to make a move on Arij. You better strike when the iron is hot, or our heads will be struck off soon after."

"I got this," I remarked. "I got this."

After my talk with Swift, I freshened up for the party and went down the stairs. Everyone—Zaragoza, Faustino, Jaipur, Swift, Toro, and Gaspar—congregated in the foyer of the house.

"Zaragoza, I'm surprised you are coming," I said.

"Why miss a party?" replied Zaragoza.

"Aren't they savages?" added Jaipur.

"Remains to be seen," he remarked with a smile. "Where have you been, Gaspar?"

"Sightseeing," said Gaspar.

"Did you find more Egyptian walls?" asked Zaragoza sarcastically.

"One or two," replied Gaspar.

"I did some sightseeing earlier," said Faustino. "I found a place with great cheesecake, but I didn't find anything Egyptian."

"In the bazaar?" asked Toro.

"No, near the gardens," replied Faustino.

"I'll have to see that one," said Toro.

"That reminds me. I did see Gaspar wandering near the gardens," said Faustino.

"Didn't stop to say hello?" asked Gaspar.

"Seemed like you were in a hurry," said Faustino.

"To find the gold of . . . What was it again?" asked Zaragoza. "Oh, yes, the gold of Retenju."

"*Retjenu*," corrected Gaspar.

The rest of us were quiet, feeling the tension in the air.

"Could you explain that to us?" asked Zaragoza. "We all feel left in the dark, Captain."

"What's there to explain?" said Gaspar.

"The wall. The gold," I interjected.

"Retjenu is a mythical gold extracted by the ancient Egyptians," explained Gaspar. "Where or how, I know not. The wall was pure coincidence. Does that satisfy your curiosities?"

"Are you after the gold?" asked Faustino.

"What gold?" replied Gaspar.

"Ret . . . Retjune? Oh, Retjenu gold," said Faustino.

"Sure. Why not?" said Gaspar.

"Here?" said Faustino. "On the island? Is gold on this island?"

"How should I know?" replied Gaspar. "Let's get to the party before we run late."

Cosimo

Scene ii: Festive Dance

◊◊◊◊◊

G ASPAR SPOKE NOTHING more about his intentions or anything
to do with the Egyptians. He was secretive, dodging every question thrown at him. Sooner or later, we would figure out his
true intentions. I would for the sake of this expedition.

As for this moment, the princess was my sole focus. Her party
was most extravagant. I had never seen or even thought a party like this
could exist.

It was held in the gardens of the palace, decorated with mosa-
ic fountains and colorful drapes on the columns. Through the garden
was a large, narrow pool of water, which ended at a grand marble staircase, leading toward the entrance of the palace. Performers and mimes
were scattered throughout the gardens, entertaining the guests with their
tricks and jokes. Better yet, there were elephants in the gardens, offering
the guests rides upon their backs. Magnificent trained exotic birds with
feathers colored teal, yellow, red, white, and purple flew above our heads
or rested on branches.

The guests were drinking wine or fruit juice, talking with one another, enjoying each other's company. Seemingly, no more than a hundred or so people were invited to this exclusive party. The guests were
dressed in dazzling robes made of the finest silks or furs of Far Eastern
fashion. Gaspar, Zaragoza, and Faustino split from our group the moment we entered the gardens to do their own bidding.

My eyes drifted to the top of the grand staircase where Arij was.
Seated next to her father, she was dressed in the most magnificent white

dress and wearing a golden crown. "There she is," I said. "Stunning."

Swift squinted his eyes to see in the distance. "She is. She is."

At that moment, Prince Sikander, dressed in his Arabian royal regalia, came from behind Arij, bringing the princess a drink.

"Sikander," I said.

"We knew he would be here," said Swift.

"What's wrong, Cosimo?" asked Jaipur.

"The princess," added Toro.

"Yes," I said. "The princess."

"How did you know, Toro?" asked Jaipur. "I didn't know."

"I pay attention," replied Toro.

"So do I," said Jaipur. "Cosimo never said anything about liking the princess."

"Love can be seen without spoken words," said Toro.

"What do I look at then?" asked Jaipur, trying to stand on his tippy toes to see in the distance. "I can't see love. Where is it? Where's the princess?"

Toro rolled his eyes, picked up Jaipur by his robe, and raised him up. Jaipur remarked, "Whoa."

"Oh, the princess looks beautiful," said Jaipur. "I must be in love, too. I'm in love!"

Toro sighed as he placed Jaipur back down.

Faustino returned to our group, holding a glass of wine in his hand. "This is great! There are elephants!"

"Where did Gaspar and Zaragoza go?" asked Swift.

"Over there, chatting with some of the guests about Spain," said Faustino. "Any action over here?"

"Cosimo wants the princess," said Jaipur. "I want her, too."

"That's private, Jaipur," I replied, annoyed.

Faustino laughed aloud. "You can't be serious."

I kept my eyes focused on Arij. "Mind your own business, Faustino."

Faustino laughed louder. "You are serious! You have no shot, monk. No shot. Stay with what you know. Stick with maids and nuns."

"How about you, Faustino? Stick with drunken rants and wine," I said sternly.

Faustino's face grew red though he kept his anger at bay. He took another sip of wine. "Your time will come soon, Cosimo. Soon."

"Have to go through me first, Faustino," said Swift.

"And me," said Toro.

"Aye, me too. Me too," said Jaipur.

Faustino took a sip of wine, eyes piercing. "Have a good time, each of you." He walked away.

Faustino angered me. I felt the heat course through my veins. I clenched my fist.

"Don't let him inside your head, Cosimo," said Swift. "Stay focused."

"Aye, agreed," said Toro.

"Right, right," I said as I cleared my head.

"What's Faustino's problem?" said Jaipur. "He looks like the kind of guy who would beat his wife, don't you think?"

"I can't say," I remarked.

"It's the wine, the drunkenness. He has a demon in him. Aye, a demon," said Swift.

"Ugh, enough of that," said Jaipur. "I'm going to ride an elephant. Anyone want to come? Toro?"

"I'm fine," said Toro.

"Come on, Toro," pleaded Jaipur. "You need to live once in a while."

"Might as well go, Toro," said Swift.

Toro shook his head. "Can I watch you do it?"

"What fun is that?" said Jaipur.

"Fine," sighed Toro. "Good luck with the princess, Cosimo."

I nodded at Toro, and Swift and I made our way to the grand staircase toward the princess. As I walked up the stairs, I could see the princess gleam at me, the same powerful gaze I saw by the river. At the sight of Arij, my heart raced, fluttering faster than the wings of a bird. Next to her at the top of the staircase was the sultan talking to Prince Sikander. I took a deep breath.

"Ready?" asked Swift.

"Yes," I breathed as we reached the top of the staircase.

"Sorry to interrupt you," said Swift.

The sultan and prince stopped talking that moment, fixing their attention on Swift and me. It felt awkward and unnatural.

"Please, you are my guests," said the sultan with a smile.

I had to get over my insecurities and stay confident. I made a slight bow and smile toward the princess, "Splendid party, Your Majesty."

"Wonderful party, Your Grace," said Swift, bowing.

"All for my beautiful daughter," said the sultan. "Thank you for coming."

"Yes, thank you," said Arij.

"Indeed," said Prince Sikander, quickly.

"Did any of you have a chance to ride the elephant?" asked the sultan.

"Two of our companions are right now," said Swift.

"You mean those two?" pointed out Prince Sikander.

We turned around and, in the distance, saw Jaipur falling off the elephant, hanging on Toro's arm. Jaipur was pulling and pulling on Toro, trying to lift himself back up. In that mayhem, the startled elephant lifted up its two front legs, and both Toro and Jaipur, hollering for help, slid off the back of the elephant, hands waving in the air.

I turned back toward the Sultan. "Not sure if I know them."

Swift looked uncomfortable. "Oh, that hurts. That hurts the back."

"I thought I saw them with you," questioned Prince Sikander.

Princess Arij laughed and laughed as she watched the scene play out from afar.

"Them? No, no," said Swift. "We came with a lot of people."

The sultan noticed Arij's happiness, smiled, and laughed along with her. I could tell he loved his daughter to the moon, the stars, and back.

"Let me go assist them," said the sultan. "Oh, don't forget. We have some of the finest cheesecake here tonight, made by my mother using her special recipe."

"I love cheesecake," I said.

"Toro will need some after that fall," said Swift.

Prince Sikander raised his brow at us as the sultan walked away.

"Princess," said Prince Sikander, gesturing toward her.

"That's a fine necklace you have, Prince Sikander," said Swift, stepping in front of Prince Sikander and Arij.

I made a quick, decisive move toward the princess. "Would you like to go on a walk, Princess Arij?"

"With whom?" she asked.

"Um, well . . . with me?" I replied.

She laughed. "I'm joking. Yes, let us go on a walk."

"Wonderful," I said.

"So how's the weather in your own land this time of year, Prince Sikander?" asked Swift, blocking Sikander's view of the princess.

"Wait, Princess," said Prince Sikander, trying to get her attention. "Princess! Can you move? Princess, wait, wait!"

"What?" questioned Swift. "I don't want to move there. No, no. Much too dry for me."

Arij and I followed the steps down and through the garden, leaving Swift preoccupied with Prince Sikander.

Cosimo

Scene iii: Dance of Winged Cupid's Strike

෴

T HE BRIGHT MOON was dressed in her glowing nightgown high in the celestial clear sky. I had Arij in that moment. My head pondered what to say, what to do. I hadn't thought I would make it this far. I said the only thing that came to my mind.

"Have you had the cheesecake?" I asked.

"Too many times to count," she replied. "My father is obsessed with it. Too obsessed with it."

"Your father's quite a character."

"What's a 'character'? I know not that word in Spanish."

"It's . . . well . . . How do I put it? It's someone with personality. Someone who's alive, who has unique thoughts, opinions, feelings."

"Am I a 'character'?"

"Of course. We're all characters in the play of life."

"Then how would you describe my character?"

"Free spirited." I paused, staring into her bright eyes.

"What are you looking at?"

"At you. I'm thinking."

"And?"

"Your thought is the finest fragrance. Your words are smooth as silk, and your soul is full of adventure."

She smiled. "I am not adventurous."

"Yes, you are. More so than I."

"Nonsense. You've seen the world, seen Europe. I've never ventured far from the palace walls and never will."

"I used to think the same things."

"What do you mean?"

"Well, I used to live in a monastery behind large stone walls under a terrible friar. I was a slave there."

"Why did you not leave?" she asked.

"Why do you not leave the palace?"

"Where shall I go?"

"Same for me. I had nowhere to go nor did I know what life was like outside the monastery walls. I was told for years that I would die out there, die without the protection of God, so I stayed."

"Sounds similar to what my father tells me every day. So how did you escape?"

"By studying nautical charts. I found a captain and a ship. I never looked back."

"Perhaps I could do the same."

"Perhaps you could."

"I could go to Europe, yes. What is Europe, your home, like?"

"It's . . . it's . . . " I thought for a moment. "It's different."

"I like different."

"Yet we are not so different."

"We are not. Your eyes see what I see."

"What do we see?"

She laughed. "I shouldn't have to tell you."

"Truly."

We stared deep into each other's eyes. No word spoken could describe the gravitational pull between us.

"I have an idea," Arij said suddenly.

"What?"

"I know a great place that serves the most wonderful sorbet. Would you accompany the birthday girl to the shop?"

"But your party . . . your father."

"And your point is?"

"We could get in trouble. *I* could get in trouble."

"Where's the adventure in your soul?"

"Front and center."

"Come, follow me. I know a secret way through the gardens."

We crept through the gardens and into the city under the cover of night as the party continued in the distance.

Swift

Scene: Dance of Festive Games

〰️

"**D**ID HE TAKE the princess?" said Prince Sikander, looking around.

"Did who?" I replied.

"Your friend," he huffed.

"Which one?"

The prince sighed, annoyed. An awkward silence followed. The prince quickly and rhythmically tapped his foot on the ground.

"Come here often?" I asked.

"May I be truthful with you, Spaniard?" said Prince Sikander.

"As truthful as one may be, but I'm English."

"Regardless, you and your captain are too late."

"Too late to catch a ship?"

"Too late for a deal. The Portuguese came here before you, long before you."

"That complicates things."

"Your own kingdom has an accord with the Portuguese, and soon the sultan of Boubazar will join us. Best you leave before the Portuguese arrive. Don't want a mishap."

"Trade deals are like promiscuous women, loyal today yet love another tomorrow."

"Ture, though this deal has an armada coming in here in a few days to finalize the deal between Boubazar and Portugal."

"Is that so?"

"Tough to broker a spice trade with six or seven men without a ship, wouldn't you say, English?"

"My name is Edward Swift."

"Since I'm thinking about it, I heard from a few friends of mine that the Portuguese were searching for a Spanish crew headed for the Spice Islands going west. If I am not mistaken, the sultan said your crew traveled west to arrive here."

"I wonder where he got that idea from."

"Yes, where did he? Further, my Portuguese friends told me they were hunting for a captain—a Portuguese captain, in fact—who turned on his country and his king to sail under Spain with the intention of finding the Spices Islands. I'd call that treason."

"I'd call that court gossip. You shouldn't trust court gossip."

"True, but the Portuguese—our ally and soon to be Boubazar's ally—are searching for this treasonous crew of Spanish pirates. You wouldn't happen to know where this Spanish crew could be?"

"Wait," I said. "You hear that?"

"Did you not hear me?"

I paused.

"This foolishness is a disgrace worth banishment," said Prince Sikander. "Worth death."

"No, no, I haven't heard a thing," I shrugged. "I cannot stand pirates. We should search for them together."

"Indeed," replied the angry prince. "We should, starting with your captain and your friend with the princess. An enemy of the Portuguese is an enemy of me; an enemy of me is an enemy of Boubazar."

"Why not start with me?" I said fiercely.

The sultan, accompanied by his personal guard, approached us. "Good men, save your energy for the athletic games. Show our guests your athletic prowess in honor of Boubazar."

"Games," I said. "I forgot about the games. May I ask what kind of games?"

"Games of agility, speed, strength, and wit," said the sultan. "The best kind of games."

"A European could never compete in festival games," said Prince Sikander. "It would bring dishonor to our tradition."

"Is that so?" I spoke.

"I beg to differ," said the sultan. "I encourage diverse sport."

"But, Your Majesty," pleaded Prince Sikander.

"But nothing," said the sultan. "Take your challenge to the games, and let the better man claim victory."

"Yes, I agree, Your Majesty," said Prince Sikander with a bow. "My companions and I will show these strangers our superiority in athletic sport so that they may return home with tales of our great strength, not only in trade but in sport."

A large crowd began to surround us. Before I knew it, Gaspar, Toro, Faustino, and Jaipur were behind me. The crowd was excited to see a challenge, cheering for the games between Sikander's companions and the foreigners.

Jaipur looked around nervously. "What does the Prince want?"

"He wants to compete with us," said Toro.

"What of the Spaniards?" asked the sultan. "Will you participate in the games?"

"What are the events?" asked Jaipur.

"Running, jumping, javelin throwing, boxing, wrestling, and *mobarezon*," said the sultan.

"*Mobarezon?*" I inquired.

"What's the word in Spanish?" said the sultan.

"A duel," said Toro.

"Yes, a duel. Sword on sword," said the sultan, excited.

Gaspar whispered to us, asking if we wanted to play the games. We all agreed. Gaspar nodded. "We'll compete."

"Good," said Prince Sikander, smiling.

"Then let the tournament begin!" said the sultan.

We walked to a large, open, circular area of trimmed green grass in front of the palace, prepared with expert care for the games. Surrounding the massive circle was wooden scaffolding five stories high composed of seats circling the grass arena, like that of an ancient Greek stadium. The field was seven hundred feet long and 115 feet wide with perfect dimensions. Large swaths of pedestrians from all corners of the kingdom were allowed to enter the stadium and watch the tournament.

We were facing a strong group of competitors. Their names were called out by the sultan: Prince Sikander, Gabir, Fazl, Juda, and Miraj. Each was a different size with a different skin shade, shape, and skill set.

Worthy opponents, they were.

I called out to Zaragoza, watching from the sidelines. "Zaragoza, are you competing?"

"Nay, I had too much to drink," he replied. "I'll watch from here."

"Don't waste your breath," said Gaspar. "Where's Cosimo?"

"On a walk," I said.

"Walk?" questioned Gaspar. "With whom?"

"The princess," I replied.

"I see," said Gaspar.

"What do you see?" asked Jaipur.

"I'm not lifting ye up again, so don't ask," said Toro.

The sultan walked into the middle of the field, followed by his guard, the vizier, and other high officials throughout the land. The sultan then announced the start of the games and set fire to a torch upon a pedestal. The crowd roared with excitement.

The rules for the tournament were simple: whichever participant won the event received a point for his team, and the team with the most points in the end won the tournament.

The first event was the footrace. Our team was composed of Jaipur, Faustino, Gaspar, Toro, and me.

"Looks like they have some fast ones," stated Faustino. "I'm not fast."

"Who's fast?" asked Gaspar.

"I am," I said.

"Anyone else?"

"Jaipur," said Toro.

"I can run," said Jaipur. "I'm quick."

"You two then. Up, up," said Gaspar.

Jaipur and I lined up on the field at the starting line. Our opponents were all men: Prince Sikander; Gabi, a tall, slender runner; Mirag, who was short and stocky; and Fazl, who maintained a medium-sized muscular frame, similar to my own.

The event started to an excited, cheering crowd. Dirt was flung into the air as we kicked our feet into the ground, moving faster than shooting stars in the sky. It was a close match, neck and neck, inch by inch. In the end, Miraj won the event. I came in second, and Prince

Sikander in third. A tough loss.

The next event was jumping to test who could jump the farthest distance. Toro volunteered and went against Fazl. Toro bent down into a running position, lunged forward, and sprang into the air. He jumped far, farther than any man could, farther than I had ever seen before. Toro won the event with ease. A point to us.

Javelin throwing followed the jumping event. Our team decided that due to his large, powerful arms, Faustino would participate and Gaspar because, well, he volunteered. Gaspar and Faustino threw against Miraj and Fazl. Each person threw far. Faustino threw the shortest by a long shot. Fazl threw the farthest, though closely followed by Gaspar's javelin. Another hard loss.

Boxing, one of the more brutal events in the tournament, was next. The athletes' hands were covered with cloth to ease the blow. The rules stated that the first man to hit the ground would lose. Gaspar volunteered again for this event. He wrapped his fingers well and practiced a few jabs in the air. He dodged left, right; he punched and jabbed. Gaspar looked lethal.

Gaspar squared up against Miraj, the short, stocky brute of Sikander's companions. Mean and ruthless, he looked. His chest and arms were covered with black tattoos of what appeared to be Arabic phrases.

I was a little worried for Gaspar because Miraj seemed to be the star athlete of the team, and this event drew blood. The event started, and the two men went at it—fists up, squared up, and focused on another.

Gaspar dodged.

Left, right, hit, hit, jab.

Blood fell from both men.

Gaspar came in strong with a left uppercut, and Miraj went down like a snapped tree. He did not get back up after that blow. Victory, it was. A point for us!

Wrestling came after. Faustino spoke up, wanting to volunteer for this event. Faustino was a tall, massive man. He could win this one for the team though after the javelin-throwing event, I had my doubts. We all had doubts, and yet, we agreed so that he might redeem himself.

Faustino removed his cloak, showing off his bronzed body, large muscular frame, big hands, and strong thighs. His opponent was Fazl of medium frame; he looked agile but maintained substantial strength in his arms and legs. The event started, and both men grappled with one another; ferocious and bloody, they were.

On their last breath, Fazl placed Faustino in chokehold. Scarlet blood began to drip from Faustino's nose. Faustino gave up and accepted defeat. Another loss.

The last event, the *Mobarezon*, was upon us. This duel between two swordsmen was worth two points due to the danger and skill involved. The rules were simple: first to give up or die would lose. We had to win this one.

Gaspar came before our group—each of us worn out, breathing hard, sweat dripping. "Who's best with the sword?"

No one stepped forward or answered.

"I'll do it then," said Gaspar.

"No, I will," I said.

"Can you win?" asked Gaspar.

"I feel confident," I replied.

Gaspar threw me his sword. I nodded.

I walked to the middle of the stadium, and there before me was Prince Sikander, preparing to duel. The prince turned to me with a smirk. "I hoped it was you."

"You won't be saying that soon," I replied.

"My last opponent said that before I killed him."

"Your last opponent wasn't me."

"No, but he was a Christian."

"Good to know he rests in the Lord's bosom. Tell him hello for me after this."

Prince Sikander removed his robe and shirt. He was fit and agile with a muscular neck, chest, and abdominal muscles. He displayed skill as he wielded his sword. On his right pec, he had a tattoo of six black lines intersecting with each other like a musical note.

"That symbol," said Toro,

"Aye?" I spoke.

"That is the symbol of a Tughra," said Toro.

"What?" I asked. "What is that?

"The best fighters in all of Arabia," replied Toro.

"Good to know," I spoke.

"You will be fine," assured Toro.

I took my robe and shirt off, revealing my defined chest, neck, and abdomen. I wrapped a red cloth around my forehead to catch the sweat, cracked my neck, and brought forth my sharpened blade. I wielded the sword in the air, feeling its weight, and cut the blade through the air.

Prince Sikander and I squared off. The crowd roared, waiting for what would unfold.

The event started. Sikander and I touched blades, then backed away from one another. He looked professional with perfect posture and maintained calm eyes.

The prince yelled and lunged forward.

"*En garde!*" I exclaimed.

Our swords clashed. I pivoted, as did Sikander. The crowd screamed for blood. Sikander and I circled one another. Then, he danced forward, lunged, leaped, struck, missed. Our swords collided.

Cling, cling, swish, swoosh, strike.

We both jumped back. Sikander gasped for breath. I could feel the sweat dripping from my forehead though it was caught by my red cloth.

I lunged forward.

Cling, cling, clung, step, step.

Sikander was light footed, quick and forceful, yet I was faster and stronger. Each of my strikes exhausted him. Side to side, we danced.

Cling, clung, twirl, stab.

Ah!

Sikander's blade pierced the edge of my arm. Then, he swung at my leg. My blade blocked it, but the tip of his blade cut my right thigh. I fell on my left knee.

"Weak," shouted Prince Sikander.

Sikander then struck down with a loud yell. I held my blade up, colliding with his.

Cling!

We both exerted great force upon each other, blade on blade, like two lions competing for a kill on a great grass savannah.

Sikander gritted his teeth as he pushed down on me with all of his energy. I held firm, feeling my right wrist ache. The bone was splitting, giving out.

Nay, nay, my end is not here, far from here. I shall return home, home sweet home. Rose, my home, my love, my love. Strengthen me! I see you, my love.

I took a deep breath and roared. I pushed my legs upward, feeling the weight of the world and my troubles upon my shoulders. I held my hand steady, steady and pushed up, up. Prince Sikander could not stop my force. I stood before him, calm and collected. I sensed fear rush through Sikander's veins, expressed on his worried face. Sikander broke from the interlock.

At that moment, I grabbed his throat with my left hand, clenching his esophagus. He tried to strike me, yet it was of no use. The prince gasped for air, causing him to drop his sword. Before the dark mist could fill Sikander's eyes, he yielded to me.

Victory.

Our team won by one point. The crowd applauded our victory as we were crowned victors at the center of the field. The sultan commemorated us in front of the crowd.

Unknown to our team, Cosimo and Arij had returned at the beginning of the games. They had watched the games next to the sultan and vizier. We shook hands with our competitors fraternally, but Prince Sikander left the field without a peaceful handshake.

I had not forgotten what Prince Sikander told me about the incoming armada. Why would he tell me that? Did he want to scare me? Was he lying? I thought we were competing for the sultan's favor, or had he signed with the Portuguese before our arrival? The Portuguese had been here before; they had been hunting Gaspar, hunting the *Valencia*, hunting us. If they caught us, they would throw us in the galleys, force us to be slaves until death.

If we were caught. If we were caught.

Scene ii: Realization of the Crew

꘠ᨒᨒ꘠

W E RETURNED TO our house after the tournament. The only one of the crew not walking back with us from the stadium was Zaragoza. At this point, the crew didn't care what he did or didn't do. He was useless to us anyway. Zaragoza lurked in the shadows, waiting for his chance to escape or find a way home without us. I knew it. Gaspar knew it. We all knew it. I didn't care what Zaragoza did by this point. I was far too elated by our victory.

The whole crew was high on victory, celebrating with laughter, cheering, and singing as we opened the door to our house. This victory brought us together and quelled some resentment among us, in particular that between Cosimo and Faustino. Tension was lightened in the room. Victory felt good like fresh, crisp air.

Once we were behind closed doors, I thought it was best to tell the crew what I discovered about Sikander. I did not want to ruin the good feelings, but I felt this was necessary information we should all know.

The crew was around me, relaxing in the living room. I gathered their attention and elaborated on what Prince Sikander told me before the games: every detail about the Portuguese, my opinion on the sultan's allegiances, and how the Portuguese were coming to the island and were after Gaspar and our crew.

The group fell silent upon hearing the information, slowly coming to terms with another obstacle, further diminishing our dreams of returning home.

"King Manuel of Portugal," said Gaspar, angered. "That rat! He refused my offer to go west. Mocked me, he did. The Portuguese won't catch me, won't catch *us*. Rest assured."

"Another worry of mine. What if the *Valencia*, that ship full of mutinous Spanish sailors, returns to Spain before us?" I asked. "To save themselves from the brig, they'll claim we, not they, mutinied. Our word against theirs. I'd wager King Charles V will be after us sooner or later, and I don't want to test my luck in Spanish courts. Oh, if an Englishman ends up in a Spanish court, I'd be as good as guilty and off to the brig."

"So everyone is our enemy?" asked Jaipur.

"Not Arij," said Cosimo.

"She could help us," I said.

"Arij would help us," stated Cosimo. "She is the closest person to the sultan, to her father."

"Gaspar, have you talked to the sultan?" asked Toro.

"I have," replied Gaspar. "He's conflicted."

"Did the sultan say anything about a ship and spices?" I asked.

"He wants my charts," said Gaspar.

"You still have them?" asked Cosimo.

"Aye," replied Gaspar. "Carried them on my back from the ship all the way here."

"Those charts are invaluable," I said.

"Everything has a price," said Faustino.

"I can't give up my charts," said Gaspar. "It's my life's work, the only thing keeping us alive."

"What if that's our only way?" said Jaipur.

"There's another way," said Gaspar.

"What way?" asked Cosimo.

"Another way," replied Gaspar.

"We could bribe the sultan," suggested Jaipur.

"With what?" said Toro. "We have nothing."

"Then we need to go, leave, run before the Portuguese arrive," said Jaipur. "Not the brig. That's a fate worse than death. I can't go to the brig."

"Sikander could be lying," I said.

"Quiet, everyone," said Gaspar. "I will persuade the sultan to help us. I will."

"That's reassuring," I said.

"We can't leave here without spices," said Faustino. "I need the money."

"I second that," said Swift.

"This would have been all for nothing!" said Jaipur, shocked.

"We'll do what we can," said Gaspar. "With or without spices, I'll convince the sultan."

"I doubt that! Zaragoza was right. We'll end up with nothing, *nothing* under you, Gaspar," said Faustino. "I'm leaving."

"What are we going to do?" I asked. "The Portuguese could be days, *hours* away. We have no ship, no deal, no allies."

We left the room, depressed, mad, scattering throughout the city, pondering what to do. Perhaps there was nothing we could do.

Prince Sikander

Scene: Appearance of a Friend

ᏫᎥᏒᎥᏉ

I COULD NOT *believe it. How could I, a prince of royal blood, lose to that . . . that . . . that Spaniard! He embarrassed me in front of all my peers—Arij, the sultan, and worse of all, my father! My father, the vizier, will be furious with me. Ruthless man, he is. Ruthless. I must compose myself, keep my feelings inside.*

A prince must have many faces to rule and stay in power. I rule by fear, as my father does, and by force. My subjects fear me; therefore, I rule indefinitely. Fear . . . Fear . . . The people fear me not, not after losing to that Spaniard! I fear my father's response more than anything.

My father summoned me to his guest house near the palace. He was sitting in a chair, surrounded by his personal guard. I approached him and bent my knee.

"You called me, Father?" I spoke.

"I did," replied Father. His physiognomy expressed anger and disappointment. "All of you leave, except my son."

The room cleared out that instant, bringing silence to the room. I could feel my father's piercing eyes look down upon me.

"Father, I did not mean—"

"Quiet," demanded my father. "You brought shame upon our people, upon our kingdom. How could you lose to a Spaniard, lose in front of the whole kingdom? You embarrassed me. By losing, you put our whole operation in jeopardy. If the sultan sides with the Spaniards, he will refuse our trade deal with the Portuguese, allowing their armada inside the port of Boubazar. No deal means the Portuguese cannot enter the Boubazar port. Does my stupid son understand these implications?"

"Yes."

"Tell me the implications."

"Without the Portuguese armada in port, attacking from the west, our armies cannot infiltrate the walls of Boubazar from the east and north."

"You put doubt in the sultan's mind!"

"I did not mean to."

"Your brother Kazi would have never lost to a Spaniard. Never. Why do you think I chose him to command our army? I made a mistake bringing you here. A mistake!"

"I do not like being compared to my older brother."

"Because he's twice the man you are?"

I fell silent.

My father began to calm himself down, exhaling and shaking his head. "You need to do something about these Spaniards now, or I'll do something. I'll do away with ye—yes, *you*. Understand?"

"Yes, Father," I remarked.

How should I kill those Spaniards? I could kill them in the shadows, assassinate them. No, that's too ugly for a prince. I could pay them off, send them on a ship, then kill them. No, they could use that against me if the sultan finds out I bribed them. What should I do? How could I convince the sultan to kill them, banish them?

If I can't convince him, oh, my father, the vizier, will execute me. I know he will. I hate my father, hate my brother Kazi, I would kill them if I had the chance.

For now I can't. I must find a way to kill the Spaniards.

I walked along the gardens, still pondering what to do. There were a few people still scattered in the garden from the party. As I was walking, a man came from the shadows and approached me. I drew my sword on him, thinking he was a thief in the night. The shadowed figure begged me to stop, revealing his face. It was a Spaniard, pleading in Spanish to me.

"What do you want, Spaniard?" I asked, sword drawn.

"I mean no harm! I want to talk," said the Spaniard.

"Why would I want to talk to you? I should kill you now. No one would know. Yes, I might do that very thing." I lifted up my sword, ready to strike.

"Wait, wait! I could give you something of value, something worth saving my head."

"Concerning?"

"Gaspar and his men."

"Aren't you part of his men?"

"No, no!"

"What is your name?"

"Zaragoza, Your Majesty."

I lowered my sword. "Speak."

"I heard you brokered a deal with the Portuguese," said Zaragoza.

"That's none of your concern."

"You want to build your empire, grow it well, play the game of diplomacy. I know court games quite well."

"Cut to the point, Spaniard."

"I offer you a deal. I could give you a trade deal with King Charles V."

"I don't care about King Charles V. The only deal I want is you and your friends banished from this rock."

"I see. I see. I want the same for Gaspar and the others."

"What do you mean?"

"I want revenge, as you do."

"You don't know what I want!"

"Yes, yes, of course, Your Majesty. What I meant to say is that I want revenge on Gaspar and his crew."

"Why turn on your fellow countrymen?"

"Gaspar and the others are not my countrymen. Traitors, they are."

"Is that so?"

"Verily so. Gaspar went against King Charles's orders, killed most of our crew. He is a treasonous pirate roaming the seas under a false pretense, a false flag. Gaspar's power and word is null and void."

"Explain yourself."

"Gaspar murdered my friends, thinking they were all against him in some plot to mutiny. The crew was forced to mutiny against him though I was caught in the wrong place, left with Gaspar and forced to do his bidding. I wanted to come to you, Prince Sikander, first before the sultan, as you looked the most reasonable."

"Yes, of course. You made the right decision coming to me first with this information," I said. "The sultan must know of these treasonous pirates."

"For the sake of justice in this new, free world, the sultan must know! Also, did I forget to mention that Gaspar still has his nautical charts to the New World?"

"You did forget."

"If one as powerful as you had those charts and a partner like me, well, he could connect the trade routes of the Eastern and Western worlds through the New World. We would gather untold riches beyond imagination. What an idea, eh?"

"Yes, enough money to buy an army, overthrow regimes," I said, staring at the night sky with a sparkle in my eye.

"Endless possibilities," said Zaragoza, his hand upon my shoulder.

"I know what we must do," I said.

"What shall we do, Your Majesty?"

"You will talk to the sultan and tell him this information."

"Would he believe me?"

"If I'm there he will," I said. "He will."

The Witch

Scene: Thought Variations I

꩜

STAR, STAR. SHOW *me, great Pole Star. Show me the light. The night air, crisp and cool, Pole Star, bright and prodigious. Show thy servant the fate of dear Gaspar and his crew.*

Horror.

Gaspar

Scene: Freedom

〇〰〰〇

WHAT IS LEFT *for my great transformation? The final piece of the puzzle, the Great Work is near—so near, so close. Let the winds rage and let the seas turn, for the ingredients are an arm's length away from Gaspar. Soon—yes, soon—I shall have the power, and my soul will morph from black gall into golden rays.*

Oh, Great Chord, show me the way. Show Thy servant Thy way. Complete my transformation. The Egyptians discovered it. The Jews labored over it. The Greeks witnessed it. The Muslims, the sultan, protect it. Gaspar will complete it.

Yes, I will complete the transformation of it and become the one—yes, the enlightened one—higher than a noble, a prince, a sultan, a king.

I sat there in my room, pondering and dreaming of the orange gold, Retjenu gold. There was a sudden knock on my door.

"Who comes?" I asked.

"It is Jaipur," he replied. "May I enter?"

"Perfect. I wanted to see you. Come, come."

Jaipur sat down across from me, twiddling his fingers.

"Sir, I wanted to talk to you about . . . about . . . about something." His voice trembled as he spoke softly.

"Speak with words, my friend," I said lightly.

"Aye, we discussed before this endeavor that I would be free upon reaching the Spice Islands."

"We did."

Jaipur took a deep breath. "I come to you to make true on that promise, the promise of my freedom. Gaspar, you have treated me well, and I thank you with my whole heart for this, but I wish to be free—free to roam, free to leave, free to be free."

He spoke with true sincerity.

I stared at him, looked into his eyes. Silent, we were.

"I knew it was hopeless," sighed Jaipur, getting up from his chair.

"Grab my brown bag on the bed," I pointed. "There."

"What?"

"The brown bag on the bed. Grab it."

Jaipur did so and handed it to me. I took out a large, leather-bound book, opened it, and pulled out an old piece of parchment. I took my quill, dipped it in carbon-based ink, and signed the old paper.

Jaipur stared at me with deep passion. "Is that . . . ?"

I handed him the parchment. "This is your freedom, signed by my hand."

"Freedom?" questioned Jaipur as he looked at the parchment. "*My* freedom?"

"I kept your deed with me for many years, brought it here for this moment. You are free, Jaipur."

A tear dripped down Jaipur's cheek, hitting the wood floor. He tried to hold back his feelings, but his tears overflowed, pouring out.

"I don't . . . don't know what to say," stuttered Jaipur. "Thank you, Gaspar."

"Do not thank me," I replied. "Rather, I ask you for your forgiveness."

"For what?"

"For enslaving you for all of these years."

"You never treated me like a slave. Well, other than forcing me on your wild adventures."

"It was wrong, though in my heart I knew the only way to reach this island was with your help."

"I'm honored, though I didn't do that much to get us here."

"You did enough, more than you will ever know."

Jaipur nodded with humility.

I continued, "One more thing. On your deed, I included a gift to you. My charts."

"Charts?" said Jaipur. "You don't mean your nautical charts?"

"Aye, I do."

"No, Gaspar. I can't take your life's work."

"If you so choose to return with us to Europe, my charts will be yours upon arrival. Granted, I will need them to return home, but the moment we step foot on European soil, my charts are willed to you. Further, if some misfortune were to befall me prior to reaching Europe, you are my beneficiary to my estate and will."

"Gaspar! Your whole estate?"

"Aye."

"You are mad, Gaspar. Mad indeed. But a good kind of mad."

"I must be. Then it is settled, I will—"

"Wait."

"Wait?"

"Your gifts are sweeter than honey, but . . . "

"But?"

"I am staying here on the Spice Islands. I seek to return home, to my *true* home, to my family. Please understand this, Gaspar."

I smiled. "I do."

Jaipur made a slight bow before me.

"If or when the time comes," I said, "you may choose who shall receive my charts. It's still my gift to you."

"Whom should I choose?"

"That's your decision."

"Well, I'll need to know where the charts are when I choose."

"You'll find them when you need them."

"You always were secretive, Gaspar."

"And always will be."

Jaipur thanked me once more and, carrying his deed, left the room. The moment he left my room, I began to pack my astrolabe, vials, food, water, books, and other intricate tools into my backpack.

As I looked around, I realized it may be a while before I would see this room again, if at all. Seamlessly and inconspicuously, I left the room and the house without a soul knowing. I made my way for the witch.

The sun began to leave her golden throne, granting me a twilight sky, revealing the stars in the celestial sphere. The time had come to begin the process, my transformation.

I knocked on the witch's door three times.

Thump. Thump. Thump.

Her door creaked open without a face to greet me.

I walked in. "Where art thou, Witch?"

"Here. Here I am," she replied, walking up from the basement.

"Are you ready?"

"If you are."

"Do you have my ingredients?"

"Took a while, but yes, I have them."

"Good."

"As you scared for what lies beyond the shadows?"

"Why should I be?"

"No man returns from the labyrinth."

"I am no ordinary man."

"What makes you different?"

I opened my brown bag, opened the flap, and pulled out a circular amulet with the symbol of Anubis on it. "This. The key to the teardrop."

Her eyes grew wider than the fixed horizon. "The Amulet of Retjenu, the conductor."

"The stars have aligned, and the labyrinth is primed," I said. "Now bring me to the entrance."

Faustino

Scene: Sudden Appearance of an Old Aquaintance

⟨ഝ⟩

I PONDERED TO myself as I sat at a table in a tavern on the far edge of the city. At least, I thought it was a tavern. It looked like a rug store to me. I was drinking *koumiss*, an alcoholic milk of sorts, from a bowl. It tasted refreshing.

Still, why did I ever come on this voyage? Why? Because I had no gold, had lost it all gambling. Why did I gamble like that, wager my life's savings like that? Why did I act like that? I had a problem, but I also had a solution. *Koumiss*. Is that the answer? My eyes stared into the bowl, searching for the answer.

What are answers? Is there such a thing as an answer or a question or a desire? I desired alcohol, desired it more than the woman I loved. My love had left me, left me because of a drinking problem. Nay, I didn't have a drinking problem. *She* had a drinking problem! If anything, she led me to this drinking problem, led me straight to it with her nagging, her nonstop nagging. I couldn't stand her any longer.

She had to be silenced, silenced by a slap.

Once, twice, thrice . . .

A drinking problem? A gambling problem? More like a nagging problem.

Then, I remembered I had no gold. That was why I was here. I was told this expedition would be dangerous though balanced by a great reward. Infinite spices, they told me. I had nothing to lose, only to gain.

Only to gain another sip . . .

As I drank from my bowl, I thought about that night, played it out in my head. After I hit her, soon after, I started to see a shadow, *my shadow*, creeping in the night. It was the shadow that led me to the recruiting table. It told me to sign up with Captain Gaspar, told me to discipline my ex-wife, told me other things . . . dark things, good things!

The shadow's voice never ceased. He told me that Gaspar would turn on me, side with that Cosimo. I had tried to silence the voice, thinking it . . . him . . . whatever it was . . . was wrong. Nay, I was wrong for silencing the shadow, for he was right. Gaspar had turned on me and sided with those . . . those pests. The shadow told me to follow Zaragoza, and look at what happened.

Damn you, Gaspar! I should discipline you like I did my ex-wife. Aye, and do the same to that Cosimo. I think I'll do that.

I turned my attention toward the door of the tavern. There was the shadow, gesturing at me to follow it. He wanted to show me where Gaspar was in order to discipline him. I knew I must follow the shadow, for the shadow knew, always knew, and always will know.

The owner approached me and spoke Arabic gibberish to me. I didn't speak pig tongue. I spoke Castilian Spanish! I then poured my bowl on him.

"Leave me alone, ye savage pig," I said, turning away from him.

In a moment's notice, four men surrounded me.

I screamed, "To hell with all of you pigs!"

They grabbed me by the shoulder, demanding payment. I punched one of them square in the face. As a result, the four men started to beat me.

Strike, punch, jab, one after the other. I fell to the ground, helpless.

They then picked me up and threw me out the door and into the mud. It took a minute for my senses to return. I groaned from the pain, flopping around in the mud. My right eye was swollen shut; both sides of my chest were bruised. I think they had broken one of my ribs.

"You are pigs, all of you!" I yelled with my fist raised. Mud covered my hair, face, and clothes.

I rose slowly and steadily, feeling the pain in my side. I noticed a full moon outside, feeling the cool night's whisper in the air.

The pain feels good. How?

I looked up and around. There at the end of the street was the shadow, gesturing for me to follow. I was lost in a daze.

Gripping my bruised side, I started to move toward the shadow. I had to catch the shadow. I had to follow it. The shadow then moved into the alley. I followed it around corners, up and down tight stairs, until I came upon a strange building decorated with two serpents eating one another.

I saw the shadow, still in the distance, right in front of the building. Next to the shadow was a beautiful woman, but why?

The shadow turned toward me, revealing its face. The shadow became Gaspar! Did my eyes deceive me? Gaspar was before me . . . with a woman.

I felt betrayed. The shadow showed me the truth. Gaspar had lied to me. He was more worried about a woman than my gold, my pay. Gaspar must be disciplined!

In an instant, Gaspar and the woman left the building, walking into the alley with haste.

No, no, he shall not leave me anymore. The shadow, the shadow . . . I shall find out where my shadow goes.

"You shall be disciplined, both of you," I muttered, keeping close behind Gaspar and this mysterious woman.

I followed them through the streets, out of the city, and into the mountainside. It was a hard trek to say the least, but I kept on them, determined to have my revenge upon Gaspar. After hours of walking, Gaspar and the woman approached an open ledge overlooking the thick bush of the jungle. I stayed hidden behind a boulder, gripping my sword, ready to pounce on them.

But then, I heard Gaspar utter words in a strange language, sounding identical to when he spoke to that Egyptian wall.

Could this be the gold? Aye, this was the way to the gold! I knew Gaspar was hiding something from me. I knew he wanted gold—gold for himself, all for himself, and not for Faustino! Good thing the shadow led me to him.

After Gaspar spoke the words, to my amazement, the rock face began to shake like an earthquake. Coming from the rock, rising upward, was a platform made of a strange material I knew not. Blue lights spiraled outward from the platform. My whole world was flipped upside down, realizing the reason for this journey. It all made sense. Gaspar had come here for this, for ancient gold hidden beneath the earth, not for the spices. I wanted the gold, needed the gold, the city of gold!

Gaspar kissed the woman on the lips, then stepped onto the platform and was lowered into the earth. The moment he disappeared, I came out from behind the boulder. The woman screamed, realizing I was there. I grabbed her by the arm before she could run away. Her face was defined; she had long eyelashes and brown skin. She reminded me of my ex-wife. I hated my ex-wife. She needed to be disciplined.

The woman begged me to let her go, pleading for mercy. Standing before us was the shadow, watching us, telling me to discipline her.

The woman turned and saw the shadow standing behind her. I felt the fear rush through her body as she screamed for help. No one could help her now as no one could have helped my wife back then on that secluded mountain top.

Strange. This seems similar, if not the same, to how my ex-wife died. Same predicament. What are the odds?

Prince Sikander

Scene: Throne Room Persuasion

ᑕᗰᗰᓯᑐ

T HE TIME IS *nigh to end this Spanish ulcer, this pestilence, so that my true plans may unfold. The Portuguese are near. The sultan must side with me and with my father, the vizier. The Portuguese must enter the harbor. With our army coming from the east, surrounding the city, the sultan would be forced to surrender the crown without a battle or drop of blood. We'll strike the moment they enter the harbor, the moment the sultan concedes. Their cannons will blow through the walls, destroy them, allowing our armies inside.*

Genius, genius! The sultan likes the Spaniards and is skeptical of me. Nay, not after now, not after he learns of their dark and treasonous ways, for I have one of their own to testify against them. Zara . . . Za . . . Gogo . . . What's his name again? It does not matter, for the moment I take the city, I'll kill him with ease. The sultan will not be able to protect any Spaniard or his precious daughter from me.

Yes, perfect.

I entered the throne room, and seated upon his majestic throne was the sultan, appearing confused and flushed.

"Great King Muzaffar, Commander of the Faithful, may I have an audience this hour?" I asked.

"Yes, you may," replied the sultan. "Come forward."

"I wanted to bring forth some—what's the right word?—some concerning information regarding the Spaniards and their captain."

"Continue."

"Wise and most gracious sultan, I am obliged as a servant to my kingdom," I began.

"Get to your point, Prince," said the sultan.

"Oh, yes. The Spaniards that have come to our shores are not under King Charles V. In fact, they are mutineers to the king of Spain, bargaining and trading under a false pretense. They want to broker a deal for a ship, for spices, under a false promise to return to your grace. They play us for fools, Your Majesty. They want to steal our goods and hospitality while putting at risk our deal with the Portuguese, who are but a day or so away.

"On top of all of these things, I came to know from a Portuguese emissary that Captain Gaspar was once a Portuguese pilot and went against his own king, King Manuel of Portugal, in the same manner as he is doing to King Charles V: mutiny and piracy. The Portuguese want Gaspar and his treasonous crew for the sake of justice on the high seas.

"Worst of all, my most loyal men have witnessed Gaspar entering the house of a witch multiple times over the past few days. Not only does Captain Gaspar offend us, but he also offends and insults Allah, the all-seeing and all-knowing.

"As a result, the Spaniards cannot be trusted, and I believe we must give them to the Portuguese to conduct justice on behalf of us and Allah. In doing so, we shall show the Portuguese good faith in our new alliance between our three kingdoms. The Spaniards must be dealt with in haste, Your Majesty. With haste."

I then bowed in respect and honor.

The sultan's eyes were sharp as he rubbed his chin, thinking. After a minute of silence, the sultan said, "How do I know the validity of these accusations? I am but a just ruler, an honest ruler."

"I thought you would ask that, Your Majesty," I replied. I turned toward the guards and gestured. "Bring him in."

At that moment, the doors opened, and Zaragoza walked into the throne room and bowed to the king. We then spoke in Spanish.

"This is Zara . . . Za . . . Za . . . " I said, fumbling my words.

"Zaragoza, Your Grace," he said.

"Yes, Zaragoza," I stated. "He brings his attestation to my claims."

"It's an honor to have an audience with such a wise king," said Zaragoza.

"Are your statements true?" asked the sultan sternly.

"Yes, they are, Your Majesty. They are," said Zaragoza. "I am the voice of King Charles V, a true blue-blooded Spaniard. I was given power by King Charles to carry out his word and rule abroad."

"What were the king's orders?" questioned the sultan.

"To determine if the western passage is a viable route for future trade and diplomacy. Nothing more than that," said Zaragoza. "Captain Gaspar and his loyalists went against the king's orders by continuing to pass through the western strait for their own political gain. They risked the lives of our men by pushing farther into the Pacific without provisions or court order. Captain Gaspar and his loyalists sought fame and glory and did so at the expense of the Spanish crew's lives. Captain Gaspar refused to turn around at the western strait, and when we tried to demand thus, Gaspar killed multiple Spanish officers and sailors who protested his decision."

"Then why are you here and not on the ship?" asked the sultan with a raised eyebrow.

"Captain Gaspar picked me and a few of his loyalists to go on a scouting mission on this island. Gaspar chose me because he thought I was plotting against him, plotting a mutiny, and thought that by bringing me the crew would not mutiny while he was on the island."

"*Were* you plotting against him?" asked the sultan.

"No, Your Majesty," said Zaragoza.

"Then what?"

"The crew took the ship while we were on the scouting mission. The crew stranded me with Gaspar and his loyalists on the island."

"So, the crew mutinied, not Gaspar?"

"No, sir. Gaspar went against the king's orders, as I've said, by refusing to turn around once the strait of the southern continent was found. Captain Gaspar killed in cold blood those who refused his order. The crew had no choice but to return to Spain."

"I see," said the sultan. He then stared at Zaragoza without a flinch or flash of his eye, pondering his decisions. After a few moments of silence, he said, "It sounds persuasive. The prince is convinced, yet my gut does not trust any of you."

"I speak in truth, Your Majesty," I said, bowing with my hand on my heart.

"Regardless, I refuse to do business with a man who associates himself and his crew with dark magic," said the sultan. "It is my duty as the Commander of the Faithful to arrest Captain Gaspar and his crew for their deceitful actions and wicked, pirate-like ways. Prince Sikander."

"Yes, Your Majesty?" I replied.

"Have them arrested, and bring them before me to testify. If Captain Gaspar and his loyalist crew are found guilty, I shall hand them over to the Portuguese. If they resist, kill them on the spot."

"I shall find them without a moment to spare," I replied.

Swift

Scene: Symbol of the Ancients

GXXXXO

I RAN THROUGH the city and hurried around alleyways, as the great lamp was diming her light above. The air was cool and dry. After a long sprint across the city, I reached our house. My clothes were drenched in sweat, and my lungs struggled for breath. I opened the door. Cosimo was in the long hallway, leaning his shoulders on one of the arches.

"Swift, you back?" asked Cosimo, smiling. "We're celebrating upstairs."

"Celebrating what?" I asked.

"Gaspar gave Jaipur his freedom!"

A wave of joy washed over me. "Wow!"

"Yes, indeed."

My happiness then fell to a black cloud as concern filled my face.

"What's wrong? You look stressed," said Cosimo.

"Gaspar," I said. "Gaspar. I saw where he goes."

"Oh, no."

"Aye. Oh, no."

Cosimo and I hurried up the stairs into the open living room.

"Swift!" exclaimed Jaipur, standing up to greet me. "Did you hear the good news? I'm free today!"

"I did, my friend," I replied. "I am more than happy for you, but—"

"I don't like that look on your face," remarked Jaipur, concerned. "Say what it is."

"What troubles you, Swift?" asked Toro.

"He saw Gaspar," said Cosimo.

"As did I, no less than a few hours ago," stated Jaipur.

"Give me some parchment," I said.

"I have *khawi*," said Toro. "Here."

Khawi was animal skin, yellow in color and higher in quality than lamb parchment to scribe on. I took the skin and drew out the sign of two snakes eating one another, the sign above the house Gaspar went into. The group huddled around me.

"I saw Gaspar go there," I said.

"Into a snake?" said Jaipur.

"This was the symbol above the door," I replied.

Each person looked at the drawing intently.

"What in this geocentric universe . . . " muttered Cosimo.

"Seen that before. The sign of a magician, a sorcerer," said Toro.

"I followed Gaspar there," I said.

"Gaspar is a dark man," said Jaipur. "Talks to himself. All of you know this. But a sorcerer?"

"There's more," I added.

"What?" asked Cosimo, examining the drawing.

"One of Prince Sikander's guards, or so I think it was, was following Gaspar," I said.

"That's not good," said Toro.

"Did the guard see you?" asked Cosimo.

"No," I replied.

"I guarantee Sikander will tell the sultan about this funny business," I said. "He wants us dead, gone, banished—any and all of the above."

"Whoa, I'm not a friend of Sikander, but let's not jump to any conclusions, eh?" said Jaipur.

Cosimo was still enthralled by the drawing, ignoring our conversation. "I think . . . I think I've seen this before, but where?"

"From what I thought, I'd wager that symbol has something to do with that Egyptian we saw in the cave," I said. "Aye, my last silverling."

"I remember now. Yes, it's an ancient symbol of alchemy," said Cosimo. "Back on the ship, Gaspar told me about his ingredients . . . about salt-fire."

We looked around, trying to understand what Cosimo meant.

"Isn't that what Gaspar sprinkled on our torches in the cave?" asked Jaipur.

"Aye, it was. It was," I said.

"We need to go to a library, one around here," said Cosimo. "Has anyone seen a library?"

"Not I," I said.

"Yes, down the street is a large one. I went there the other day," said Toro.

"I didn't see you go there," remarked Jaipur.

"I did it after my morning prayers to Allah while you were sleeping," said Toro.

"Where are Zaragoza and Faustino?" I asked.

"Gone," said Toro.

"They're always gone," said Jaipur.

"Let's get to the library," said Cosimo. "I feel our answers to this puzzle will be found there."

Cosimo

Scene: Dance of the Library

⟨ᘓᙏᙖᖇ⟩

E made it to the library a couple streets over from our house. The library was built out of marble, constructed with massive golden arches supported by light blue columns. The library seemed to have an infinite number of shelves filled with scrolls, books, and parchments of all shapes, sizes, and languages and from different time periods.

"What are you looking for?" asked Toro as we walked past rows and rows of shelves.

"Practical chemistry . . . transmutation of metals . . . mystics," I said.

"We'll need help finding that one," said Toro.

Toro looked to one of the librarians, spoke to him in Arabic, and asked for assistance finding scrolls on these topics. The librarian nodded and walked us through the tall shelves until we came upon a large wooden door. The librarian handed each of us our own candle, and we descended down another row of dark corridors until we reached a section of shelves hidden away by time. This section was surrounded by spiderwebs. The librarian told Toro this was the correct section and then walked away.

"This place needs a deep clean," said Jaipur.

"I like the feel of this section. It smells old, looks old," I said. "I like it."

I began to browse the shelves filled with numerous stacked scrolls. Each of the scrolls was marked in Latin. After a minute or two of searching, I found a scroll with information on ancient alchemy.

"Latin scrolls? Here?" asked Swift.

"Muslims were keen on acquiring knowledge from around the world," I said as I read through the scroll. "This may take a moment."

I peered through the scroll, trying to understand this enigma of alchemy in all of its complex concepts. Then, I stumbled upon the symbol of the serpents.

"Yes!" I yelled. "Here! The two serpents."

"What does it mean?" asked Jaipur.

"Hold on," I said.

I continued to read and analyze the scroll. My eyes found the words *prima materia*, the prime material, surrounded by Egyptian hieroglyphics. Why would Gaspar want this, this *prima materia*? What would a seafaring spice trader want with *prima materia*?

"Those hieroglyphics look similar to the paintings on that wall in the cave," said Swift.

"Yes, yes," I said. "Listen to this. *The Egyptians found a mysterious chaotic rock from a faraway land. They called this rock Gold of Retjenu, said to contain power beyond the celestial sphere, power from the heavens.* But wait . . . "

"Faraway lands?" added Swift.

"That's the gold Gaspar spoke of!" exclaimed Jaipur. "Gold of Retjenu."

"You are right," said Swift.

I continued to read aloud. "*The stone, red in color, must be transformed and mutated, like the raw state of Adaman to unlock its true power.*"

"Sounds like Adam," said Swift.

"From scripture," added Toro.

"You mean Adam from the Bible? As in God?" asked Jaipur.

"Adaman means 'red earth' in Hebrew," said Toro.

"Toro, where do you learn this stuff?" stated Jaipur.

"I read a lot," said Toro.

I continued, "*God grew angry at Adam, cursed the red earth. In order for the material, for mankind, the soul to be redeemed, man must go through a transformation to be free from saturnine mud.*"

"'Soul'?" said Swift. "I thought you said 'stone.'"

"Soul and stone, intertwined, stuck in mud," I replied. "*To free one's power from the mud, the material, the soul must go through a labyrinth of transformation, transmutation, called the Great Work.*"

"I've heard Gaspar say that more than a few times," I remarked.

"I'm lost," said Jaipur. "I have no clue what's going on now."

I continued, "*The labyrinth corresponds to the signs of the zodiac, of the stars aligned in such a way that the only way to enter and navigate the labyrinth is by the stars.*"

"Wait, wait. I'm starting to understand," said Jaipur. "Is this labyrinth real or a metaphor perhaps?"

"Could be real," said Toro.

"I agree," said Cosimo.

"If it's real, who could build something that size, and where could they build it without anyone knowing about it?" asked Jaipur.

"The Egyptians?" added Swift.

"In the earth below the surface," said Toro.

We all looked to Toro, shocked, realizing the labyrinth could be below the surface.

"I think you are right, Toro," I said.

"Keep reading," demanded Swift.

"*Once the* prima materia, *called Gold of Retjenu, undergoes the labyrinth of transformation, the material shall become drinkable gold, giving the soul and body power to see the heavens.*"

"Can't be possible. Can't be," said Swift. "Would Gaspar really be searching for a mythical labyrinth now? Here? On this island? We're here for spices, not fairy tales, unless . . . "

"Unless he never came for spices," said Toro.

"Oh, I felt that one," said Jaipur. "I'll say this: Gaspar did not come for spices. No, sir."

"Where . . . Where does it say the labyrinth is located?" asked Swift.

I rolled down the scroll, and there at the bottom was a rough sketch of the world with a star on a large island off the coast of India, labeled with a hieroglyphic phrase of some sort. Based upon my maps, it looked to be near our location, if not our exact location. My mouth dropped upon seeing the star on the scroll, realizing our situation, the dishonesty, and the secret before us.

"Gaspar . . . No," said Jaipur. "He wouldn't come all this way here for a stone. He sailed across the world for spices. Men died for those spices. I almost died for those spices."

"He promised King Charles those spices," said Swift. "What will the king make of this? Of us? Of our expedition? He might believe those mutineers!"

"Right now, I fear the sultan's reaction more than that of King Charles," said Toro.

"He'll believe Sikander," said Swift. "Better yet, the sultan would believe the incoming Portuguese over us. They can't wait to wring us by the necks."

"We need something—*anything*—to prove our innocence!" said Jaipur.

"Wouldn't it be a strong move if Gaspar found the stone . . . the rock . . . whatever it is and used it as a bargaining tool?" asked Swift. "That would be something, eh?"

"As a matter of fact, I think Gaspar *is* doing that," I said.

"You think so?" said Swift.

"I would say so," said Toro.

"Let's plead with the sultan for mercy," said Jaipur.

"Instead of pleading, what if we searched for the stone ourselves?" suggested Swift.

"What do you mean, Swift?" I asked.

"We're enemies of the Portuguese, right?" said Swift. "And if Sikander is right, they'll be here soon. That means they have an accord with the sultan."

"Yes," I said. "That's true."

"Even if we plead with the sultan for mercy," said Swift, "I bet he still would hand us over to the Portuguese as a matter of good faith in his newfound alliance with them and Sikander. You see my point?"

"Aye, your point is we're hopeless," said Jaipur. "Gaspar has abandoned us."

"Gaspar might have abandoned us, but what if we could find this material, this rock for ourselves and bargain with the sultan, bargain for our lives?" asked Swift.

"That's a long shot, Swift," I said.

"It be our only shot," said Toro.

"You mean to say we should search for a mythical labyrinth in hopes of finding a stone inside that labyrinth in order to bargain with the sultan for our lives," said Jaipur. "Am I correct?"

"Not only for our lives," said Swift. "Perhaps also for spices and a way home."

"I can't imagine Gaspar picking up and leaving us," said Jaipur. "Or maybe I could too well."

"We'll soon find out," I said.

"See where the labyrinth is on the island," said Toro.

I flipped through the scrolls, reading, reading. Then, I came upon an ancient map, showing the different points on the island.

"Look, the gate we encountered in the cave was labeled as an entry point to the island," I stated.

My finger followed the river, which cut into the mountain. Inside the mountain, the scroll showed a drawing of a large gate leading into a sketched labyrinth.

"The river near the city will take us to the labyrinth," I said.

"Does it say any more?" asked Swift.

I scanned the parchment, searching for any remaining indications, legends, anything. But time had worn away any other words. Then, I came to a barely legible phrase at the bottom of the page.

I read it aloud. "It says, 'Beware the shadow and beast.'"

Shadow . . . shadow . . .

Faustino had spoken of a shadow. I'd heard Gaspar speak of the shadow. I had seen a shadow, the shadow on the ship. No, no, that couldn't be the same shadow. What was the shadow and beast? A fearful chill crept up my spine.

"To hell with that!" said Jaipur. "I say we run—run, swim, fly to another island if we have to. We'll run from them all, all of our enemies!"

"I'm not running away when the spices are this close," said Swift, "for a shadow, beast, or any other fairy creature."

"Then you can go down in the dark. Not I. Not I!" said Jaipur.

"If we don't find Gaspar, then we have no other choice but to descend into the labyrinth," I said. "Not even Arij could help us by that point."

"I vote we go back now, back to the house," said Swift.

"I am meeting the princess after this," I said. "She might know of the rock, of the gold."

"It could be a trap!" said Jaipur.

"No," I said. "No, it's not."

"She could help us and tell us what her father is thinking," I said.

"We'll go back and see if Gaspar has returned," said Swift. "In case something happens, if anything happens, let's meet at the waterfall, the place where we first met Arij."

"Good idea," said Toro.

"Aye. Good, Swift," I said. "That's where I'm meeting Arij."

"I have a feeling we'll be right behind you then," sighed Jaipur.

"Godspeed, Cosimo," said Swift.

"Godspeed, all of you," I said.

Swift

Scene: The Book

⌒℧℧℧↺

J AIPUR, TORO, AND I returned from the library with the utmost speed. We approached the front of the house, and Jaipur said, "People were here. Candles are lit inside."

"You are right," said Toro.

"The question is who?" I spoke.

"Sikander's men?" asked Jaipur.

"Might be," I said. "Keep your sword ready."

We opened the door and peeked inside; no one was there. We heard rustling on the floor above us. I signaled for us to be quiet, then pointed up. Toro and Jaipur nodded and tiptoed up the stairs. My heart began to beat rapidly though I had to stay calm. We reached the next floor, and the living room was a disaster; chairs were knocked over, furniture was ripped up, and parchment was scattered across the floor. The room appeared as if a storm had mercilessly blown through it.

Then, I heard shuffling coming from Gaspar's room. We looked to one another, understanding the fight to ensue. I took a deep breath and gripped my sword, and we approached Gaspar's room.

Inside Gaspar's room, the candlelight illuminated on the wall a shadow of a man as he rummaged through objects. Toro and I made eye contact. He then nodded, and I gestured my head for him to make the move.

Toro then moved into the room quickly. Jaipur and I charged fearlessly behind Toro.

We all stopped, realizing who the culprit was.

"Zaragoza?" I asked.

Zaragoza turned to us in a flash and tried to make for the window. Toro picked up a white plate on the ground and threw it at him. Zaragoza fell to the ground, gasping in pain.

"You scoundrel dog!" exclaimed Jaipur. "We should kill him here and now."

I picked up Zaragoza by the collar. "You cleaning up the place, eh?"

Zaragoza panted. "Swift, Toro, Jaipur. Nice to see you. Didn't think you would be here."

"Good thing we were," said Jaipur.

I punched Zaragoza in the gut. "What are you looking for? Why did you do this?"

Jaipur looked around the room and sighed. "My head. That plate hit my head."

"Explain yourself, Zaragoza," said Toro.

"Explain what?" said Zaragoza.

"I'm done with this," I remarked. I threw him on a wooden table. "Hold out his arm."

Zaragoza resisted, but Toro punched him square in the face, almost knocking him out cold.

"I see cheesecake, cheesecake," said Zaragoza, delusional from the punch. Toro grabbed Zaragoza's arm, forced it out, and nodded.

"You don't talk, you lose your arm," I said, holding up my blade that glistened in the candlelight.

Zaragoza's eyes widened, and sweat poured from his forehead. "Fine! Fine! Not my arm. Nay! What do you want to know?"

"The room!" yelled Jaipur.

"I'm searching for something," said Zaragoza.

"For what?" I asked.

"I don't know," said Zaragoza.

I then slashed his leg, cutting the top portion of his thigh. He shrieked. "For the charts! Gaspar's nautical charts!"

"Why?" I asked. "Who wants them? Tell me, or I'll take the whole arm clean off!"

"Prince Sikander!" said Zaragoza.

"You made a new friend, eh?" I spoke.

"He was always social," said Jaipur. "Social on the *Valencia*, too."

Zaragoza chuckled to himself. "Social enough to mutiny. Too bad Javier left me with ye savages."

"I knew you played a part in it!" exclaimed Jaipur.

"That matters not now," I said. "Tell me of Sikander. What did you promise him in return for the charts?"

"He will save my head when the Portuguese arrive and give me a stake in our new trade deal," said Zaragoza. "All of you are dead men. The sultan knows you are a bunch of treasonous pirates who meddle in dark magic against Allah. Oh, ho! He, not I, will hand you over to the Portuguese upon their arrival. Nay, not I!"

"We do not partake in dark magic," proclaimed Toro.

"Aye, but your captain does. Captain Gaspar," said Zaragoza. "You should have spoken against him on the *Valencia*. Aye, you should have!"

"Glad I didn't," said Jaipur.

"If you did," said Zaragoza, "I would have made you a slave of mine, serving me in my future palace. You go to the brig now!"

"I am no slave," said Jaipur. He then punched Zaragoza right in the nose.

"Ah!" shrieked Zaragoza as blood poured from his nostrils. "My nose! I bet you broke it! You'll hang for that, savage. Prince Sikander will hang you for that!"

"We need to leave," said Toro. "Get out of town before the guards come for us."

At that moment, Zaragoza punched me in the stomach, pulled a knife out from under his white shirt, and cut Toro in the arm. I reached for my sword. In a flash, Zaragoza jumped through a two-story window and landed through a broker's stall, breaking his fall.

"He's on the run!" said Jaipur.

"Leave him," I said. "Are you okay, Toro?"

"Aye," said Toro as he wrapped his bleeding forearm in a purple cloth.

"If Zaragoza's right, the sultan's guards are looking for us as we speak. We can't outfight them," said Jaipur.

"Wait, what about Gaspar's nautical charts?" I asked.

"Gaspar gave them to me," said Jaipur. "Well, he willed them to me."

"Where are they?" asked Toro.

"I'm not sure," said Jaipur.

"Not sure?" I questioned.

"Gaspar said when I want the charts, I'll know where to find them," said Jaipur.

I thought for a moment, repeating to myself what Jaipur said and looking around Gaspar's room.

I then said, "Where? Here? Under the bed? No. Where would Gaspar hide them?"

Toro checked the drawers. "Nothing here."

We searched the white room through and through like a bird searching from above the green tree line for her dinner on the forest floor. I looked inside the closet, finding nothing but women's robes. We looked around the marble house, inside cabinets, under rugs, even in the tightest of places where not even a mouse could fit. Stil, we found nothing.

"He must have burned the charts," sighed Jaipur, slumping into a wooden chair.

"I doubt that," said Toro, "but we have not the time to keep searching."

"Regardless, I have no idea where the charts are. There. Simple as that," said Jaipur.

I rubbed my chin, pondering where the charts could be. "Jaipur, did Gaspar give you anything before he left?"

"Not that I know of. No, wait. Yes. Yes, he did! The deed to my freedom," said Jaipur.

"Give it here," I said.

"Why?" questioned Jaipur.

"Give it here, please," I insisted.

"Good eye, Cosimo," said Toro.

Jaipur hesitated but opened up his brown bag and handed me an old piece of parchment. I began to scan the deed.

"Have you read it?" I asked.

"Can't read," replied Jaipur. "Never learned."

"Here! On the back of your deed!" I exclaimed.

"Something there?" asked Jaipur.

I continued, "It says you, Jaipur, own the nautical charts, and they are located under the stone floor near the bed."

Our eyes each looked to Gaspar's bed and noticed one stone grayer in color. We rushed over the tile, picked it up, and moved it to the side. Hidden in the floorboards was a brown bag filled with thick, leather-bound books. I pulled out the bag and opened one book.

There before us were the nautical charts of the known globe, charted by Gaspar. The book was filled with degrees, zodiac signs, constellations, and magnificent maps of the world painted in light green, pink, gold, and teal blue. Other pages were of drawings of armillary spheres, nocturnals, celestial spheres, exotic animals and their anatomies, and much more.

The last few pages were incredible scenes of the heavens above and the Lord seated upon his throne, surrounded by angels. Below His feet was the Garden of Eden with Adam and Eve in perfect form. Next to them was the Tree of Life with strange, glowing orange apples hanging from the limbs. At the foot of the tree was a teal serpent with dark red eyes, lurking in the shadows, staring at Adam and Eve. Below the Garden of Eden—the terranean surface—was the place of fire where monstrous, horned beasts fell into the red abyss below. It was the most amazing drawing I had ever laid my eyes on.

"This was a collaboration," I stated. "This book, these charts, this nautical work of art."

"Looks to be a connection between the study of the natural world, art, and religion," said Toro.

"That's over my head," said Jaipur.

I reached the end of the book, and there were three signatures: Gaspar, Cosimo, and one other. An Italian name.

"Whose name is that?" asked Toro

"I think the signature reads Michelangelo," I spoke. "He must have done the drawings. He's pretty damn good from what I know. Damn good."

"I've seen better," said Jaipur.

Toro rolled his eyes at Jaipur.

"You like it, Swift?" asked Jaipur.

"Very much so," I replied. "Very much so."

"As do I," said Toro.

"It's yours. Have it," said Jaipur.

"Jaipur!" I exclaimed. "This is priceless."

"And it's yours now," smiled Jaipur. "Consider it a token of friendship. Take good care of it."

"Jaipur," I said, humbled. "Thank you."

"Wait," said Toro. "You hear that? Guards. Down below."

"We need to leave!" exclaimed Jaipur.

"Give me a second to think," I said. I scanned the room, and my eyes drifted to the closest. I pushed a chair and table, blocking the closet, and opened the door. Inside the closet hanging on a rack were women's robes and veils of many different colors, styles, and sizes. I turned to the others. "We could wear these robes. The veils would cover our faces."

"You mean dress up as women?" questioned Toro.

"Aye, we must talk in a high voice, keep our faces covered," I said. "No one would suspect a thing."

"I'm not good at acting," said Jaipur.

"You are today," I said. "Hurry."

Toro

Scene: Dance of the Mimes

꙰꙰꙰

MY DRESS IS too big," said Jaipur. "It's dragging."

"Looks fine to me," said Swift.

"Keep quiet," said Toro.

We continued down the cobblestone street leading away from our house. Behind us, a whole regiment of guards surrounded our house and stormed inside, looking for us. We missed them by a minute.

"That was close," said Jaipur. "Why is it always so close?"

A guard shouted in Arabic to us. "Wait! You three, come here."

"What did he say?" asked Swift. "I don't speak Arabic."

"This is the end. Oh, this is it," whispered Jaipur.

"Let me do the talking," I said.

The guard ran up to us. He was a burly man with a deep voice and outfitted in black armor. We slowly turned around.

"How are you ladies doing tonight?" asked the guard, smiling.

I answered with a high-pitched tone. "Praise be to Allah. What are you doing to that house?"

"Oh, yes. Praise be to Allah," replied the guard. "We are looking for Spanish men. They are dangerous magicians conspiring against Allah and the sultan. Very dangerous, they are."

"Oh, my," I replied. "Good thing we have such strong and buff guards like you to protect poor, innocent women like us from such danger."

"It is rather tough, tougher after those morning workouts."

"I can tell."

"You can? I have been working hard on my arms. See this one?" He cleared his throat. "Uh, well, have . . . have ye seen them, the foreigners?"

"No, what do they look like?"

"They look different from us. They dress differently though this city is full of different people. They dress like magicians. Yes, like magicians. I think there is one tall, ebony-skinned man, a short islander man, and a few white men from Europe. They all speak Spanish."

"Here? In Boubazar?"

"Yes, we've arrested a bunch of mimes with white painted faces already."

"You mean the mimes from the festival?"

"Correct. They could be magicians, Spanish magicians, with those painted faces. One mime tried to put a silent box around me. He tried to box me in, scared me; I had to arrest him. That mime must have been a Spanish magician. Must have."

"Oh, the mimes. So scary."

"I would never let them hurt a lady with as beautiful a voice or eyes as yours. Never."

"So true, so honorable. Praise be to Allah for your service."

"I do what I must," said the guard, placing his hand over his heart and bowing. "I'm Saladen. Perhaps we could meet again. What is your name?"

"My name?" I spoke.

We all looked at one another.

"Yes, your name?" said Saladen, smiling.

At that moment, the guard was pushed to the ground. Six or seven men and women with white painted faces and black outlines ran past us in silent motion, their intricate red robes flowing behind them. Their clothes looked like what a magician might wear.

"Mimes!" yelled Saladen, struggling to get up due to his heavy black armor.

One of the mimes bent down and made a funny facial expression with his tongue out toward Saladen. Then, he ran down the cobblestone street.

"I'll get you, you Spanish magicians!" said Saladen.

Ten other palace guards stormed past us in pursuit of the mimes.

One of the guards helped Saladen up, patted him on the back, and joined his brothers in arms.

"I must go, my sweetness," said Saladen.

"Go, go," I said. "Before they get away."

"May Allah align the stars and bring us together once more," said Saladen. "Goodbye! Goodbye!"

Silence then filled the street. Swift looked down the road, making sure all of the guards had left.

"What the . . . " said Jaipur. "Those mimes?"

"Don't ask," I replied.

"We're clear. No one's around," said Swift.

"Good," I said.

"That was a great performance, Toro," laughed Swift. "Sophocles would have put you center stage after that audition. You would be Sophocles' new Antigone."

I rolled my eyes.

"You did theater, Toro?" asked Jaipur. "When did you play Antigone?"

"What? No," I remarked. "I'll knock both of you out if you talk of this to anyone."

"So you didn't do theater?" said Jaipur.

"No, Jaipur. I have never done theater," I replied, annoyed.

"You should," exclaimed Jaipur. "You are a natural."

"What did the guard say?" asked Swift.

"They were looking for us. That's all," I said.

"Where will Cosimo meet with Arij?" asked Jaipur. "Did he say?"

"You forgot? said Swift.

"Must have," said Jaipur.

"The waterfall in the forest," I said. "Where we first met Arij."

"Good place to meet," said Toro. "Secret."

"Well, I'm not waiting for him to return to the house. No, sir," said Jaipur.

"We won't," said Swift. "Let's get to the meeting point by the river. I pray he's there."

Princess Nur-al-Arij

Scene: Love, Duty

⟨∞⟩

M Y HEART, MY *heart, my newfound heart. Could Cosimo be the one for me? Allah has sent me a sign. Fell from the heavens, Cosimo did. Like an angel. I can't move too fast, extend my heart too far, but my heart beckons me to do so. Why does my mind contradict my feelings? Why? Is it because Cosimo is different from Prince Sikander? Is it his different beliefs and customs? Am I scared of different?*

Nay, I love different, for I am different. I want different—a different life, away from here, away from this palace. A life far away to a place where dreams are made, a place beyond these palace walls, a place in Cosimo's arms.

My father should understand my intentions, should understand me. My father wonders why I seek a life beyond the palace, beyond him. I seek that life because I've been locked inside my room far too long, reading, reading. I am tired of reading. I want to experience these things I've read for myself. I want to see them with my own eyes and live the adventure, not read the adventure. Cosimo could be my companion on that adventure.

My father would never allow it. He would never allow Cosimo and me to be with each other, never in a thousand and one years. I know what my father wants, what he desires. He wants to betroth me to that awful Prince Sikander. Sikander is terrible and terrible for me. The look in his eyes says it all. He would hurt me, beat me, and tell me that I am stupid and to remain quiet. I've been quiet my whole life. I will not be quiet, not a moment longer! I know what I want, the life I want, the person I want, the love I want. I could escape my father if I had to. I could do it with ease.

Cosimo. Oh, Cosimo. Your sweet smile, your gentle heart. We aren't so different. Nay, we both know high walls. Yet no wall is too high for us to scale. I must talk to my father right away, tell him my thoughts, my wants, my needs, and my dreams.

I thought of all of these things as I paced around my room, my dungeon. I looked out my window at the setting sun.

I must confront my father.

What if I fold in front of him? Why is it so hard to talk to him, to tell him my true feelings? What if he screams at me?

I don't care. I must have courage. I have courage. I must do this now before time runs out.

I opened my chamber door and rushed through the corridor, down the stairs, and into the throne room. My father was there, seated upon his golden throne, talking with an emissary, what looked to be a white European. But he was not speaking Spanish. Nay, the emissary was speaking Portuguese.

My father noticed me at the far end of the hall and gestured for the Portuguese emissary to leave.

"My daughter, Arij," said the sultan. "Please. Come, come."

"Father," I said.

"I'm glad you came. I was talking with Prince Sikander and his father . . . What's wrong, Arij?"

"Who was that emissary?"

"Don't worry about that, my child."

"I do worry. Who was it?"

"That's what I want to talk with you about." He exhaled deeply. "Prince Sikander . . . "

"I don't like him, Father."

"It's not a matter of liking him, my child. It's a matter of longevity, stability, and tradition."

"No, Father. He's—"

"Let me speak."

I bowed.

"I have signed an agreement with Prince Sikander, the vizier, and the Portuguese to form an alliance between our three kingdoms. I believe it's best for our kingdom."

"No, no," I said with sadness.

"If you would marry Sikander to complete our unification, he . . . he" stuttered the sultan. "Don't cry, my child. I do this for us, for our kingdom, to protect you. Prince Sikander would take good care of you. More and more Europeans are seen in our waters, encroaching on our borders. We are not as strong as we used to be, my child. We need this alliance. I wanted to give the Spaniards a chance, but I have no choice. "

"You always have a choice, Father."

"Then who would you choose? That Spaniard named Cosimo? We need protection. *You* need protection. What can he offer you?"

"Love."

"Love? You love him?"

"Yes."

"You can't be serious," said the sultan angrily. "They . . . they are . . . Christian! European!"

"Does that matter?"

"Yes. Yes, it does. This kingdom was built by Allah, built by your ancestors who fought and died for us—for our customs, our language, our birthright. For you."

"The world is changing, Father. Each day, it grows more interconnected through trade, just as you said. The future is here at our doorstep."

"Your future is with Prince Sikander."

"Why close yourself off to this idea?"

"No daughter of mine shall marry a white European, a Christian. Understand that."

"Why? Because they are different?"

"That marriage would never work."

"Because you say it wouldn't work?"

"You are too young to know."

"To know that if we close ourselves up in this palace, behind these walls, then the world, the future would pass us by. These walls do not protect. Nay, they inhibit us."

"Stop this nonsense! You must marry Prince Sikander. I have already signed the deal with the Portuguese and Sikander. This is your duty as my daughter to do this for Boubazar."

"Duty? My love is a duty?"

"Your mother, if she were still alive . . . Your mother did her duty."

"You talk of love like it's a trade, a deal, something to bargain with."

"You know not what you speak."

"Love is not to know but to feel, to listen to, like our mysterious Allah. No man, not even a sultan, could say what love is and what love is not."

"I can say you will love Prince Sikander, just as your mother learned to love me."

"I don't want to be my mother. I want to be Arij, free as a bird to fly, to sing, and to love."

"You are selfish," said my father. "I do this for you, for my love, to protect you for when I leave this earth!"

"By signing me away to Sikander. He will turn on you, on me, on all of Boubazar."

"The is the real world, Arij. It's not some tale about fairies and jinn like in your books. You will understand with time."

"If the Portuguese are arriving, then what will happen with Cosimo, Gaspar, and his crew?"

"Gaspar is a renegade who deals with the devil through witches. He insults Allah and me by his actions. More so, Gaspar and his crew went against King Charles's orders. As a result, Gaspar's word is null and void."

"Who told you this?"

"One of his men."

"And you believe this?"

"Prince Sikander and the vizier verified the claim's authenticity."

"Your vision is so clouded."

"The Portuguese will be here tomorrow. They have a bounty on Gaspar and his men. I believe it's best, in good faith with our new alliance, to hand Gaspar and his men over to them."

"They'll kill them!"

"It's none of my business what they will do with the Spaniards. If they are renegades, then . . . "

"I'm not going to let you do this," I exclaimed. "I am not!"

I then turned on my heel, back toward the door. There waiting for me were two massive guards blocking the door. I looked back at my father with tears dripping down from my eyes. "What are you doing,

Father?"

"I can't let you tell them," said the sultan. "You must stay here. It's safer that way. I demand you go your chamber right now."

I shook my head, and the guards led me up the stairs and back to my chamber, locking me inside. Tears continued to fall from my eyes at the thought of Cosimo's dying.

I could not give up. I needed to save Cosimo and the Spaniards. I had to get out of the room, out of the palace, and warn Cosimo before it was too late. I had to leave at that moment. We were supposed to meet by the river soon.

I can escape. Yes, I can get there. But how?

I looked around my room, thinking, planning. Then, an idea came to me. I took the sheets on my bed, tied them together like a rope, and anchored them to my bed frame. I double checked the tightness of the knots, then hoisted myself through my window.

Cosimo

Scene: Pursued

∽ⱳⱳ∾

I RETURNED TO the forest, to the river, to the place where I first laid eyes upon Arij, enraptured by her long-lashed, bright brown eyes. The moment I left the library, I hustled across the city, past the walls, and into the forest. I did my best to remember the way back to the river. It took an hour or two to get there as I moved through the thick shrub to find the spot—our spot—along the riverbank. The telltale sign of our meeting point was the waterfall, the place where we were flung from the cave into the river.

The sun began to set, still yielding some light, enough light for me to find my way around the forest. I heard the waterfall in the distance and followed the sound to the river. I hid myself near the waterfall behind the brush. I was tired. My lower back was sore, my clothes were soaked in sweat, and my feet ached with blisters. It was no casual Sunday stroll to get here, more like an intense trek.

There was a crack, a snap of a twig, in the forest. I looked around, looking for any movement. There before me, holding a torch, was Arij, beautiful as ever. I couldn't help but smile. Yet she looked distressed.

"Cosimo? Cosimo?" called Arij, looking around the pool.

"Arij, I'm here! Over here," I replied.

"Praise Allah you are alive," she said as we hugged one another,. She felt like a warm fire on the coldest night. Her veil was gone, revealing her sparkling face.

"Your veil?" I spoke.

"I forgot it, though it matters not for Allah would understand," explained Arij.

"So sweet art thou, Arij. Why . . . Are you . . . Look at you. What's the matter?"

"We must leave Boubazar. Both of us."

"Calm down, calm down. Tell me what happened."

"I don't . . . don't . . . My father . . . He . . . he wants to give you up to the Portuguese. He said Gaspar and his crew were renegades, outlaws to all nations, for dealing with dark magic. I told him it was not true, couldn't be true. Tell me it's not true."

"It is not true, Arij. Who told your father this?"

"Prince Sikander and his father, the vizier."

I looked to the ground, lost in my thoughts. "I had a feeling it was Sikander."

"And a Spaniard. One of your own."

"Zaragoza. Aye, it must have been him. That rat. Ugh! That . . . that rat!" I bit my tongue, holding back all the curses in my heart.

"We'll run away, run to Europe, run to the west, run to your own land, away from here. We can forget about all of this."

"You can't run, Princess."

"I can do whatever I please."

"Do you think the sultan could be swayed if we prove our innocence?"

"Not with Prince Sikander and the vizier in his ear. Worse, the Portuguese are said to arrive in a day or so."

"Aye, you right."

"Gaspar could persuade him. I think . . . I hope he could bring truth to these accusations, these lies, and turn my father's eyes away from the Portuguese."

"Gaspar is gone."

"Gone? Gone where?"

"Well, I have a strong conviction he's gone."

"What do you mean?" asked Arij.

"I believe Gaspar left us to find . . . find . . . You wouldn't believe what I say."

"Try me."

"Gaspar went to find a material . . . a stone, a mythical rock."

"Named? What is the property's name?"

"It has many names, not one. But the Egyptians called it the Gold of Retjenu."

Her eyes flashed. She repeated the name to herself.

"You know of it?" I asked.

"I've read about it. Orange gold. It resides in the famed labyrinth, the Labyrinth of Pandemonium."

"Pandemonium? That's a Greek word."

"As you said, it has many names. In Arabic, we call it the Labyrinth of Hutamah."

"Hutamah?"

"It means 'that which breaks to pieces.'"

"Like a stone breaking."

"Or a soul breaking."

"Then what of the Gold of Retjenu?"

"The stone has power, great power, inside of it. To unlock the power within, the stone must be mutated, transformed to open a gate between us and the heavens to obtain the last ingredient, or so the legend says."

"The Great Work. Yes, it makes sense now but . . . but a direct connection with heaven? Which ingredient means heaven or . . . or is it in heaven?"

"No one knows," said Arij.

"No one knows. Well, I bet Gaspar knows, and he's after it now."

"Sounds like Gaspar is playing with fire, with dark magic. Oh, my father was right."

"Though we should not suffer for what Gaspar does. Look, I found this scroll in an archive," I said, digging inside my backpack and pulling out the scroll from the library. "Here. The scroll says where the labyrinth is located."

Arij took the map and analyzed it, reading every piece of it. She was brilliant, more than brilliant.

I continued, "It seems the only way to save our lives at this point is by finding this stone, this Gold of Retjenu, and offering it to the sultan as a gift, as a trade for our lives. If my crew and I return to Boubazar empty handed, the sultan will give us to the Portuguese, but if we return with this gold, this powerful gold, he might offer us safe passage home in return."

"Your plan is far too daring. Even if, by Allah, you find the gold, that does not guarantee my father will offer safety to you and your crew."

"Nothing in life is guaranteed, but that gold is the best chance we have for striking a deal. I can't return without it. I can't."

"I pray to Allah you are right."

"Me too," I said. "Me too."

Arij looked at the map of where the labyrinth was said to be located.

"You know where the labyrinth is?" I asked as she analyzed the scroll.

"Based on this, down the river and inside a mountain. In fact, I've been to this place, to the entrance, when I was a child. I had no idea then what it was. We must go there now. You are right. We go into the labyrinth, for us, for your crew, for our future. I have a boat down there along the river. I use it all the time."

"By Jove, that would be perfect, but we need the others. Oh, I hope they weren't captured."

"They could be. My father has sent guards for them."

There was a crack in the woods. I unsheathed my sword and gestured for Arij to hide. I slowly walked to the brush.

Crack, snap.

I gripped the hilt of my sword, my heart pounding.

"Cosimo. Cosimo, it's me, Swift, with Jaipur and Toro."

"Good Lord, you scared me," I exhaled. "It's okay, Arij. They're my friends."

Jaipur, Toro, and Swift stepped out of the brush and into the torchlight. They were dressed in women's robes and veils.

"What are you?" I asked, stupefied. "Women?"

"Is that a new look?" laughed Arij.

"Don't say anything," growled Toro.

"We had to escape," said Jaipur. "Lots of guards were after us."

"In women's clothes?" asked Cosimo.

"It worked, didn't it? stated Swift.

Each of them took off the feminine robes, revealing the old clothes underneath.

"My father," sighed Arij, shaking her head.

"The others? Faustino? Zaragoza?" I asked.

"No, Faustino and Zaragoza betrayed us, sided with Prince Sikander," said Swift. "We caught Zaragoza looking for Gaspar's nautical charts at Sikander's request."

"Arij brought me up to speed on Zaragoza," I replied.

"We need to keep moving," said Toro.

"I'm with Toro on this one," said Jaipur eagerly. "The guards were behind us, scouting the area. They were looking for us and now, obviously, the princess."

"Let's take my boat down the river. We can reach the labyrinth that way," said Arij.

"She knows of it?" asked Swift, surprised. "The labyrinth?"

"I know much about it," said Arij.

"You can't leave. Think of the sultan," I said. "And the labyrinth is far too dangerous. No place for a princess to be."

"I am not going back to the palace, not when you need my help," said Arij.

At that moment, I heard sounds of galloping moving fast toward us. I checked around the brush to see if I could see the incoming horsemen. They were there, coming down the dirt road toward us. It was a regiment of armored guards carrying torches. The guards were following the sultan, who was at the head of the formation, followed by Prince Sikander, the vizier, and Zaragoza, all at the sultan's side. The formation stopped for a moment.

"Put out the torches!" I spoke.

"Zaragoza," stated Swift.

"Traitor," said Jaipur. "Traitor to us all."

"Come quick," said Arij. "Follow me to my boat, right up here."

"Right behind you," said Swift.

We hustled through the forest, watching our footsteps, watching out for sticks and twigs. We moved quietly, quickly over roots and around trees. We followed the river to a wooden dock where a few dhows were docked. Overlooking the river was a flat-roofed, cream-colored house.

Arij gestured for us to be quiet as we walked along the wooden dock. The wind was strong, and the river was rough. We boarded Arij's wooden dhows. Each was roughly sixty feet in length, fifteen feet in width, and maintained one mast and one sail. It was a simple ship, a perfect ship for the river. Arij untied the knot and pushed off from the dock.

"Arij, what are you doing?" I spoke. "You must get off, return to shore."

"I know these waters. You need me to navigate," said Arij. "I'm coming with you."

"She has a good point," said Swift.

"What if something were to happen to you?" I spoke. "I do not know the land. How could I save you, bring you to safety?"

"You won't have to, for I am strong," said Arij. "I would never allow into danger the one person I hold dear when I can help, when I can save him."

"She made her decision, Cosimo," said Toro.

"Thank you, Toro," said Arij.

At that moment, the sultan's large armed forces emerged from around the forest bend. They began to shout at us in Arabic. Prince Sikander rode to the dock, shouting at us. Arij and Sikander exchanged words as our ship was taken by the strong river current.

Prince Sikander then began to yell at us in Spanish. "Dock your ship! We'll spare one leg if you do!"

"Daughter, please. This is foolish," said the sultan from a distance.

"We mean no harm, Your Majesty!" yelled Swift. "We seek justice and safe passage. That is all."

"You are pirates loyal to no flag," screamed Prince Sikander.

"You took my daughter!" said the sultan. "Let her go!"

"We have not, sire!" I returned.

Our boat continued to move with the current, taking us farther downriver, farther away from the sultan and his men. We then unlatched the sail, gaining wind behind our backs and increasing our speed twofold.

"We'll find you and kill you!" yelled Prince Sikander.

"My daughter. Please give her back," yelled the sultan. "Please."

"I assure you, Father. Sikander has bad intentions for our kingdom. I know this, and I will not return until you listen to me!" yelled Arij as we floated farther downriver and out of sight.

Prince Sikander

Scene: Thought Variations II

☙✦❧

THOSE INFIDELS GOT *away! How could I let them take the princess? Hypnotized her, Cosimo did with his dark magic. They are magicians, treasonous pirates that must be dealt with in the most severe manner. Yes, then the sultan would have to consent to our alliance and would have to allow the Portuguese armada into the port of Boubazar.*

Our armies, my father and brother, are waiting, waiting for the moment to strike. The sultan would never expect a thing, for his mind is preoccupied with these Spaniards, with his daughter. Yet this stress may change his view on the Portuguese and put off our deal.

I can't let that happen. Nay, my father will kill me if I do not solidify the deal. My father, the vizier, has already killed one of my brothers for displeasing him. I'm next on his list, next in line for the sword. I despise that man, my father. He won't take my head. Nay, he won't!

I know what I must do to maintain the sultan's trust and allegiance. Yes, I must save the princess from those pirates, those magicians, those Spaniards. If I save his daughter, I would gain his trust and unfaltering allegiance. Therefore, the sultan would let the Portuguese into his harbor without a fear or doubt in his mind. In fact, the sultan might let my army march through the gates of Boubazar without a fight, without a drop of blood, without the shot of a cannon—all because I saved his daughter and because he would trust me like a son, like the son he never had.

I could take over Boubazar from the inside out, like that Greek myth. What was it again? Ah, yes, the Trojan Horse. I am the Trojan Horse. I am Odysseus.

I am a genius! I'll take the city for myself, take Princess Arij for myself, make the sultan bend at the knee. Then, in the future, I'll make my own father, the vizier, bend at the knee.

With Boubazar in my hands and the Portuguese armada in my rear, I could take over my father's kingdom. Yes, yes! From there, I could take over all of Arabia from Baghdad to Cairo. Oh, yes. Have I forgotten about Captain Gaspar's nautical charts? I could take over the New World with Gaspar's maps, charts, and calendars and use the armada to venture west. Genius! I could take over the world with those resources. No man is smarter than I.

Slow down. Slow down, my thoughts. Slow down . . . I need the princess, must have the princess. Then, Boubazar will be mine. I will follow the river, follow the Spaniards, for I have scouts on every corner of this island.

The magicians cannot escape. Nay, they cannot, will not escape me.

Princess Nur-al-Arij
Scene: Thought Variations III

ᏇᏇᎧ

W E CONTINUED SAILING downriver with a strong wind behind us. It was peaceful on the river, feeling the boat sway from side to side, feeling the crisp wind kiss my cheeks. Pleasant, it was.

Cosimo, Jaipur, and Swift slept as Toro steered the boat. I couldn't fall asleep—thinking of my father, thinking of Cosimo, thinking of this mess we were all in. I stared at the night sky, gazing at the twinkling stars above, thinking.

I must find this gold, for it can save my new friends, save my dear Cosimo. My father cannot refuse us, refuse me. Perhaps this gold could sway him away from Sikander and the Portuguese. Does that matter? Nay, all that matters to me is Cosimo's safety and the safety of his companions, even if . . . even if he leaves the island, leaves my arms, leaves me forever. At least, by Allah, he would be safe. That I can live with.

One day, one day far from this day, I could visit Europe, visit Cosimo when all of this had settled down. I wonder what Europe looks like, what Italy looks like, what Rome looks like. Cosimo speaks well of Rome. I want to see this Colosseum, these large aqueducts.

More so, I want to see Cosimo. The gold will give them safe passage, even if my father rejects them, the Spaniards. They could get a ship on their own and make way for home on their own though dangerous it may be with the Portuguese in the waters.

Oh, Allah. Help us. Help me. Help Cosimo. Help my father see.

My father is blinded by Sikander and the vizier. Nay, I will never be with Sikander. I know Sikander seeks my father's kingdom, yet my father will not listen to me. My father has good intentions in protecting me, he does, but his overprotection and strong conservatism are blinding him from seeing the truth of Sikander.

This gold, this Gold of Retjenu could change my father. I do not know how, but I feel in my soul that it would. If the stories of the labyrinth are true, could there be such a rock with unimaginable power contained inside of it?

I've seen this place, the place of the supposed labyrinth, the entrance. I saw it when I was a child; rather, I fell upon it while wandering on a wooden raft.

As children, we were told stories about the labyrinth to scare us from being bad; we were told in a way that if we acted up, we would be thrown into the labyrinth and our souls would be feasted upon by the leviathan, a terrible beast that roamed the labyrinth.

A small shiver crept up my spine as I pondered; if the Gold of Retjenu existed, then the labyrinth existed. Therefore, the leviathan within the labyrinth existed.

Oh, Allah, send Your angel Gabriel to guide us through the labyrinth and protect us from the beast within the maze.

ACT III

Cosimo

Scene i: Dance of the Ancients

〜

O UR BOAT CAME to a fork in the river. Arij told Toro to steer the ship to the far right and hug the bank until we reached a small crevasse leading into the mountain. Arij was spot on: soon after she said so, we came upon the cliff with a cavern composed of narrow and jagged edges protruding from below the surface and on the cavern walls.

Swift was at the wheel, steering the ship with methodical precision, avoiding sharp rocks on all corners. His skill was unprecedented. No wonder Gaspar chose him to be our naval pilot. We lit our torches and, carried by the flow of the river, went into the mouth of the dark cave.

After a few moments of silence and darkness, we moved around a bend in the river, and there it was: a piece of land next to the river, surrounded by cavern walls. The ceiling was the open sky. The moon and stars were full and bright, illuminating our surroundings and this open-air cavern. Our ship drifted to the bank. The cavern appeared like a man-made dome.

"Is that it?" asked Swift.

"Where's the labyrinth?" interjected Jaipur. "I see only rocks."

"Yes, this is the entrance," replied Arij.

"Looks man-made," I said, looking around the cavern.

"There! On the rock surface," pointed Swift. "What's that?"

At the center of the small bit of land below the night sky was a mysterious stone structure; it looked like an ancient charting device. It had a circular top piece held up by a stone pillar no more than four feet high.

"It's nothing that I remember," I said.

We docked our ship and walked up to the circular rock piece. I examined it closely, focusing on the details.

What could this be? I had seen these before in a book. I couldn't remember the name, but this device looked like an ancient sundial or an ancient nocturnal, a tool used to measure the constellations. On the dial were strange symbols and multiple languages—hieroglyphics, ancient Greek, Hebrew, and Arabic all meshed together in sporadic phrases. Bending over, I felt the smooth circuital dial, looking under it and over it, thinking.

"Let me see it," stated Swift. He analyzed the dial from top to bottom. "Measures the sky. How, though, I know not."

"The inscriptions are faint, too worn down by time to read," said Toro.

"No one on the island could figure out how to read it," said Arij. "It's far too old to be able to see anything."

"Maybe the labyrinth is somewhere else?" suggested Jaipur. "This could be the wrong place."

"No, you said labyrinth," I said. "I looked at the scrolls. This is where it is. I know it."

I continued to stare at it, pondering the dial's ancient, cryptic, mechanized ways. I looked up at the night sky, seeing a grand view of the cosmos.

"It's not a sundial," I said. "No."

"Looks like a table, a simple table," said Jaipur. "Nothing more than a gambling table."

"Not a table," I said.

"Never could solve its riddle as a child," said Arij.

"Tide volvelle?" said Swift.

I wiped the object with my hands. "It has numbers on it and letters in ancient Greek."

"Greeks? Here?" replied Arij, astonished. "Impossible. They never made it this far east."

"Who said the Greeks or Egyptian came from the east?" I added.

"Nonsense. How else would they get here?" asked Arij.

"West. They came west," said Toro.

"As we did," said Swift.

"That . . . that . . . would be," stumbled Arij, "profound."

I looked deeper into the object, and I figured that the top part of the device was a measuring disc. I could make out a design etched into the stone, a design of a dragon with two intersecting points, like a dual-ended wind rose outlining specific points on an armillary sphere. One point was on the head of the dragon, and the other point was on the tail. I then attempted to move the disc, but it would not budge.

"Give me a knife, please," I asked.

Toro pulled a dagger out of his belt loop and handed it to me.

I began to work the tip of the knife into the groves of the disc. Still nothing.

"Won't budge," I said aloud.

"Keep trying," said Arij.

I studied the device once more, wondering, pondering. At last, an idea, a revelation hit me. I exclaimed, "Eureka! The Pole Star! This drawing is of the Pole Star. Here, and these lines on the edge of the disc represent degrees, longitude and latitude."

"You mean the North Star?" said Arij.

"Yes, yes," I replied, excited, taking off my backpack and pulling out my mobile compass. "Which way is north? . . . Ah, here. That way. The Pole Star is facing the wrong way on disc. Let's . . . uh . . . "

"What? Do what?" asked Toro.

"Move it?" said Swift.

"Yes," I said. "Each piece must move in succession with the next. If we move this piece in the right direction, then we could move the next piece."

"A big puzzle," said Jaipur. "We move one piece to unlock the next piece. That seems easy to do."

"Right!" I said. "Let me try to turn the outermost ring of the Pole Star this way."

I pressed down on the outermost ring and positioned it where the Pole Star faced north.

"How do we know where the other rings go?" asked Jaipur.

"From the stars above," I said.

"I see," said Swift. "This point of the dragon shows when the Pole

Star is directly north. Then, this disc is the night sky, and each ring represents the degrees of each star's position when the Pole Star is at this point."

"You got it, Swift," I said.

"That's confusing," said Jaipur.

"But . . . but . . . " I said.

"What?" asked Arij.

"I don't know the exact degrees of other stars when the Pole Star is at this point," I said. "I have no way of knowing that information, those calculations."

"Unless . . . " said Swift.

"Unless what?" I asked.

"With Gaspar's nautical charts, we could find those degrees," said Toro.

"You . . . you have them?" I asked.

"Gaspar left them to Jaipur before he scooted out," said Swift.

"You jest," I said.

"Nay, he's right," said Jaipur.

"Means we're in business," smiled Swift.

I cheered.

Swift took out the nautical charts with star positions from every day of the year. We found the exact alignments and measurements and adjusted the rings to meet those specifications. The moment the last ring was set in place, we heard a click.

Nothing happened.

"Well, hmm," I said. "Maybe this? Or . . . ?"

At that moment, a powerful wave of light emitted through the air, like a pebble dropped in a pond, followed by a large sound. Arij grabbed my hand, holding on to me.

A blue electrical light stemmed from the pillar of the disc, rising upward like scarlet blood through veins. The teal blue light began to outline the languages and symbols etched on the disk.

My hair stood up, floating in the air. What power was this? I looked around. Their hair was doing the same as mine, rising upward. Out of nowhere, sparks of blue, purple, and yellow lightning flashed around us, crackling through the dry air.

"Dark magic! Dark!" said Jaipur, covering his head.

"I think . . . I think it's energy," said Arij.

"An amazing amount of it, too," I added.

Blue lights extended outward from the disc down to the floor, illuminating the surface beneath our feet and revealing strange patterns and designs. The device then lifted out of the ground in an advanced mechanical fashion.

"This knowledge," I said, dumbfounded. "How? By what?"

Out of the ground, the disc rose, bringing forth a large platform underneath it as it rose to the surface. The platform appeared to be bronze or some similar metal, working in a pulley system. Attached to the platform was a series of mechanical wheels pulling the platform to the surface.

What source of energy could power this mechanism? Could it be that gold, that hidden gem deep inside this mountain, this fabled labyrinth?

Transform, the scroll had said. *Transform the gold to unlock the gates of the heavens, to unlock the power within, to transform the soul.*

Was Gaspar after this gold, this power? Why?

I remembered he mixed chemicals on the *Valencia* that night to make . . . to make . . . What?

The ancients—the Egyptians, the Greeks, the Hebrews, the Arabians and who knows what other civilization—knew of this rock, knew of this power. I wondered if the power could be harnessed to build incredible structures, such as the Pyramids of Giza, the Colossus of Rhodes, the Hanging Gardens of Babylon. What if even the Tower of Babel?

What secrets did this labyrinth hold?

Cosimo

Scene ii: The Descent

⌒ℳℳ⌒

"I'M NOT GETTING near that . . . that thing," said Jaipur. "Don't ask me to."

I approached the platform in a slow, methodical motion. I touched the smooth metal railing around the platform, then stepped on it. The platform was six feet in width. Inscribed on the platform in the middle of a collection of hieroglyphs was ancient Greek text. I knew these words, had seen these words before. I translated them aloud: "To the Beginning."

"Looks like a one-way trip to hell," said Swift.

"Hebrew and Arabic text here," said Arij, examining the platform.

"Many, many civilizations have come hither before," I stated.

"If it's a labyrinth, how are we going to find a way through?" questioned Swift. "Last time I checked, we don't have a magic thread."

"You are right," said Cosimo.

"Don't you have the Latin scroll?" asked Arij. "That could offer us a clue, a way through."

I nodded, pulled out the Latin scroll, examined it, and read aloud, "*To find your way through, look to Koblach as your guide. Maintain that direction to see the light.*"

"No stars under a mountain," said Jaipur.

"True," I said. "Koblach, the Pole Star. Maintain that direction."

"The Pole Star is the North Star," stated Arij.

"Yes," I replied.

"Then what if we follow the North Star?" asked Arij.

"But there is no way to see the night sky in a mountain. Hmm . . . "
I spoke. "Our charts are useless without the sky."

"No, no, I see what she is saying," said Swift. "We go north. North
leads us the right way through the maze. We remain north at every opportunity."

"Right!" said Arij.

"Oh, yes, yes," I said, still pondering. "To do that, to keep our direction north, we could use my mobile compass! You are a genius, Arij!"

"Oh, please. I am not," said Arij, blushing.

"Good, good," I remarked. "That solves our direction though the
maze."

"What do we do if we find Gaspar?" asked Jaipur.

"Demand gold," said Swift.

"Let's cross that bridge when we get there, eh?" I spoke.

We all agreed.

"Are you all sure about going down?" I asked. "I know not what
lies below, what lies beyond this platform. I cannot promise that we shall
return with gold or our lives, but I'm going. I have to go."

"Are you mad?" asked Swift. "You think I'll let you have all the fun
down there? Nay, I'm going."

"You said gold. I'm not going back without some," said Toro.

"Don't even try to dissuade me from going," said Arij.

"I won't. I've learned my lesson," I said. "And what of you, Jaipur?
Do not feel obligated to come."

"Aye," said Jaipur nervously. "I don't want to go, yet my soul pulls
me. You are the only family I've had since I was taken many years ago. I
must help you, all of you, my family. I know this, I feel this, and I want
to do this. Trust me, I'm scared—very scared—but I can't let my family
do this alone, no matter how scared I am."

"Well said, brother," said Swift.

"You are part of my tribe, Jaipur," said Toro, bowing.

"May Allah bless you, Jaipur," said Arij.

"For all of eternity," I added. "Tie yourself to one another with rope
so that we may not lose each other in the darkness."

We tied a rope around our waists and connected it to each another
like a chain. Then, we stepped onto the platform. I took a deep breath

and pushed the lever, and we descended to the subterranean world below.

I could hear the pulley system working—*ching, ching, crack*—and down the platform went. Down, down, down.

The blue light illuminated our way, granting light on the way down. I extended my hand outward and touched the rock wall, which felt moist with water. The air around us was feeling warmer, rising in temperature as we continued our descent.

A painted panel, detailed with an Egyptian style, appeared on the rock face in front of us. The panel was of a garden, a beautiful garden with a man and woman.

Still, we continued downward. Then, another panel came before us. Then, numerous panels appeared in successive order, one after the other. The next panel was of a serpent in a garden, tempting the man and woman to eat an orange fruit. This appeared to be the story of Adam and Eve.

The next panel was of Eve conversing with the serpent, taking the fruit and giving it to Adam. The following panel showed God in divine form, casting Adam and Eve out of the garden.

After that, God cast the serpent into an abyss of fire deep beneath the earth.

Following that panel was a panel with an army of angels, constructing a labyrinth to keep the serpent from leaving the abyss or, rather, keeping man from entering the abyss.

The next panel was of an ancient Egyptian boat sailing in the ocean, looking to the stars above for guidance.

Following that panel was one with the Egyptians stumbling upon an island, exploring it, and descending into the mountain at the center of the island. There, the panel showed the Egyptians discovering a strange labyrinth, the same labyrinth the angels built prior. The Egyptians ventured into the labyrinth and came across a garden, the same magnificent garden from the earlier panels. Inside the garden was the same tree full of reddish orange fruit. The Egyptians took the fruit and brought it back to the surface.

The following panel was of the serpent from the earlier panels, killing and devouring the Egyptians on the island.

Following that was a panel of Greek ships, but this panel was painted and designed in ancient Greek artistic fashion, much different from the Egyptian style. The panel showed the Greeks following the North Star as they sailed the ocean. The Greeks found the island, ventured into the mountain, and stumbled upon the labyrinth and the stone, as did the Egyptians before them. Inscribed in Greek on the bottom of the panel was a word.

I translated the word and said it aloud: "Minosium." The group was confused.

Following that panel was one of a Greek sorcerer, a magician of some sort, taking the fruit from the tree, and adding it and other properties into a large, teardrop-shaped furnace located next to the tree. Once all the properties were mixed, it showed a winged entity offering a new fruit to the magician.

The panels stopped after this one, but the platform continued to descend.

"The magician picked something from the tree. It looked like an apple," said Jaipur. "That must be some kind of apple."

"And mixed the apple with salt-fire," I stated.

"Did anyone forget to mention the part where the Egyptians were eaten by some sea snake?" said Swift.

"Only panel that caught my eye," stated Toro.

"It's called the leviathan," said Arij.

"Levi-who?" asked Jaipur.

"You mean the Hebrew monster spoken of by Job in the Tanakh?" I asked.

"Yes," said Arij. "In the legend of the labyrinth, my local communtiny's version, we were told as kids that if we acted up, we would be sent to the labyrinth to be feasted upon by the leviathan, the feared serpent of the deep."

"Sounds like King Minos and the minotaur to me," interjected Swift.

"Seemes all these stories were taken from the same place, the same one story," said Arij.

"What story would that be?" asked Jaipur.

"The story of creation," said Arij.

"Ah, forgive my many questions," said Jaipur. "Gaspar forgot to pay for my schooling, but then where does King Minos come into this?"

"It's a Greek myth," said Swift. "King Minos built a labyrinth to contain his deformed son, a minotaur, half man, half beast."

"The Greeks called the rock minosium," I said. "Minos . . . minosium. There's the connection, and that must be their version of the story."

"In all of them, there's a beast to encounter," said Toro. "A beast I fear we'll encounter."

"So how did the Greeks deal with the beast in their story?" asked Jaipur.

"The hero, Theseus, killed the beast, the minotaur," said Swift. "Found his way through the labyrinth by a thread."

"We'll find our way through my compass," I said.

At that moment, we descended past the rocks walls and into a gigantic cavern, multiple leagues wide in every direction. This immense cavern seemed capable of fitting a whole mountain, island, or continent inside of it. The cavern was illuminated by scorching red lava spewing in the distance and by the blue light, weaving through the infamous labyrinth.

All of us were silent, witnessing the endless mythical labyrinth. The labyrinth was made of exquisite black rock, so black that light seemed to bend off of this mysterious stone material. Even stranger, like water poured through cracks in a stone, weaving in numerous directions, blue light still weaved through the labyrinth.

The labyrinth appeared to have an infinite number of corridors, extending high in the air. More bizarre, I saw forests, trees, and vegetation in certain areas of the labyrinth, defying all logic of life. I could not make sense of any of this.

"What's that?" pointed out Jaipur.

"Where?" said Swift.

In the distance, flying above the labyrinth, were large, winged creatures, appearing like monstrous bats. I knew then there must be many creatures of this size in this obscure, mind-bending world beneath our own.

The platform continued to descend, bringing us to the bottom of our destination. We hit the floor.

Pum, cling, cling, puff.

The platform stopped inside an enclosed spherical room. Inside this room were three exits, one next to the other, leading into different corridors of the labyrinth. The room was constructed with pure gold with walls filled with painted hieroglyphics. The room was supported by Greek Ionic columns. Above each exit were multiple inscriptions of Hebrew and Arabic text. There was another language below the ancient Hebrew, one I knew not. Perhaps Sumerian or Akkadian.

What a wonder this place was! Many civilizations and ancient peoples had come before us and had left their mark, yet where were they now? Why did they leave? Why did the world not know of this?

I felt a winged flutter move through my stomach, for I knew I would soon find out why, whether I wanted to or not.

I pulled out my compass and gauged our whereabouts. Above the archway to my far right was a painting of a large star, coursing with the blue light, sparkling like a diamond.

"That way," I said. "North."

Jaipur

Scene: Enter the Labyrinth

ᏬᎳᎳᎾ

I WAS SCARED but kept it hidden; I had to look tough, tough like Toro. He never showed fear, much less emotion. I couldn't let them know my innermost thoughts. I had to be strong and courageous for them and for myself.

Where am I? I'm deep in the earth, in a maze, in a labyrinth built by the ancients, searching for some mythical stone. It's guarded by what? A beast? This is not what I expected, yet what did I expect? After all those years living with Gaspar, was this labyrinth that wild, that strange?

Yes, this was strange. And scary. Yes, scary.

At least I can see with this blue light. How is it powered? I'm not going to question it.

We passed under an archway and followed the winding stone corridors into the endless maze. The corridors in the labyrinth were diverse with some parts open, some closed in. The surface moved up, down, right, left, zig-zag, and diagonally—in every way imaginable. At one point, I looked up and saw a corridor above my head and upside down! Yes, upside down! What was the point of an upside-down corridor? Worse, I started to feel that I was upside down, walking upside down. We encountered stairs going up, and the corridor above us had stairs going up also, mirroring our corridor.

I am going crazy. Crazy. My brain is ready to explode! I cannot handle this mind-bending place. Cannot.

I was hot and felt my thirst worsening in my dry throat. I had packed a few things in my backpack, some bread and a sack of water, though Cosimo told me to conserve it.

My mind is running with thoughts, of that thought . . . of that thought . . . of a thought within a thought. Wait, what's that? A shadow? My shadow?

"What is it, Jaipur?" asked Toro. "You are frozen in place."

"I thought I saw a thing . . . a thought . . . a thing. I thought I saw a dark thing," I replied.

"Oh, no," said Swift. "You need to rest. We need to rest."

"You saw a shadow?" asked Cosimo, raising his brow.

"Aye, shadow. Yes, down the corner he ran, or so I thought," I said, worried. "You saw him, too? Thought it, too?"

"You saw a shadow, Cosimo?" asked Swift.

Cosimo paused for a moment, silent.

"This place plays tricks on the mind," said Arij. "Dangerous tricks."

"I saw a shadow on the ship," I said. "Well, jumping off the ship toward this island."

"A man went overboard?" asked Swift. "You never told me that, or did you?"

"I can't remember if I did or not, but it was not a man," replied Cosimo. "It was a shadow of a man. Faustino was there. He said he knew of the shadow, and the shadow knew him."

"Faustino knows only the bottom of a bottle," said Swift. "Let alone his own shadow."

"Reminds me of a jinni," said Arij.

"Is that a fairy?" asked Swift.

"No," said Arij. "A dark spirit, a demon cursed by King Solomon."

"The shadow could be a jinni. Could be," remarked Cosimo as he stared at the ground, lost in thought. "Pay no attention to it, Jaipur."

"I agree with Arij," said Toro. "Spirits roam this place, these corridors. I feel them." Toro grabbed his necklace, kissed it, and spat on the ground.

"What does that do?" I asked Toro.

"Keeps the bad spirits away," remarked Toro, "and keeps Allah close."

We continued through the winding corridors. Time felt nonexistent here. I could not tell if it was day or night, only that I was tired. My feet began to blister. I heard something once more. It was a voice from whom or where I knew not—just a creeping voice in my head. The voice was like a whisper, soft as paintbrush upon a canvas.

The whisper called out my name.

Jaipur. Jaipur.

I covered my ears and tried to block out the voice. I felt the black corridor walls caving in. Up was down; down was up. Each wall was the same, the same as the one before, the same around every corner.

Dark, wide, the corridor, the whispers, the shadowed call.

My stomach fluttered; I was losing touch with direction. I was slipping away from reality.

The voice whispered to me, persistent. "Jaipur, Jaipur. This be your mother, Jaipur."

"You are not," I said, staggering and feeling drunk.

"What did you say?" asked Swift, concerned.

"Nothing. Nothing at all," I replied, smiling.

"Jaipur, you are pale," said Swift. "Too pale."

"Not I. You are white. You are pale," I replied. "Not I."

"Hold up!" said Swift. "I said hold up! Jaipur needs a break."

"We can't stop now," said Cosimo. "We must make headway. Our supplies are low."

"I say we stop!" said Swift. "I need a break."

"We can't, Swift," said Cosimo, agitated.

"Who said so?" asked Swift.

"I, the second-in-command after Gaspar," said Cosimo.

"Be calm, Cosimo," said Arij. "A break might do you good."

"No one is in command. Leadership rotates per situation," said Swift. "I say we sit."

"I don't need a break. No," I remarked, gesturing for them to move forward.

"You look green," said Swift. "Sick."

"He's fine, Swift. We are all fine," said Cosimo. "Let's continue."

"Are we fine?" said Toro.

"We are," demanded Cosimo.

"Watch yourself, Cosimo," said Swift.

"Watch your own self, Swift," said Cosimo.

"Aye, watch your own self, Swift," I said. "Watch . . . watch . . . myself . . . watch."

Our walk went on.

Where were we even going? Where are we? I feel hot. Am I the only one hot? Why am I breathing so heavy? This never-ending walk.

Right, right, left, right, right, right, right, another right, another right, right, right!

My heart pumped fast.

Bump, bump, bump. Right, right, right. Why so many right corridors? Why not left corridors or those above us?

The voice continued. "Jaipur. Jaipur. It's your mother, Jaipur. Come with me. Come. Be free with me. Come home. Come home to me. Be free. Leave them. Come. Leave them. Come. Come!"

I whispered, "No. No, I won't come to you, not to you. Where to you? Mother? Is that you? I am tired, so tired."

The voice continued, "Come to me. Leave them. Be free. Be free."

I turned my head down the left corridor, and at the end was a silhouette of a shadow, a spirit. I could feel the spirit. I could smell a familiar smell, the smell of home, the smell of my mother. It was my mother, exactly how I remembered her the day I left. Yes, from the day I left home, the day I became a slave. My mother was a slave, sold. Yet here she was before me.

I don't have to find her after this. She's here, here before me. I made it home, made it home as a freeman. I will free her, free my mother.

A tear dripped down from my eye.

My mother is here, calling for me. I must free her from slavery.

The voice said once more, "Come, my son. Come to me. Free me, and be free. Rest easy in my bosom. Rest easy under the palm tree. Rest your weary head. Come, come, come to me!

I replied, "I shall come to you, my mother, and we shall both be free forever and ever."

Toro

Scene: Disappearance of a Friend

೧ⅢⅢ೨

THERE WAS NOT a nudge, not a pull, nothing behind me. A weightless feeling. I stopped, stopping the whole group—a group tired with one another, mad at one another. I turned around and felt the rope.

My intuition was correct. The rope was cut, and no one was behind me. Jaipur was not behind me.

I felt the weight of sadness fall onto my shoulders. I struggled with it, for I knew the truth, just as I had known what those bandits did to my family. They were gone, gone forever.

And Jaipur was gone forever, too.

"Jaipur is gone," I said, emotionless.

The whole group turned around, quick and confused.

"Impossible," said Cosimo.

"Cut the rope, he did," I said. "Cut it without a pull or stop."

"No! That . . . that can't be," said Swift, "Jaipur! Jaipur! Can you hear me?"

"Jaipur!" yelled Arij. "He could not have gone far. Nay, not far. I pray not far."

"Maybe he slipped back there," said Swift. "There . . . there was water on the ground. I stepped in it myself, slipped. Or maybe a break. Jaipur needed a break."

I shook my head. "He found an eternal break."

"How could you let that happen, Toro?" questioned Cosimo. "Jaipur was right behind you the whole time, attached to you by the rope.

Were you that negligent?"

I bit my tongue. "Not my fault. He chose."

"Don't blame Toro," said Swift, sadness in his voice. "This is your own doing, Cosimo. *Your* doing."

"My own doing?" said Cosimo. "Toro should have watched over him, as a brother would do. Like you told him, Swift."

"Stop it, all of you!" said Arij.

"It was no one's fault," I said, firmly.

"Nay, Cosimo gave him no break," said Swift. "Jaipur needed that break. Jaipur! Can you hear me?"

"Jaipur can't hear you!" said Cosimo, filled with sadness.

"Then what can he hear?" asked Swift.

"I made a choice," said Cosimo. "Aye, I made a choice for us all. If we stop here in this labyrinth, we die here. We all know this."

"So, Jaipur's gone forever? Just like that? He dies with no burial, no last words. He dies like a savage?" asked Swift, angered.

"We can't go back," said Cosimo.

Swift squared up to Cosimo. "We can't go back? You are going back. Oh, yes. You are going back." Swift then slapped Cosimo in the face. "It's your fault. You are going back! You are going back to bury him!"

"Please! Stop it!" screamed Arij. "The labyrinth, the shadow wants division among us."

Cosimo punched Swift in the face. Both of them began to wrestle with one another. They were brutal and unrelenting—punching, grunting, and yelling at one another, each blaming one another for Jaipur's disappearance.

I had to put an end to it. I penetrated the fight, pulled them off one another, and threw both of them to the ground.

"Stop fighting! Stop!" I yelled.

Cosimo and Swift were red in the face. Both of them were cut and bruised from the fight, still trying to catch their breath.

"We can't fight now," I said. "The only way through this is by coming together. We must work together. I loved Jaipur, for he was part of my tribe, was my brother. But what has happened has happened. Do not point fingers at another, blaming one another like children. Be men, work together, and move forward."

There was a minute of silence, of reflection, of consideration.

"I . . . I'm sorry, Swift," said Cosimo. "This place . . . this . . . this thing. I don't know." He wiped away a tear. "I don't want to leave Jaipur either. I don't. I don't." Sadness broke into his voice. "What's wrong with me? I care for my friends, my family. What's wrong with me?"

Arij wrapped her arms around Cosimo and laid her head on his chest.

"I'm sorry, too, Cosimo," said Swift. "You were thinking only of what was best for the group. May God care for Jaipur."

"That shadow," said Cosimo. "He saw the shadow. The shadow took him."

"Be not afraid of it," I said. "Keep your faith."

At that moment, the sound of a loud horn echoed through the corridor. The horn sounded like it was nearby as if it was in the next corridor over.

"A horn?" said Arij. "Here?"

"People perhaps," added Cosimo.

"That means we're not alone," said Swift.

"Never were," I remarked.

"Keep your swords close," said Swift.

I turned around, looking down the dark corridor where we had lost Jaipur. "Jaipur, may your soul rest with Allah."

The others stood next to me and made their own condolences to Jaipur.

"Goodbye, Jaipur," said Swift. "Goodbye, my brother."

"May he rest in Abraham's bosom," said Arij.

"May you have your freedom," said Cosimo.

I said my own last words inside my heart. Jaipur annoyed me, angered me. Yet I loved him. I was with him for months, for years. Jaipur told me when this expedition was all over, I could stay with him in the Spice Islands and live a life in paradise. We would form a partnership and trade spices across the world and accumulate wealth and freedom beyond imagination.

May Jaipur ride upon an elephant into paradise . . . and this time not fall off. I pray to Allah that I myself do not fall off at the gates of paradise.

Cosimo

Scene: Blasphemous Dance

⟨∽⟩

W E LEFT JAIPUR there and continued on our journey. The echo
of the mysterious horn was near, a corridor away.

"Look! Light in the distance," said Swift. "At the end of
this corridor."

"It must be magma," said Cosimo.

"Terrible heat," said Arij as droplets of sweat fell from her face.

"Here, my dear," I said, offering her my sack of water.

Arij took the sack of water and shook it. "You are low on water.
Nay, you shall need it."

I pushed the sack of water away from me. "I'll be fine. Drink."

She nodded reluctantly and drank a few sips.

I took out a piece of cloth and wiped the sweat from her face.
"There. All better?"

"Yes," she said, smiling.

"We ready?" asked Swift.

"I am," said Arij.

"Please, all of you, speak up if you feel the need to rest," I said.

We then entered another large cavern, feeling the scorching heat
as if we were on a beach on the hottest day in Naples. In the distance, I
noticed massive clouds of smoke hovering in the air. Out of the clouds,
purple lightning struck, followed by loud crashing thunder. On the surface of the cavern was a gigantic lake of magma, boiling up and bubbling
with fire.

"This place feels familiar," said Arij. "As if my soul but not my mind or body knows of this place, this lake of fire."

"Didn't think this would be here," said Swift. "See that in the distance?"

"What?" I said, squinting my eyes. "Where?"

I looked around this subterranean surface and witnessed massive rock arches, towering to unbelievable heights. Past the rock arches were wide canyons cutting through rock structures as large as mountains. All was illuminated by the lake of fire at the center of the cavern. Down a winding rock path extending to the right over the lake of fire was a building, circular in shape with a dome.

Where had I seen a structure like that? In one of my books of drawings? It resembled the Pantheon in Rome and, on second thought, it looked almost identical to the Hagia Sophia in Byzantium. It had an incredible black dome held up by an arcade of a hundred or so arched windows.

Why? Why was it there in a mountain? It made no sense, absolutely no sense, though nothing made sense in the labyrinth. Was it a trick, a figment of my imagination? There was only one way to find out.

"That building," said Swift. "Looks Greek to me."

"Byzantine to me," said Arij.

"That's what I thought, too" I added. "Byzantine."

"I don't like this place," said Toro. "Not at all."

"I agree with Toro," said Arij. "This place burns my soul. Reminds me of a story I read once before."

"What did it say?" asked Swift.

"There was a lake of fire surrounding the Palace of Pandemonium—the throne of evil, the council of hell—where the Devil and council made their decisions from hell."

"Did the story say what kind of decisions?" asked Swift.

"For the Devil to uncover whether Allah was creating a new world, a physical world, with a new being to live in that world," said Arij.

"Adaman," I muttered. "Red Earth."

"Mankind," said Toro.

I looked up at the archway of the last corridor we came from, which led into the lake of fire. Inscribed on the corridor frame was an ancient Greek word, sketched with haste.

I said it aloud: "Chaos."

"Looks like chaos to me," remarked Swift. "Does your compass point this way through the lake of horrible fire?"

I looked at my compass, and it pointed straight ahead through this terrible cavern.

I replied, "Yes. Yes, it does."

Upset, Swift shook his head. "Of course, it never was easy, never will be easy. It will not deter me, my love. I will return to you. No shadow, no prince, no lake of fire shall block me from you." A tear fell from his right eye. "I will make it back. I will. By God, I will."

The same rift of sadness entered my own heart, wearied by Jaipur's disappearance. My emotions were shot; all of our emotions were shot. At a certain point, I could not hold back the pain, the sadness, inside of my heart. This whole trip, these past weeks, this time in the labyrinth—all were breaking me into pieces.

"My soul is weary," I said. "My shoulders hurt, and my feet ache. My whole being is tired. I'm tired." I slumped to the ground next to Swift.

"Great Allah, help us," said Arij. "Help us through this maze of life when our souls can't move. The mountain is high, and our faith crumbles like a landslide. Help us, Allah."

"I have nothing left in me," I uttered. "Nothing."

"Nothing? Nay, you are strong, Cosimo," said Arij. "Stand up and push on, push on through the fire, through the pain, through the suffering to light at the end of the corridor. For it is there. There it is. We are strong together—in here and in my heart. Look up. Keep looking up to the heavens, to the stars. Never give up; never stop believing. Look, stand up! Quit your moping and your crying. Stand up, for I am not dying in here."

Is Arij right? Do I have it in me to keep going? My legs hurt; my calves hurt. This spot where I sit feels good . . . so good.

No, no, no! I can do this. I can do this, but the way is so long, so tough, so painful. No, I can do this. I will make it out of here. No way is too long for me. No wall is too high; no mud is too thick for me to escape.

Yes, I can do this. I have to do this. I will do this!

I took a deep breath and lifted myself up. I then turned to Swift and extended my hand to him. Swift with his purple sunken eyes nodded, then firmly grabbed my hand. I pulled him up.

"Good men," said Toro.

I turned to Arij with a reinvigorated soul and smiled. "Thank you, Arij. Thank you." Warm, fresh tears rolled down my cheek.

At that moment, she hugged me with her whole being, a hug that felt stronger than any force on this earth. I looked into her sparkling, shining, gorgeous eyes. I felt the pull, a pull I'd never felt before. A pull of true love. I pulled her close to me, and I kissed her on the lips. Our kiss was true, honest, and beautiful.

"Keep the theatrics for the stage," interjected Swift. "We better get walking."

"Save it until after we find the stone," said Toro.

We left one another's embrace with a smile. Then, we looked at the others and nodded.

The way through the lake of fire was on a stone path that led to the structure in the distance. We descended down the walkway and out of the corridor, which spiraled toward the lake of fire. The path was held up by rock arches. After a while of walking in the heat, we came upon the palace.

The building was composed of a black dome of the same material as the labyrinth. Large marble colossi of men and women from different cultures and civilizations were constructed around this pantheon. One colossus was styled like an ancient Egyptian woman in royal regalia. Another colossus appeared like Athena. Yet another was constructed like a Chinese warlord in full armor. Each physiognomy was horrific, appearing demonic in form and maintaining terrible smiles and screams. The stone path led right through the center of the structure, forcing us to go through this black pantheon.

"Why would any sane person build here?" asked Swift.

"Not a person," said Toro.

"I do not think a living person is here," I added.

"A jinni," said Arij. "A demon."

"We can't bypass the pantheon. It seems we must go through it," said Swift. "Best keep swords ready for anything."

The palace came upon us. Not a soul or living thing was around us. Each colossus appeared to be over three hundred feet tall, as if all of these were the size of the Colossus of Rhodes. Above the archway leading into the pantheon was a phrase inscribed in multiple languages: hieroglyphics, Greek, Hebrew, Arabic, and other Far Eastern languages.

I read the phrase aloud: "Palace of Pandemonium."

The moment I spoke the word, a chill crept up my spine, causing the hairs on the back of my neck to stand upright.

"The story was true," said Arij.

"Palace of the Devil," said Swift.

"Allah protect me," said Toro.

"What kind of labyrinth is this? This lake of fire, this devil palace," said Swift. "This is hell. I say, hell. Am I dead?"

"You are not dead," I said. "Are we dead?"

"I say not," said Arij.

"There is air in my lungs," stated Toro. "Therefore, we're not dead."

We entered into the great pantheon. It was composed of black marble floors, black columns, and black walls—all illuminated by the blue light from the torches. The archway led us into the most amazing assembly room. It was constructed like an ancient amphitheater in a full circle, like the Flavian Colosseum in Rome. The floor of the assembly room was not the black rock but a mixture of glowing purple, red, and orange stone. This crystal was unlike anything I'd ever seen.

"This stone . . . the floor. Do all of you see this?" I stated.

"Not rubies," said Arij.

"I bet . . . Yes, I bet this is the—" I said.

"Gold of Retjenu," said Toro.

"Aye, minosium," said Swift.

"Must be," I remarked.

"Enough to fill a palace. It must be rich in the mountain," said Swift. "Enough to get us home, enough to change any man's mind. It's beautiful. Look at the way it sparkles, like lightning in a bottle."

"I'm more concerned about why this . . . this place is here," I said.

At the center of the assembly center, there was an elevated throne made of red, orange, and purple minosium, glowing with beauty. In front of the throne was a circular table.

"Someone's up there!" exclaimed Arij.

"Where?" said Swift, drawing his sword.

"The table," said Toro, urgently.

"It's a jinni," said Arij. "No sword works on a jinni."

A shadowed person arose from the table. I could not make out his appearance. I thought it could be the shadow. My heart began to beat rapidly.

The figure turned around. "Please, come in. Come in."

"Faustino?" said Swift. "Is that you?"

The man came out of the shadows. Lo and behold, it was Faustino, dressed in a fine red robe. Yet he looked sick and pale and carried an aroma of death.

"Not possible," I said. "Not possible at all."

"An illusion," said Arij.

Faustino laughed as he carried a bottle of wine in his right hand. "No, no. It's me, still flesh and bone."

"How did you end up here? Speak plainly," said Swift, sword still drawn.

"Crewmates, we are friends. No need to draw on me," said Faustino with a dry smile.

"I've seen enough in here to know anything is possible," said Swift. "Now, answer my question."

"I have nothing to hide," said Faustino. He ran his finger along the circular table. "I followed Gaspar here, for he opened the gate. I walked in, just like that."

"Gaspar?" I interjected. "Have you seen Gaspar in here?"

"Ask not, Cosimo," said Arij. "A jinni has him. The eyes tell all."

"Oh, he's here in paradise, wandering and looking for the Garden," said Faustino.

"Garden?" questioned Swift. "There's no garden below the earth."

"Not in the land of the living," said Faustino.

"What garden then?" I asked.

"Of Eden. Genesis. The transformation," said Faustino.

"From . . . from . . . Wait, from the Bible?" asked Swift.

"*Bereshit?*" said Arij with a raised brow.

"Aye, in the beginning," said Faustino. "*On the rock in the garden, combine the eagle with dragon's fire to open the gates of heaven and retrieve my soul's desire.*"

Combine the eagle with dragon's fire? What did he mean? I remembered reading that, but what did that mean? Combine . . . combine . . . what two things? Gaspar combined . . . combined what?

"Back away," said Swift. "Take not a step closer. You have crazy eyes, black eyes. You won't eat me!"

"I have more than enough food here, enough for you, Swift," said Faustino with a smile.

"What are you thinking, Cosimo?" asked Arij.

"Faustino, do you mean sal ammoniac, as in the eagle and salt-petre? As in dragon's fire?" I asked.

"I mean many things," said Faustino.

"That's where Gaspar is," I said. "Where he can combine them with . . . with . . . minosium in some sort of contraption. He needs a furnace. Yes, a furnace. How do you know this, Faustino? Who told you this?"

"That's why he brought all of you here, brought me here, to tell ye of his wonderful things," said Faustino.

"You refer to the shadow, yes?" I spoke.

"He led us here, Cosimo," said Faustino, "Remember that night on the ship? We both saw him, both chosen for his service. He's marked you, Cosimo. No man or woman can escape his mark. Only by death will you be free."

"You tell him or whoever he is that I don't want whatever he's offering," said Swift. "I bet that thing took Jaipur."

The strongest, loudest roar resounded throughout the assembly hall, so loud that it shook the foundation of the palace. My heart began to beat with fear.

"He's here," said Faustino. "He controls the beast, controls the world. All of you, besides Swift, can join him, join him like me. Each of you could live like an emperor, like me."

"I'll kill you right where you stand," said Swift.

"Imagine, Toro," continued Faustino, walking around our group. "Imagine if you had enough gold to buy a whole new herd to replace your family who were massacred by bandits because of your negligence. Toro, you left them there to die alone in the desert."

"Quiet! Quiet, you devil!" yelled Toro.

I had never seen Toro with this much emotion or passion.

"A shame," said Faustino.

"You are wrong," yelled Toro. "I had no choice. No choice. Oh, my poor boy . . . " His speech cracked with sadness and tears.

"You have a choice now," said Faustino.

"Don't listen to him, Toro!" said Arij.

"Arij, you have a choice," said Faustino. "Leave the yoke of your father. Join me. Join the true king. Live free or become a slave like your mother, beaten by Prince Sikander. You know your father doesn't love you. If he did love you, Arij, then why would he give you away to Sikander? Your father cares not about you. Look in your heart. You know this."

"My mother was no slave," said Arij.

"You are a slave behind palace walls," said Faustino. "Sold off like cattle for a price."

"I am no cattle!" said Arij.

"Do not fall for his words, Arij," I stated.

"My words," laughed Faustino. "You are no different than cattle, Cosimo. your parents gave you away to the monastery. You are worse off than Arij. You have no one, and no one cares for you."

"Who told this to you, Faustino?" I asked.

Faustino continued, "Up above did not care about you, Cosimo. That's why He locked you away in a monastery to never experience love. I stand corrected. You would experience love, love from that Friar Marzano. Oh, Marzano would sleep with you. Whip you, too. Marzano loved to whip Cosimo. All little Cosimo could do to escape Friar Marzano's forbidden love was run to the library. Marzano will be the only person to ever love you, Cosimo, unless you join my king who will always love you."

"Aye, I was ashamed of what Friar Marzano did to me, ashamed of it. I hated the Lord above because of it," I said.

"Love my king, Cosimo," said Faustino. "Have your revenge. You deserve it. Let my king help and avenge you."

I closed my eyes and took a deep breath. "I am not scared of my past, of what Friar Marzano did to me, of what I thought of myself. I know my self-worth, and I have found someone who loves me, a family who loves me, and a Lord who loves me. He has liberated me from bondage and brought me to my real family."

"My love," said Arij.

"My brother," said Toro.

"Aye, and my friend," said Swift.

"My family," I said, smiling at each of them. "Move aside, Faustino, for we have somewhere to be."

With a dry, mysterious smile, Faustino stood motionless in front of us.

"Aye, Cosimo said move, so move!" yelled Swift.

"Swift, the jester," said Faustino, "who came across the whole world to save his love."

"You know not my heart's desire," said Swift. "I'm tired of this back-and-forth nonsense. Move!"

"Spices to pay for the treatment to cure her sickness," said Faustino. "Too bad Rose has died, Swift. She's here in this place. All this effort, all this journey was for naught."

"Never say her name aloud. Never!" yelled Swift. "Move now, or I'll cut you to pieces."

Faustino stood there with a blank stare, refusing to move out of the way. True to his word, Swift lunged forward and drove his sword into Faustino's chest. Faustino did not cry out or shriek. He looked at Swift as the sword cut through his tendons and muscles.

"Bad move, Swift," said Faustino.

"This is real dark magic!" said Swift, watching with horror.

Faustino grabbed Swift by the shoulder and threw him across the room with otherworldly strength. Not a drop of blood came from Faustino's chest.

Faustino continued, "Join the true king. Achieve riches and immortality. All it takes is one sip from the saturnine wine." Faustino took the sword lodged in his chest, threw it to the side, and gestured toward the center of the table. There on the table was a bowl of black liquid coursing with purple energy moving like lightning through the bowl.

"What is the name of your king, your shadow king?" I asked, slowly backing away from Faustino.

"Beelzebub," said Faustino.

"It is the devil!" said Arij.

"We must cut him down," yelled Toro. "Devil! Devil!"

Another terrible roar echoed through the assembly hall, sounding like that of a large monster. I had to think fast.

"His child comes," said Faustino. "Leviathan comes."

"The beast!" cried Arij. "The beast!"

I witnessed an enormous tail of a reptile moving around the pantheon behind the window arches. Judging by the size of his tail, this beast was larger than a mountain. I could not see the whole creature. I prayed to the Lord to help me.

"You must drink. You must!" yelled Faustino.

"Or what?" I asked.

To my amazement, I began to hear loud chanting spiraling around me. Seated in assembly seats were dark souls, demons of the most horrible complexion. Each was different from the next; some had horns while others had yellow eyes glaring at us. These dark creatures were of all shapes, sizes, and colors.

"If you decide not to drink, Cosimo," said Faustino, "you shall die here, for the king has spoken."

"Where is your king?" asked Toro.

Faustino smiled and looked up to the throne above us. The figure of the dark, haunting shadow bypassed us and walked up to the throne. At last, there before me was Faustino's king—the king of the underworld, the biggest fish in the sea of fire, Beelzebub.

The Dark King was adorned with a golden crown. He had long red horns, yellow eyes, and decaying black skin. He was dressed in a red robe and had magnetic flashing eyes of a mystery that no human word could ever describe. The shadow then entered the Dark King. At that moment, the Dark King stared down at us. His terrible yellow eyes of death pierced right through my soul. I felt fire—the burn, the pain, the agony, the feeling of a thirst never quenched, a feeling of hopelessness, the feeling void of love and God.

The feeling . . . the feeling . . . the feeling of mystery.

My thoughts turned into a circus, as the Dark King's power penetrated my soul and body. I struggled to maintain control of my being, of my thoughts. I thought only of doubt, of pain, of suffering. I had to take control.

I can't. I can't resist him. What choice do I have? Can we escape this, escape him? Escape a thought? Of what thought? Whose thought? His thought . . . my thought . . . we all thought? Black, blue, orange, zig-zag, up, down. Give up, give up, give up, five, seven, give up.

No, no, I won't!

Yes, yes, I can escape.

No, no, I can't, can't.

He offers me riches, power, to avenge myself, to kill friar Marzano.

Kill, kill.

No, no.

Only love, love, love, forgiveness, and love! Yes, the Dark King will not take me, for I forgive. I forgive my mother and father. I forgive Friar Marzano. Forgive, forgive me, Lord.

Toro then grabbed me by the shoulders and shook me violently. "I'm here. Don't lose yourself. It's me! Toro!"

"Toro. Yes, Toro," I said, coming back to my senses as sweat poured off my face. "I am here. I am here!"

"What happened, Cosimo?" asked Arij, worried.

"You felt the king's power, Cosimo," said Faustino. "Now, drink the bowl—the answer you seek, the revenge you seek."

"I will," said Toro.

"No, Toro," I said.

"We have no choice," said Toro.

"Not that, Toro," pleaded Arij.

"Toro, good," said Faustino with a smile. "Drink. Drink, and all your worries of your family, of your cattle, shall dissipate faster than a shooting star in the night sky."

"Toro," I said. "Don't."

Toro looked at me with eyes filled with courage, honor, and love. Then, he nodded and walked up to the bowl.

"I do this for my family," said Toro.

The chanting continued to roar around us.

"Drink for them, for their freedom," said Faustino.

Toro looked into the bowl, closed his eyes, and took a deep breath.

Toro then hit the bowl, throwing the black wine to the floor. He drew his sword and sliced right through Faustino's right arm, cutting it clean off.

Toro then turned to us. "Run!"

Swift then kicked Faustino in the chest, knocking him to the ground.

"That's our cue!" said Swift. "Time to leave."

I grabbed Arij's hand, and we sprinted as fast as we could to the other side of the pantheon to the other exit leading out of the palace of fire. Swift was right next to us, limping.

All of the dark creatures seated in the audience descended upon us. The large archway leading back into the labyrinth was coming into sight. The demons crawled on the ceiling and on the walls and sprinted toward us. Toro was the farthest behind our group.

"Keep running!" proclaimed Swift. "Up ahead. Our way out!"

"Do not stop, Arij," I yelled, gripping her hand.

"Toro!" said Arij.

I turned around. Behind us, the large mass of demons was gaining on us, inching closer and closer to Toro. A large stone wall began to close in the distance, like the one from the river, closing our only way out.

"We won't make it," said Arij, trying to catch her breath.

Closer, closer the army of the dead descended upon us by the thousands, by the tens of thousands. More and more of them came from under the floor, coming from the arched windows, coming from every corner of the pantheon.

Arij, Swift, and I then reached the end of the pantheon, sprinted under the closing wall, and made it back to the labyrinth. Toro was still behind, struggling with his leg, too far behind to make it to the closing wall.

"Toro!" yelled Swift. "Hurry!"

"He's not going to make it," I said.

"No!" shouted Arij. "Toro, no!"

"Yes, he can make it," said Swift.

I could see Toro smile. Then, he stopped.

"What's he doing?" said Arij

"Oh, no. He's making a stand, a final stand," said Swift.

Toro drew his sword and turned to face the incoming mass of demonic entities descending upon him. Toro decided his destiny for his family. We all yelled to him, yelled for him to try to find another way, as the wall continued to close. We lay on our stomachs to see the last sight of Toro as he planted his feet, sword raised.

Then, he swung his sword.

The wall closed.

Swift

Scene: Genesis

B Y THIS POINT, I was numb on the inside. An occasional thought of Toro and Jaipur came into my mind. Yes, I was saddened, but I was also numb.

The only feeling left was for my love, for my Rose. I knew in my heart she still lived. She was all that I had left in me. I had to be strong. I could mourn once I have left this terrible place, this hell. Yes, Jaipur and Toro would want me to move on. I would make it out of there. By God, I would.

"We must keep going," I said.

"Another one," said Cosimo. "Another one dead."

"He will rest easy," said Arij. "Rest with honor."

"I know," said Cosimo. "I was so close, so close to drinking the wine. So close."

"But you didn't," I replied.

"Because of Toro," said Cosimo.

"No, you did not drink the wine, for you knew the wine was bad," said Arij. "You cannot put old wine in a new bottle, or it will break. In that moment, Cosimo, you became a new bottle."

"What do you mean, Arij?" I questioned.

"Faustino—that shadow, that Dark King—spoke of our old wine, our old feelings, our past," said Arij. "We did not drink of the old wine because our souls were filled with new wine, the lifegiving wine, a new future, a new beginning. You cannot put old wine into new bottles, for the bottle would break if you did."

"You are wise, Arij," said Cosimo.

"Black wine! I'm trying to get home to my love," I said. "Didn't want to get drunk off of bad wine, eh."

"Aye," said Cosimo. "Would have tasted like vinegar."

"Terrible vinegar," I said with a smile. "So where to now? I have a feeling Gaspar made it to this Garden."

"For the transformation," said Arij. "For the gold."

"Right," said Cosimo. "The Garden must be where the transformation takes place—where the *prima materia*, the minosium, can be found.

"Come to think of it, I bet the Garden is our way out of here," I said.

"Adam and Eve found a way out," said Arij.

"And so shall we. Let's go," said Cosimo.

We continued into the maze, around each corner, following Cosimo's compass north around the black corridor walls.

After many hours of walking, we came upon another opening where more light, different than the blue light, was shining at the end of the corridor. I could hear water flowing in the distance. My mouth was parched. I licked my lips at the thought of refreshing water.

Out of the darkness, we stepped onto soft ground. It was mud and grass instead black stone. I looked around with increased excitement. *Have we escaped the labyrinth? Have we found our freedom? Wait, no. Is this . . . is this the Garden? The Garden of Genesis?*

Wind brushed against my arm and face. A relief. The wind whooshed around and through the trees, causing them to sway back and forth. I closed my eyes to hear the wind whisper in my ears.

"Have we escaped?" I spoke.

"This must be the Garden," said Cosimo.

"Amazing," said Arij. "The night sky is above us, lit by the moon's glow. This is an opening in the mountain, in the labyrinth."

"Let me fall into your night's embrace," I said.

"Sleep not, for I hear something," said Cosimo.

"What do you hear?" asked Arij.

"I hear it, too" I said. "Sounds like a man."

"Sounds like Gaspar," said Cosimo.

Cosimo

Scene: Waltz of the Garden

〜

W E MOVED THROUGH the thick forest in haste. I noticed flowers of all colors blooming from the ground, green vines hanging from trees, and buzzing insects jumping from leaf to leaf. Unfortunately, I stumbled on a tree root protruding from the ground and fell into a briar batch. I bit my tongue to keep quiet, but the thorns pierced deep into my arm. Arij did her best to remove some of them.

After an hour of walking, we came upon a small hill next to a pleasant, still lake. On the hill was a white gazebo, constructed in Greek fashion with five Ionic columns holding up a dome. Adjacent to the gazebo was some type of mysterious metal, bronze in color, arranged in the shape of a water droplet, a teardrop. Smoke puffed out the top of the teardrop mechanism. I knew what this teardrop was: it was the furnace, the furnace from the scrolls, the furnace to morph the properties into eternal gold.

"Look at the flowers on the hill," said Swift. "They glisten like gems. Might be gems, I'd say. Numerous gems."

"Wow," I said.

"The buds of the flower," said Arij. "I know my gems, and those are rubies, emeralds, and sapphires. See there? That flower bud is a diamond."

"That'll get us home, sultan or not," said Swift.

Right then, a man came out of the forest from the other side of the hill. It was Gaspar, carrying a large sack toward the furnace.

"Gaspar," I uttered.

"I say we catch him," said Swift. "Bind him to a tree and demand answers."

"Nay, violence is not the answer," said Arij.

"We'll soon find out the answer, eh?" said Swift.

Gaspar noticed movement in the shrubs and grabbed his sword in a haste. Incredibly, his sword appeared to have green energy, like lightning, flowing around it. How was this possible? Did Gaspar capture lightning from the sky?

"What magic is on his sword?" asked Swift.

"Back away, you shadow!" yelled Gaspar. "One strike of my blade, and you shall evaporate into infinitesimal pieces."

"It is Cosimo," I yelled, "with Swift and Arij."

Gaspar laughed. "I am not easily deceived, shadow. They remain up top. No life other than my own ventures down here."

"Listen to me, crazy one," shouted Swift. "We came a long way to find you. A long, long way."

"Tell me something only you would know," said Gaspar, still pointing his sword in our direction. The shrub still covered our faces.

"You recruited me, Cosimo," I said. "You came to Florence, helped me escape the monastery, and took me on a great adventure across the world."

"Too bad this adventure was never about spices, Gaspar. You lied to us," yelled Swift. "Tell us. Was this whole journey about some stone, some gold?"

"Aye, you are truthful," said Gaspar, lowering his sword. "If any of you interrupt my transformation, I will kill you. Now come out of the forest."

"We're coming out now," I said.

The area was surrounded by flowers and large trees whose branches extended to the ground. There was one modest-looking tree at the center of the hill. Hanging from the tree's thick limbs curling to the ground was a gem, a glowing red-orange stone in the shape of an apple. I could not take my eyes off of this mysterious, mesmerizing glowing stone apple. Swift looked to the flower buds under the tree, which contained different types of gems. Swift bent down and picked up the bud of a white flower, enthralled by the flower's glittering splendor.

"It's a diamond," said Gaspar.

"Never seen one before," said Swift. He took the diamond from the bud and placed it in his bag. Then, he did that with another gem, then another, and another.

"What is this garden?" asked Arij as she looked at the tree with glowing orange fruit.

"The beginning," said Gaspar. "Eden."

"Gaspar, Gaspar," I said, staring at the fruit of the tree. "You left us, lied to us. Tell me the truth, please. As a friend, tell me."

Gaspar sat down on a smooth boulder under the tree. The night sky was clear and crisp, and the moon was full, surrounded by her twinkling brothers and sisters. It was cool here; I could see my breath in the air.

"Aye, the truth," said Gaspar.

"Yes, the truth," said Swift as he continued to pick gems.

Gaspar nodded. "Many years ago, I was part of a Portuguese crew bound for the newfound Spice Islands around the southern tip of Africa. As we drew near to the Spice Islands, a terrible storm came, which shipwrecked me alone on an island quite like this one. For many days and nights, my only company was the stars above and my love, Luna, until one day I came across an old, crippled man on the beach shore. The old man had tan skin and a long white beard; he wore simple cloth and walked with a cane. He spoke my language, spoke Portuguese. The old man told me to follow him into the jungle. He led me to a secluded cave on the island. This cave was hard to access, for it was up high, surrounded by jagged cliffs that could impale you if you were to slip. As you could see, this cave was far too difficult for a man with crippled legs to climb though not too difficult for me. When we reached the cave, the old man instructed me to find and bring back beautiful, priceless gems from inside the cave.

"I thought the old man was mad, mad indeed, though I did what he said. Why not? I entered the cave and climbed down the cavern, and before my very eyes were numerous glowing purple and red stones stacked in a pile. The old man was right; right he was. Stranger, on the cave walls were many paintings, drawings, and sketches. Adjacent to each painting were inscriptions, written in multiple languages—ancient Egyptian hieroglyphics, Greek, Hebrew, and Arabic.

"Below the inscriptions were paintings of full scenes, adorned in different colors and details. The first scene was of the Egyptians using the stars as guidance to navigate the seas. Next to this painting was a sketched map, a nautical chart outlining the Egyptians' journey across the sea. Interestingly enough, the Egyptians did not go east; they went west around the unknown southern continent, the same one we went around earlier in our expedition.

"There on that rock wall, I discovered the existence of the western route. Better yet, there was another painting on the wall, an important painting. It showed the Egyptians uncovering this stone, this orange fruit known by many names, from a tree. The Egyptians called it Gold of Retjenu, the Greeks called it minosium, the Romans called it *prima materia*, and the Jews called it Red Adaman. The list goes on; the names are endless.

"I took the purple and red gems from the cave and gave half of them to the old man as we had agreed upon. After that discovery, the old man revealed nothing of the stones' origins or of the paintings on the rock walls; silent he was on the matter, stone cold silent.

"The old man then asked me to help him return to a port city, wanting me to assist him and to carry the gems. The stones were quite heavy. I agreed and did so. On the last night before we reached the port, the old man brought forth fine wine for us to drink to celebrate our newfound riches and splendor. He pulled out two cups from his satchel, poured the wine in both, and handed a cup to me. I thanked him, but before I drank the wine, I sniffed it. It smelled strange, like that of a metal. I acted like I drank it, wanting him to believe I drank, though I poured it out when he was not looking.

"Soon after our celebration, we fell asleep; rather, he thought I fell asleep, but I had one eye open. After a few hours, I heard the old man move toward me. I was anticipating his move, waiting for him to strike me. I had a rock in my hand. At that moment, the old man attempted to strangle me with a rope, yet I was ready for him. I took the rock and bashed his head open, killing him.

"When I looked to take the stones and the minosium from his satchel, it was all gone, except for one small purple stone and a book. It was a mysterious leather-bound book filled with secrets—secrets of the stars, of alchemy, of history, of minosium. I then checked my own bag, and all of my minosium was gone, vanished. I know not how or where it went.

"I reached the port city the day after, broke up the one purple stone, and sold some of the pieces for a way back home to Portugal. The rest of my story leads us here, to the ending, to the transformation."

I wondered to myself what secrets that book had held. Were these secrets in the book he gave to Jaipur?

"All of us men, Gaspar," said Swift, "we would have returned home with nothing. Men, good men, died to get here."

"Jaipur and Toro among them," I added.

Gaspar looked down and shook his head. "I loved Jaipur. Damn. I had to leave it with him. None of you here would have supported me. Not a king or sultan would have supported my endeavor to uncover this mythical stone unless I said that spices were involved, for the world revolves around the trade of spices. I said and did what I had to do, and it worked."

"You left us to die, Gaspar," said Swift, "die by the hands of the sultan."

"Nay, the sultan would have never turned away from this stone. No man could resist this stone," said Gaspar. "I tried to appease the sultan, but he wanted to send an emissary to Spain before a deal was struck between us, before we received any spices for our troubles. Do any of you know what that would mean for us?"

"We would have returned empty handed," I said, sighing. "King Charles would have reaped the benefits, not us."

"My father would have given you, all of you, your fair share," said Arij.

"I wish that were so, Princess," said Gaspar. "Many kings have told me one thing and have done another."

"I see your point," said Arij.

"I knew we would face this dilemma," said Gaspar. "I knew King Charles or the sultan would try to undercut us, outright cut us out of the deal, as King Manuel of Portugal did to me in my past life. I had to find this stone for us—for our riches, our deal, our freedom!"

"I wouldn't have undercut you, Gaspar," said Arij. "I believe in fairness and truth."

"That's why you shall be a great ruler one day, Arij," I said.

"Poetic, but not realistic," said Gaspar.

"We did gain gems, a bag full of them," said Swift.

"Aye, and much more," said Gaspar.

"What now, Gaspar?" I asked. "If you have the stone, the minosium, why this furnace? Why the garden? Why not just leave?"

"Only the fruit of the tree, the most powerful of all minosium, may provide the right ingredient to create the eternal stone," said Gaspar. "I made it this far, and I'm not leaving here without the true material, a property with a never-ending source of power."

"No man should have that power," said Arij.

"No *ordinary* man," said Gaspar. "Back away now."

"Where's the way out, Gaspar?" asked Swift. "I need no other stone. I have enough to save my love and buy the king of England."

"The ladder," replied Gaspar. "I'll lead you there after the transformation."

"I would like to know where it is now," said Swift.

Gaspar picked up his sword and pointed it. "When my property has been created, the ladder shall open, and we shall walk the way of the ancients to the surface."

"Let him do it, Swift," I said, hesitant. "We have no other choice."

The clear night sky was above as Gaspar opened the top of the teardrop furnace and held up different vials. "My Luna, my dearest love, the hour has come upon us. Grant me your power; evoke the celestial order and the Great Work to complete the labyrinth of transformation. I now pour gold mixed with antimony, sulphur, mercury, fire, water, and air. May these elements unlock the secret properties."

The furnace began to emit flames.

Gaspar continued, "Turn white, turn red, sublimate, and separate the pure from the filth, from the saturnine mud. At this moment, I shall add the key, the Amulet of Retjenu to the mixture—the final ingredient, the final tool, the Amulet of Retjenu!"

He held up a circular purple and gold amulet, pulsing with a fire red glow, similar to how water cuts through rock. Gaspar put the amulet inside of the teardrop furnace. "Combine. Solidify to where no fire can destroy the universal red tincture in my ancient teardrop. Come forth!

Come forth!"

The wind began to roar more strongly than a monsoon, and the earth began to shake and sway like an earthquake. Sparkling in the air surrounding the furnace were bolts of energy, like lightning swirling around the furnace, colored red, green, blue, and yellow.

"St. Elmo's fire," exclaimed Swift. "That's it! That's St. Elmo's fire!"

"I don't know what that is," I said, worried.

The process started to pull us closer to the furnace like a gravitational pull.

"Hang on to me, Arij," I said, holding Arij's hand firmly.

"Your Great Chord!" shouted Gaspar as the wind roared and swirled around us.

A large stroke of purple energy then lashed out from the furnace, striking the forest and evaporating a tree from its powerful force. Our hair began to rise above our heads as the energy around us grew stronger and stronger. A large burst of energy extended from the furnace, like a pebble dropped in a pond. The energy morphed into some type of force field, shaped in a perfect circle around us.

Floating in this field were small balls of energy in perfect spherical shapes, floating like planets in the solar system. These circles of energy were composed of many different colors, bright as the sun, hovering and rotating around the teardrop furnace.

Another burst of energy emitted from the teardrop, bringing forth an opening like that of a rift between existence. It came forth from the top of the teardrop, followed by the large sounds of booming thunder and crashing lightning.

What was going on? An opening, a rift of energy like a crack in the rock face, appeared above the teardrop. The rift extended, stretching above our heads. I looked up into a bright, magnificent light and saw white clouds surrounding Greek columns made of marble, extending upward toward the heavens. Beings with human forms, dressed in splendid robes, were flying in all directions, vibrating with immense, glowing energy. Flying in all directions, they had white wings like those of eagles.

The rift appeared to be a throne room constructed in immaculate ancient architecture, a mixture of Egyptian, Greek, Roman, and Islamic. These beings could see us! These winged humans must have been angels.

This rift of energy was breaking through our plane of existence into another: the other side. I witnessed a throne room with golden balconies filled with angels playing stringed and brass instruments. At the center was a staircase guarded by winged cherubim.

Gaspar held strong to the teardrop, staring up at the heavens. Coming down from the throne at the top of the stairs next to the cherubim was a massive white glistening cloud radiating with fire and lightning. The cloud moved, revealing an awesome figure seated upon the throne. This figure was the most immaculate being of pure multi-colored energy, so bright I could not look at it.

From the cloud came forth four multi-colored beings appearing like mixtures of humans and animals. Each of the beings had a form resembling that of a human with wings. The faces of the beings appeared like men and women of the most gorgeous physiognomy. The sides of the angels'—I assumed they were angels—faces looked like either oxen, eagles, or lions. The angels were wearing majestic, gold-plated armor, etched with vibrant purple-white designs, glistening like diamonds.

They stood next to a sapphire throne. Seated upon the throne was a king appearing to be in the form of a man with the shine of an electrum. Around this king was a large, spherical rainbow mixed with fire.

One of the angels pointed down. I looked down, and below my feet was the most horrible scene of a lake of fire where thousands upon thousands of dark souls were falling into the fire, screaming for mercy.

On a rock overlooking the lake of fire, watching all of this play out, was the same creature I witnessed at the Palace of Pandemonium, the Dark King.

He had long horns, dark yellow eyes, and black skin; he was seated on the same black throne. His face appeared to be decaying, like necrotic flesh. The Dark King then looked at me, and I felt his horrible power run right through me. I could not stare at him any longer.

I then looked to my right and saw another rift forming. Through the rift, I could hear two men speaking to one another as if these two men were right next to me.

One of the voices was that of a younger man with white skin and brown hair. I could see him through the rift. The young man was searching for something in the Garden. He looked like he was in rough shape, for his was face was full of dirt and his arm was bleeding.

Then, I heard another man through the rift; he yelled the word, "Cypress." In that instant, I could see the younger man stare at me through the rift. He could see me, and I could see him!

The young man called out to me and ran toward me, but the rift closed at that moment. Once the rift closed, I saw thousands of lit torches, like those of an army, coming toward us through the forest.

My attention then turned back toward the teardrop, to the heavens above. Gaspar was walking toward the rift. To my amazement, one of the angelic beings with a small stone in his hands was at the entrance of the rift that led upward to the heavens. The stone appeared like a diamond in the shape of an apple, glowing with many different colors. The being extended his other hand through the rift, pointing behind us. The moment the being's hand broke through the rift, a golden line of fire extended from his hand and into the forest, weaving through the darkness.

Gaspar paid no attention to the line of fire, for he was wild with excitement as the angel held the stone. Gaspar approached the angel and the rift, eyes fixated on the glowing stone. The angel nodded at him, then Gaspar moved his hand through the rift and grabbed the stone.

The moment Gaspar touched the stone, he evaporated into infinitesimal pieces, glowing like embers in a fire. The angel then took back the stone, and all of the rifts closed that instant.

Prince Sikander

Scene: Thought Variations I

❧

I CAME UPON this place of Genesis, the place where Faustino and the shadow had led me. I found the entrance to the labyrinth, found it through my scouts. The Spaniards forgot to shut the door on the way in, so I stepped right in, taking Zaragoza and ten of my personal guards with me. We took the platform down and ventured into the deep unknown.

Strange place the labyrinth was. Strange indeed. Some of my men began to vanish, disappearing into the dark abyss, while others went mad. We killed the mad ones, even though we were mad ourselves.

My men and I were on the verge of death and of killing one another until one of those Spaniards, Faustino it was, came out from the dark and brought us to the palace, the palace of the Dark King.

There in the palace, Faustino offered me a way to defeat the sultan, to defeat my father, to obtain everything I could ever want: power beyond imagination. Faustino offered me the black wine, the black elixir.

I drank it all in one gulp. After that, my eyes were opened to a whole new world I never thought existed. My thoughts moved faster than comets in the sky. Further, my thoughts were structured, uniform, and compiled like a magnificent architectural design. I was able to see things more clearly. The Dark King was clearly the answer, the way, the life, and the hate I so desired. Life made sense.

What did the black elixir help me to see? My eyes had a wider view of the color spectrum; I was able to see shades and colors once hidden to me. Rock was not gray in color but a mixture of black, green, and gray coalescing with one another like on the canvas of an artist. I could see details and energy waves once invisible to the naked eye. I looked at my torch and could see a ray of light illuminated around the flame, extending outward.

The strength in my arms, hands, and all across my body felt stronger than that of any lion, tiger, or bear. My movement was quick, mirrored by my fast thoughts. I was a different being once I drank the black elixir.

It was funny; Zaragoza, the Spaniard, refused to drink the liquid as did two others. Zaragoza said he would "sit this one out." Zaragoza received his wish, and he would now sit out for the rest of his life, six feet underground with the other men who refused to drink the Dark King's wine. Zaragoza learned a valuable lesson: refusing refreshments in a king's house was rude, for we were his guests and must act accordingly.

My time to take over Boubazar had come. It was my time to take over my father and take over the new world as the Dark King had instructed me to do.

All I would need to fuel my war machine was the gemstone of knowledge, minosium. With this powerful gem in my hands and the Dark King in my ear, no man, no father, no king, no sultan, no army, no country, no God could stop me!

Cosimo

Scene: Dance of the Prince

⚭

ASPAR, OH GASPAR, disappeared he did, evaporated into dust like the unfortunate Israelite who touched the ark of covenant. I looked and I looked, and Gaspar was nowhere to be seen. The only remnant of him still left were the robes he wore and his sword pulsating with energy.

"Did he . . . ?" asked Swift. "Where did Gaspar go?"

"Gone," said Arij.

"And . . . and . . . those shiny people, those shiny angels?" asked Swift.

"The heavens," I said, staring at the teardrop furnace, "and hell."

"Oh . . . oh, hell," said Swift. "I might need to pray a few Act of Contritions. Aye, more than a few."

"Those two men . . . did any of you see those two men?" I asked.

"Which two men?" asked Arij.

"I don't know what I saw," said Swift.

"I heard a word, a name," I said, thinking. "Christoph."

"Must be linked to the stone, to the fruit, to the furnace," said Arij.

I nodded, then walked over and picked up Gaspar's sword, which was vibrating with green energy swirling around the blade. I looked inside the teardrop, and there was a large bronze bowl filled with a dark liquid bursting with sparks of energy of all colors. Strangely, the amulet had disappeared and was nowhere to be seen.

Where were the stone and the amulet? The angel took the stone. I looked at the large sacred tree with its limbs filled with sparkling blood-orange minsoium. This tree . . . Could this have been the tree from which Adam and Eve picked the fruit? Was minosium the fruit, the knowledge, the answer? Was the creation story a metaphor, or was the story real? Did it happen in the very spot I stood? Where did the heavens, hell, and those two mysterious men fit into this infinite mystery?

"I did not take one of those gems," said Swift. "A second banishment didn't sound too appealing."

Arij walked over to the fruit, examined it, and picked one off. "Could this have been the fruit of knowledge?"

"I don't know," I said. "No man should have this power, this fruit." I looked at my feet, noticing a heated glow below me, a trail of fire.

"I saw the fire burst from the finger of the angel," said Arij. "He pointed that way, the way of the fire."

We looked in the direction of the fire trail as it cut through the dark forest in front of us.

"A way out?" asked Swift.

I pondered, thinking of the trail of fire, of my past. "This tangled maze, this labyrinth of life . . . this is my—nay, *our*—journey through this difficult life. Some fall along the way, but we go onward with faith, free of saturnine mud. We look up to the stars and to the heavens for guidance, for a way through our own maze of life below the celestial spheres."

"Amen to that, brother," said Swift.

"Thanks be to Allah," said Arij.

A loud horn then echoed through the forest. Behind us were a mass of lit torches, drums, and yelling in the far distance but coming toward us. It was a legion of demons, for they must have heard the commotion.

"Swift," I said quickly. "Give me your blade."

"Why?" asked Swift.

"No time. Give it here," I demanded.

Swift tossed his blade to me. I caught it and stuck the blade inside the liquid in the teardrop furnace.

"What are you doing?" asked Swift.

"Giving you an upgrade," I remarked.

Crack. Snap.

There was movement in the woods. My ears pricked, and out of the shrubs came forth a terrible nightmare.

"My friends, what a pleasure to see you here in this wonderful place," said Prince Sikander. His skin was pale, his eyes completely black, and his veins protruding from his skin.

"You must be joking," said Swift, shocked. "Keep the fun going. Let's go."

"Same way all of you are," said Prince Sikander with a smile.

"The devil has your heart, Sikander," said Arij.

"You drank of the black cup, eh?" I remarked.

"I did. I did," said Prince Sikander. "I'm amazed. The Garden of Eden, here before my very eyes."

He stepped toward us, gripping his blade, a different blade made from the same dark black rock as the labyrinth. The blade was long and supported by a red-horned hilt.

I held up Gaspar's sword. "Back, Prince of Darkness! Back!"

Prince Sikander laughed. "Seems your captain did not make it. Tisk, tisk. A shame Gaspar will not be able to partake in this fruit from the tree of life."

"What do you want with it?" I asked.

"Why would any man want it?" said Prince Sikander. "Power."

"Don't do this, Sikander," pleaded Arij. "Think of the repercussions. My father . . . "

"I don't care about the sultan!" said Prince Sikander. "He will be dead by tomorrow."

"What do you mean?" asked Arij, her voice cracking.

"Might as well tell you before you meet your grave," said Prince Sikander. "You should have drank the black wine. It could have saved you."

"I don't need to be saved," said Arij.

"Ah, you do. We all do," said Prince Sikander. "You think I came here, to your island, for a peace talk? For an agreement between our two kingdoms?" He laughed. "No, no, my dear. I came to take your father's kingdom. It shall be the beginning of my expansion."

"I knew you were an enemy," said Arij. "My father would never allow it. Nay, our walls are high, high enough to keep our enemies out."

"Or keep them in," said Prince Sikander with a smile.

"What do you mean, Sikander?" asked Arij.

"What do I mean?" said Prince Sikander. "Tomorrow, the Portuguese with their great armada will surround the port and batter Boubazar's walls with their unrelenting cannons while my army attacks from land. The sultan's army will have nowhere to rally or escape. They'll be trapped, for the sultan and his army will be stuck behind their high walls. I will not have to raise a sword or risk a life because my army will burn Boubazar from the inside out. The sultan will be forced to give the city to me, or I will burn the city and all its inhabitants to the ground. Genius, isn't it?"

"You mean your father, the vizier, will burn the city, right?" interjected Swift.

"I am more powerful than my father and brother shall ever be!" yelled Prince Sikander. "And soon, I will have the Portuguese armada at my disposal and the power of minosium in my hands. With them, I shall kill my own father and assume my throne. Nay, I will not stop there. After Boubazar, I shall take over all of Arabia, China, Europe, and the New World. In a few years' time, the world will bow to me, to King Sikander, Emperor of the World!"

"Sounds like a plan," said Swift. "A bad plan."

"You will never win, Sikander. Not like this," said Arij. "Listen to me, I know the feelings you have, the feelings of resentment, of hate toward your father. But by becoming like him, by becoming your father, you will start to hate yourself. If you truly want to change your father, yourself, and the world, then fight for love and forgiveness, not for violence and hate. Do not become your father. Nay, be yourself, your true self, and you shall be more than your father ever was or ever will be!"

There was a flicker in Prince Sikander's eyes, a flash of light, a flash that brought forth his original, true self. In that moment, he saw what could be.

Then a shadow, a black mist in the figure of a man, spoke into his ears.

"The shadow," I said.

Prince Sikander's eyes then returned to a pitch black. "The disrespect, the mockery. Death. Death to them all. Death!"

"No, Sikander," pleaded Arij. "You have a choice. Don't do this."

"I've made my choice," said Prince Sikander.

"As I still breathe, you will not have this fruit," I said, standing firm.

"My love, my love," said Arij, pulling on my shirt. "He shall kill you. Nay, run. We must run!"

"Your end has come, Spaniards," said Prince Sikander as he raised his black sword.

"I am not Spanish," said Swift, drawing his sword.

"Arij, listen to me," I said in the most serious tone. "Follow the fire through the forest, and tell your father all that has happened. Be quick, understand?"

She grabbed hold of my arm. "I can't leave you. Come. We'll sail away, sail to Europe like we said!"

"We will, my dear," I said, smiling softly. "We will."

A tear cascaded down her cheek. She murmured, "I love you, Cosimo."

I then pulled her close to my chest and kissed her with all the love in my heart. "I love you truly. Now go!"

Arij then sprinted into the forest and followed the line of fire to safety far away from here.

"The Dark King wanted this," said Prince Sikander as he removed his cloak and shirt, revealing his muscular frame. "The Dark King is watching. He wanted to give this kill to me."

Swift took out a red cloth from his bag and wrapped it around his forehead. I picked up Gaspar's sword, which flowed with purple and green energy.

The three of us moved toward the large Greek gazebo at the center of the garden. The floor of the gazebo was made of white marble. We stared at one another, focused. Prince Sikander roared, sounding like a lion and revealing his sharp fangs.

"*En garde!*" I yelled.

Our swords clashed, energy like lightning sparking from each strike. Sikander's strength was immense and powerful. His first strike propelled Swift backward into the air. Sikander was quick, moving with elegant motion. The fight ensued.

Strike, strike, lunge. Slash, step, step. Clash, step, hit. Spark, spark.

Hit, slap, jump, step.

Sikander's blade interlocked with mine. He opened his mouth, showing his sharp fangs. Then, he bit my shoulder. I shrieked with pain and pushed him off. Blood began to trickle down my arm. The pain radiated from the bite.

Swift then swung at Sikander, and their blades collided.

Strike, spark, spark, slash, jump, step, step, twirl, jump, hit, hit, hit, slash, jump, cling, cling, spark, strike, slash, back, up, up, down, back, back, strike!

Swift struck down, cutting into Sikander's right arm. Sikander roared in agony, then grabbed Swift by the throat and threw him to the ground, knocking the wind out of him.

"Die now," said Prince Sikander, raising his sword.

I jumped toward the prince and thrust my blade into his back. He grunted from the pain and pivoted. Our blades collided.

Slash, swing, up, down, side, side, hit, hit, up, down, pivot, lunge, hit.

At that moment, the prince lunged forward and thrust his sword right into my chest, right into my heart.

"No!" yelled Swift, trying to stand up.

I fell to the ground as his blade left my body. Swift pulled himself up, and screamed, "Here, Prince. Here! For it all!

Their two blades collided.

Slash, slash, hit, up, down, pivot, pivot, up, hit, spark, spark, hit, lunge, block, block, block, strike, block, block.

In that instant, the prince slashed Swift's leg, then grabbed him by the throat. The prince raised his blade as life was escaping Swift. With all the strength Swift had left, he thrust his sword into Sikander's heart.

Sikander dropped Swift to the ground as he clenched the vibrating sword in his heart, trying to remove it. As he was catching his breath, Swift picked up Gaspar's sword and, with one fluid motion, cut through Sikander's neck, decapitating the prince. He split bone, and scarlet blood dripped from his lips as the bright life left his decaying body.

Swift

Scene i: Apotheosis

⌒ınnɔ

I stood over Prince Sikander's motionless body.

All of this struggle, all of this pain, this whole journey, the ones I loved, the ones I lost . . . It all ends here, yet does my journey ever end?

"Swift," said Cosimo, softly.

"Cosimo," I said, turning to him. "Oh . . . Oh, Cosimo."

"Shh," whispered Cosimo, calmly and gently. "All is fine."

"It doesn't look too bad. I've seen worse."

Cosimo smiled. "Listen to me, Swift."

"I can pick you up, bring you out of here. We'll find a ship, a good ship. Look at these stones I've found, not to mention Gaspar's charts. He . . . "

"No, listen, Swift." Cosimo struggled to speak. "You . . . you must leave me . . . here."

"Are you mad? I can't leave you here."

"My time has come for . . . for the gates of heaven were opened to me . . . my transformation." Cosimo stared at the night sky above us. The stars twinkled, the moon glowed, and his eyes contained the truest sparkle of light. Cosimo smiled at the cosmos above as his soul began its transformation to enter heaven.

With broken sadness, I continued, "Nay, not yet. I shall carry you on my back, out of this labyrinth, and to your home."

I bent down to pick up Cosimo, but he pushed me away.

"I nev . . . nev . . . never knew why God kept me locked up in that monastery. Now, yes, now I understand . . . So, so beautiful." Tears flowed from his eyes as he continued to watch the night sky.

"Stay with me, Cosimo."

"You shall make it home, Swift. Your . . . your love, your Rose, will see you."

My own tears trickled down my cheeks. "You shall join me in London and meet her, meet Rose. All three of us—nay, Arij will be with us, so four. We will go shopping at the market, smell the spices, buy new clothes, drink the finest wine, and commiserate over a fire about our past wonderful adventures. How does that sound, Cosimo?"

"Splendid," said Cosimo. "Splendid, Swift."

Grunting, Cosimo started to cough up blood.

I grabbed, held him, and hugged him.

"I see the heavens once more. I see it. I see it all. It all makes sense, all of it."

"What do you see?"

"Tell Arij, I'll al . . . always be with her. Just look to the stars to find me."

"I will, my brother."

"And I'll be with her . . . with her."

"And me?" I said, gently smiling.

"You also," said Cosimo. "Make it back, Swift. Make it back."

"If God allows me to, I will."

Cosimo looked starry-eyed at the dark sky. I could see the reflection of the celestial bodies above glistening in his eyes, reflecting in his irises. There, I saw bright stars, the glowing moon, and for a moment a shooting star with her long tail projected across the dark night sky.

Cosimo said, "Finished."

At that last word and his last breath, dark mist covered his eyes, color left his lifeless body, and his soul ascended into the celestial heavens.

I stood up and stared at his lifeless body. "Goodbye, my friend."

At that moment, there was a growl, a roar so loud that it shook the gazebo.

"Leviathan," I said.

I looked at the forest, toward the sound of the roar, and saw a legion of numerous lit torches and heard resounding drums, marching toward me. I could not wait. I had to move, act that instant.

I picked up my sword and my bag and followed the golden red fire through the black forest. I moved quickly around trees, shrubs, and bushes until I reached a corridor leading back into the labyrinth.

I then felt the earth vibrate like an earthquake rattling the ground. I looked back into the forest, and in the darkness, I saw massive golden eyes glaring at me. It was the beast, the leviathan. I sprinted into the labyrinth following the fiery line, my only guidance, around the twists and turns of the maze.

I reached one corridor intersecting with another corridor. Coming from the adjacent corridor were two of the most terrible demons, wielding black swords with veins of fire coursing through the blades like magma. They were in full black-plated armor. The demons had horns on their heads, granite black faces, yellow eyes, and a body like that of a man and animal with claws, hooves, tails—terrifying components.

The demons screeched upon seeing me. They lunged at me, shoving me against the wall. I punched one of them while the other demon growled in my face, trying to bite me with its fangs.

"You can't escape, Swift!" hissed the demon in a sinister, snake-like tone. "Your soul is doomed to stay here with us."

I grasped my blade, which vibrated with purple and green energy, and thrust the blade into the demon. I kicked the demon off of my blade and turned to the other one. Our blades collided, sparking with energy. I pivoted and slashed right through the dark creature. Both of the demons started to dissolve like embers in a fire, leaving only their armor and weapons on the ground. With no time to spare, I kept on my way.

The fire trail led me through numerous zig-zagging corridors until I reached one that had light gleaming at the end of it.

Light! Could it be a way out? It must be a way out! Fail me not, angelic fire.

The moment I reached the end of this corridor, the line of fire disappeared. I looked up to see where I was, where the fire had led me. Before my eyes was an enormous cavern surrounding a crystal-clear, teal hot spring larger than a lake, steaming from the magma below it. Around the hot spring were gigantic deposits of red and purple minosium crystals, sparkling with magnificence.

Everywhere I looked, there were minosium crystals of all shapes and sizes, protruding from the hot springs, the cavern walls, everywhere. Over the hot spring was a arched stone bridge leading toward a ladder. It was no ordinary ladder but one made of a vibrant glowing metal, illuminated with the colors of the rainbow like that of the heavens. The bridge was situated at the end of the ladder, ascending upward to the ceiling of the cave.

By God, the ladder to heaven, the ladder out of here, the ladder to my love . . . let's go!

I heard marching, screaming, and yelling from behind me. It was a legion of demons coming for the labyrinth.

I sprinted across the bridge toward the vibrant ladder. A second later, the army of demons poured out of the corridor—firing arrows from bows, throwing spears, jumping, crawling, and running toward me from all sides of the cavern.

As I continued to sprint, I saw the beast moving in the hot spring below the bridge. The leviathan was a massive, dark green reptile—larger than a ship, two ships, three ships, larger than all those ships combined. The leviathan had a long jaw and a body like that of a crocodile, yet it slithered like a snake with its gleaming golden eyes poking out of the water.

The beast sprang from the water and with its gigantic tail destroyed the ladder and sections of the bridge. I began to panic as I saw cracks form on the bridge, shaking it and breaking it apart. Stone pieces began to fall into the hot spring. I ran to the edge of the bridge as it shook and clung to the rock wall.

What do I do? Think, Swift. Dammit, think! There's some ladder left about midway up. I can't reach where it is. Nay, it's too high up. I could try to climb the rock. Where's a good point to climb?

I turned around and saw that motionless behind me was the Dark King in front of the legion in the middle of the bridge. Next to him was Faustino, waving at me with a smile.

There was nothing left for me to do. What could I do? Would I die on this bridge at the hands of that beast?

No . . . For my love, no.

I closed my eyes and said a prayer to my last hope, to the Lord above. "I know I've remained silent for years and have done poorly in

Your eyes. I do not deserve Your help. But oh, Lord, have mercy upon me! Save me from this hell."

At that moment, a rope fell upon my face, a golden rope of a mesmerizing glow. I could not believe it! I tugged firmly on the dangling golden line. I looked up, and there, lo and behold, was Toro, gripping the rope on a ledge next to the ladder.

"Toro!" I yelled.

"Climb!" said Toro. "Climb!"

I grasped the rope and pulled with all of my might. Toro pulled and pulled, and I climbed and climbed. I reached the ledge, greeted by Toro's hands. I grabbed him by the wrist, and Toro pulled me up.

"Praise be the Lord!" I shouted. "You are not dead, Toro."

"If we stay here, you and I shall be dead," said Toro seriously. "To the ladder!"

I gripped the ladder and climbed upward, moving with the utmost speed behind Toro—a foot there, a hand there, pull up.

Then, my foot slipped! I held onto the ladder with one hand as my right foot dangled. I looked down and saw the Dark King staring right at me, piercing my soul with his gaze as his demonic army began scaling the rock wall toward us. I rebalanced myself and continued upward as fast as I could.

At the top of the ladder was another black corridor with bright light shining forth at the end of the tunnel. Sunlight! I sprinted and dove into the light, and I landed on soft grass. I was blind for a moment as my eyes adjusted to this new light. I heard an object roll, and once my sight returned, I saw Arij and Toro pushing a stone wall in front of the corridor.

The oval-shaped stone was a door with Egyptian hieroglyphics painted across it. Arij and Toro slid the stone door into place, covering the corridor. A blue light came forth from the stone, illuminating the hieroglyphics; with another flash of the blue light, the stone door clicked, clung, puffed, and descended back into the mountain, moving downward. Dust exploded the moment it was fully submerged in the mountain. It was quite the scene.

Toro sat on the ground next to me, panting. I looked around and saw that I was on top of a small mountain on arid land.

"I can't believe . . . " I said. "Toro?"

"Thank Allah for sending Gabriel to help you," said Toro. "As the darkness flung themselves upon me, I prayed to Allah to save me. At that moment, His messenger, Gabriel, came to my aid, threw me a golden rope, and pulled me up into another corridor away from the darkness below. The rope led me to the ladder. That same rope saved you, Swift. Before I reached the top, I noticed Arij coming from the labyrinth, so I helped her. Arij told me everything that happened, so I waited for you in case you needed a hand."

"I could give you a kiss, Toro," I exclaimed. "You saved my life. I'm in your debt."

"Not in mine, but Allah's," he said with a smile.

"Where's . . . " stuttered Arij.

"Cosimo . . . " I paused. Then, I exhaled and shook my head.

Arij understood the truth and did not question it. Tears cascaded down her cheeks. She did not speak. I pulled Arij close to my heart and gave her the only thing I could offer her: a hug.

"It is done," said Toro.

Swift

Scene ii: Final Waltz

⟨ШШ⟩

N OT LONG AFTER we left the labyrinth, we found a way back to Boubazar by following the river. We were much closer than I thought. I wanted to leave, to catch a ship sailing back to Europe. I didn't want to deal with the Portuguese or the sultan. I had my gems, had enough to return home. Why would I care about the sultan?

Yet I did want to help Arij and help save her kingdom. If it weren't for her help, I wouldn't have retrieved these gems to save my love, Rose. Further, I hated the Portuguese, plain and simple. They had been hunting me for years now. Why should I stop here and not deal a blow to them before they feel the need to fight England? Worse, what if the Portuguese captured me on my trek back to England? I'd be thrown into the brig. A slave I'd be for the rest of my life. I would lose my gems and Gaspar's priceless nautical log.

I weighed out my options and concluded that if I didn't stop the Portuguese here in Boubazar, I would have to deal with them in the future on more unfavorable terms. Best deal with the Portuguese now with some advantage. Oh, but another fight . . .

The great lamp shone bright, revealing her luscious locks as we approached the city of Boubazar. I was more than tired, but I had to pull it together to save my head and the city. Outside of Boubazar's walls, I could see the Portuguese armada sailing toward the port with the sun rising upon their backs. Their naval fleet was large, the largest in the world. Time was running out. Arij, Toro, and I had to tell the sultan of the vizier's plans before the Portuguese entered port.

The moment we stepped foot in the city, Toro and I were arrested. Put in chains, we were, and brought in front of the sultan and the vizier for an instant trial and explanation.

I was smart, smarter than sultan, for I knew he or his guards would take my bag of goodies. So I had given it to Arij to hold and to care for and, perhaps, to use it as proof of our story. She would keep it in a safe place in the palace until we would need it.

Once in front of the sultan, Arij told her father the whole story, the whole truth, from beginning to end of everything that we witnessed—from the labyrinth, to Prince Sikander, to our discovery of minosium, to our encounter with the Dark King.

Toro and I interjected our thoughts and opinions on the story when asked, giving our own side of things. Once our story was fully explained, Arij demanded for the vizier to be captured and thrown in jail and for the Portuguese to be destroyed before they attacked Boubazar.

The vizier was insulted; he demanded respect and justice for our actions and lies against him. The sultan had trouble believing us, believing our story until Arij showed my precious bag of gems—gems of all shapes, sizes, and colors—to the sultan. The moment the sultan saw the magnificent gems, he ordered for the vizier to be arrested and for his army to prepare for battle against the Portuguese and the vizier's army waiting just beyond the walls of Boubazar. Toro and I were unchained that instant.

The sultan called for his whole naval fleet to prepare an attack against the Portuguese. The sultan was sly and told his commanders to appear as friends, to fool the Portuguese, then fire upon them and obliterate them. Once the vizier's army, concealed behind a mountain adjacent to Boubazar, heard of the vizier's capture, his army fled to the countryside while the sultan's cavalry chased them to the shoreline.

The battle with the Portuguese on the sea was a fierce fight. The sultan granted Toro and me a chance to fight for him under his banner. We accepted his offer and fought with honor—fighting from ship to ship, sword against sword, resembling the Battle of Salamis between the Ancient Greeks and Persians on the Salamis strait.

Many men were lost on both sides, but at the end of the long day, we were victorious. As a token of gratitude, the sultan awarded Toro and me great medals for bravery and honor in the fight against the Portuguese. It seemed my efforts after such long years of hardship on the journey had come to fruition at last, thank the Lord at last. The sultan smiled upon us and granted us a room to stay in the palace for as long as we needed.

Over the next few days, Toro and I splurged on fun, relaxed in hot baths, reminisced over wine about our lost friends, and thanked the Lord (Allah for Toro) for the great blessings He had granted us.

One day as things were settling down around the kingdom, the sultan called Toro and me into the throne room. Arij was there, appearing mournful and quiet, though rested with an air of completeness about her.

"You called us, Your Majesty?" I spoke.

"I did, for I wanted to tell both of you the truth," said the sultan. "The real truth."

"What is left to be said, Your Grace?" asked Toro.

"This, my dear friend, Toro," said the sultan. "My family has concealed the labyrinth for many generations—many, many generations. My family has known of the labyrinth's whereabouts—of the evil, the gold, the minosium, the garden, everything. You see, this island, this secret, has been passed down from civilization to civilization, starting long before the ancient Egyptians. As both of you can see, the island is now in my hands, my family's hands, Islamic hands.

"Long ago, a great war was fought amongst the Islamic nations, fueled by extracted minosium from here on this island, from the labyrinth. Both sides used the minosium to their advantage and to their destruction. It was the worst mistake that recurred far too many times in history. Each civilization that inhabited this island and utilized minosium's power ended up utterly and completely destroying itself. In doing so, they left the island for the next civilization to do the same to itself in an endless cycle—one great civilization after another, destroyed. I fear one day this stone, this rock, this minosium will destroy the world if we are not careful in preserving its secrets and protecting our race from the stone's destructive power and the evil surrounding it.

"I know we are different with different customs, faith, and rules, but we all share one thing that unites us. We are humans who love, who persevere, and who live. We—united by love regardless of our origins, the color of our skin, or our beliefs—must come together in order to break this cycle of destruction and protect our people from this stone, from minosium. It is the only way. My time is coming to an end. You are the future. She is the future. Learn from me, from my mistakes. Take from the ancients and never let this stone, this gold, this minosium destroy us.

"Why do I say this to each of you? As it was my duty to protect mankind from this stone, from the evil inside the labyrinth, I now pass the torch to you to guard and protect our fellow man and to never let the evil from within the labyrinth reach our united world."

"With that said, Toro and Swift, I shall give you a ship filled with spices, accompanied by my emissary, and a trade deal with King Charles V of Spain."

"Such wisdom, Your Majesty," I said. "But . . . but how could we ever repay such a debt?"

"By swearing under Allah to keep your lantern lit and your eyes open and to guard mankind from evil, from the secret within the labyrinth. Be diligent, my friends, for we know not when that hour may come. Be ready for when it does. Be ready. Do you, Toro, and you, Swift, agree to this proposition, to this duty, to this honor?" asked the sultan as he extended his hand toward us.

"Yes," I replied. "I accept your deal, and I swear before Allah with Arij, Toro, and Sultan Muzaffar as my witnesses to guard mankind from the evil inside the labyrinth, to protect the secret minosium. Not only shall I but also my numerous descendants from hence forward shall defend the secret and shall defend mankind from the evil lurking inside of the labyrinth in order to preserve peace, prosperity, and love in this world."

Toro then said, "I, Toro, before Allah's presence, swear to you and King Solomon, that I and my descendants will preserve the secret of the labyrinth and minosium with my life."

"As shall I, Father," said Arij. "I will be steadfast in watching over the labyrinth for the sake of mankind."

"Come, all of you," said the sultan, gesturing with his hands. "Kneel before me so that I may grant each of you my ultimate blessing."

We knelt before the sultan as he brought forth a golden sword, vibrating with golden energy swirling around the blade. He held it over our shoulders and blessed each of us.

The sultan then said, "Great Allah, grant Your servants and their descendants strength, wisdom, and patience to keep Your Word through this maze of life. Let Your angels on high play Your Great Chord to help Your servants defend the secret of the labyrinth and to keep the evil within at bay. Help them connect to Your world through love and unity and not by war and division. Grant Your soldiers perseverance to never give up as the dark night descends upon their hearts. Be their star, their bright star in the night sky where they shall always look up to see You and never look down toward their feet. Be with us always, Almighty Allah."

The sultan nodded his head and smiled. "Let us now celebrate in Your Name!"

I couldn't believe the party after that. The sultan opened up the palace gates to all citizens of Boubazar. Young or old, rich or poor, slave or free, woman or man—anyone and everyone was welcome into his palace gardens for the most special celebration.

The palace gardens were draped in red cloth with tables to eat at and massive bowls of fruit juice to drink. For the more adventurous, the sultan had a special bowl filled with fine wine for all to enjoy. The food was seasoned with all Far Eastern exotic spices and flavors—ginger, cardamon, cloves, mace, curry. The list—and the deliciousness—went on.

There was even cheesecake, a cheesecake tower six feet tall with red swirls. Toro and I each took a slice of the delectable yellow cheesecake, smiled, and stared out across the courtyard in pure bliss. To my astonishment, there were performers with painted white faces, dressed in black robes. They were the mimes from earlier in our adventure, and here they were, doing their bizarre show.

The sultan has figured out the mimes aren't dark magicians . . . or are they?

I then heard an elephant trumpeting right by my ear! My heart skipped a beat, causing me to drop my cheesecake. It was Arij, riding on an elephant.

"I see you found the cheesecake," she said with a smile. "Rather, you dropped the cheesecake."

"Very funny," I said, sarcastically.

Toro laughed aloud and took a bite.

"I see you found an elephant, Arij," I replied.

"My daughter needed one," said a familiar voice, coming from behind us. It was the sultan, happy as ever, helping his daughter off the elephant's back.

"I heard both of you are leaving tomorrow," said Arij.

"We are, Princess," I said. "The sea beckons us once more."

"Your ship is ready, stocked to the brim with spices and a crew," said the sultan. "My diplomat has set the departure for tomorrow. I look forward to a prosperous trade deal with King Charles V."

"As long as I'm dropped off at London afterward," I remarked with a wink.

"London?" questioned Toro.

"Yes. Aren't you coming with me?" I spoke.

"I suppose I am then," said Toro as he bit into his cheesecake.

"The ship follows your orders, Captain Swift," said the sultan, smiling.

"Cap . . . captain?" I asked.

"Yes," said the sultan. "None better than you."

"I'm honored, Your Grace," I said. "Is the princess coming as well? We could use another hand on deck."

Arij laughed, then looked to her father. They gleamed at one another, understanding one another. "Maybe next time."

"Next time then," I said.

"I'll miss you both," said Arij.

"As will I, Princess," said Toro.

"Me too," I added.

"As shall I," said the sultan.

"I have a feeling we will see each other once again," I said.

"We can only hope so," said Arij.

"Goodbye, Princess," I said with a formal bow, "and you, Sultan Muzaffar."

"Till we meet again," said Toro as he bowed.

Arij then grabbed us and hugged us both. "Goodbye, Spaniards."

"May Allah bless you to the moon, to the stars, to the heavens, and back," said the sultan. "Goodbye, my friends."

"How about a ride on the elephant, Father?" asked Arij.

"I am not so sure. My back has not been well," said the sultan.

"You can ask Toro about riding elephants," I said, laughing. "Rather falling off of them."

Toro sighed, then stuffed the cheesecake in my face. "I like that much better."

One of the mimes standing next to us and eating cheesecake made a silent, sad face toward me, acting like he was crying. Arij, the sultan, and Toro laughed at the mime's silent, theatrical expressions. I wiped the cheesecake from my eyes and face, starting to boil up with anger, but then I began to laugh with everyone.

"Father," said Arij. "One ride. That is all I ask."

"Well, um . . . actually, I would love nothing more than a ride with you, my daughter," said the sultan.

"Wonderful," cheered Arij.

Arij and the sultan climbed on to the back of the elephant and sat on a majestic blue chair mounted on the elephant's back. Arij then steered the elephant upward in a sudden, fast motion.

"Whoa now!" said the sultan as held onto his white turban.

"You are fine, Father. Stop worrying so much. Be adventurous for once in your life," said Arij.

"I'll try my best for you, my love," said the sultan.

Swift

Scene iii: Lover's End

༄ᶦᵐᵐᵍ

∽∽∽

T HE EXPEDITION WAS full of twists and turns through dark passages of the unknown and the unexpected. I felt the love lost for faces I would see and feel only in the night sky, glimmering and shining in their glory above, as they looked out for ole Swift, guiding me with their glow. I felt that I had found why Gaspar fell in love with the moon. I couldn't say how or why he did, but I felt the unspoken answer inside my soul.

Perhaps Gaspar wasn't so mad after all. He might have been onto something. Well, nay, he was mad but a wild, genius mad that I felt the world needed. I respected Gaspar in retrospect—admired him, in fact—for the world told him "no" at every opportunity and still Gaspar set out across the world with a dream and with a love. By God, he found that stone, found his answer against all odds even if it killed him or, rather, evaporated him.

I took Gaspar's lesson with me: dream big, believe in yourself when all others do not, look to the stars in order to navigate through your own maze, and go forth relentlessly. The catch, the one thing to this lesson, was to not let your dream evaporate you in the end. But hey, there are no guarantees in life, and evaporation would be a hell of a way to go out, I'd say.

As for Toro and me, we returned to Spain accompanied by Sultan Muzaffar's emissary on a ship filled with spices. The moment we entered Seville and the city realized who we were, the people welcomed us with a huge, rip-roaring applause.

I found out that King Charles V and the people of Spain were told by those lying Spanish mutineers that Gaspar and his loyalists turned into renegades and pirates who perished at sea. Thankfully, the sultan's emissary was quick to fix our image, verify our story, and tell the world of our valiant efforts in defeating the Portuguese at Boubazar for King Charles V. Further, the king told us that he was honored to have Toro and me in his court and ordered for the real mutineers to be rounded up and thrown in prison, starting with our old friend Javier.

Better yet, from the amount of spices the sultan granted us, we were able to pay back King Charles V in full—thrice over! Did I forget to mention the fabulous trade deal between Spain and Boubazar that followed? I heard years later that the trade deal between Boubazar and Spain was so profitable for Spain that it paid the way for numerous Spanish voyages headed west.

I think it was safe to say Spain would colonize the New World in the coming years due to this wonderful trade deal with Boubazar, tipping the tides in favor of Spain over Portugal in this great age of discovery and trade.

In truth, none of this would have happened if not for Gaspar, Cosimo, and Jaipur. I told King Charles thus, and he said monuments would be erected in their honor, and their families would be credited with their fair share of the wealth acquired from our voyage. Who would have thought things would have turned out so perfectly?

The last and most pressing thing on my mind and heart was to save Rose, to be able to pay for the treatment she needed.

I tried to convince Toro to join me in London, but he wanted to return to Timbuktu to resolve some unsettled business, as he said. I understood, and we said our goodbyes in Seville. I never saw Toro again after that day though I knew in my heart that he was off somewhere enjoying the most wonderful cheesecake with his loved ones nearby.

In remembrance of this great journey, I wrote down the whole of our journey—of the *Valencia*, of Boubazar, of our passage through the labyrinth, and of my friends—in Gaspar's (and now my) nautical Journal. I hoped and prayed that one day this priceless book of art, science, and history would offer truth, love, and light to the world when darkness returned from the depths below.

As for me, I finally returned to London after many months at sea. I returned home to my love, to my Rose.

Carriages moved to and fro in the streets on this bright summer's day as I stood outside my small, simple townhouse on the edge of the city. I was quite nervous. Why, I knew not.

I had not heard from my wife in so long. What if she remarried? What if the sickness had caught her, brought her to ash? Was this still my house, or was it sold off when she died? How long had it been? Was it two years? Oh, two years too long. No, no, she was not dead, for I would have known. I would have felt it. She lived, waited for me.

I still had my brown bag full of gems and my nautical works. I kept them very close over these past months. I took a deep breath and walked into my house. The wood floors creaked as I stepped on them. The living room looked exactly how I left it two years ago. Sunlight shone through the open window, illuminating the house with light. A large black pot was boiling over my brick fireplace in the back of the living room. There was my simple wooden table, and my four wooden chairs with red cloth draped over them. It was a modest house, a good house.

She must be home. Yes, yes! She must be cooking. How do I look?

Wait, wait, Rose never felt well enough to cook, yet this pot is cooking. This must not be my house. Nay, this must be someone else's. Oh Lord, please let that not be the case.

I then heard a door open in the back of the house. I froze in place, hearing footsteps, stomping, and singing—beautiful singing. I recognized that voice, that tune. I peeked over, and there she was, the most beautiful woman in the world. It was Rose with her long brown hair, her sharp nose, and her perky smile, dressed in blue. She carried a basket full of fruit.

"Rose," I said delicately.

Startled, she looked up at me and dropped her basket of apples, which rolled in all directions, to the ground.

"It's me, Rose," I said. "I'm here."

She looked at me, wide-eyed and inert. "Ed . . . Ed . . . Edward?"

"Yes."

Tears began to cascade from her blue eyes, past her red blossom cheeks. She said with broken words, "Can't be . . . can't be you . . . Edward?"

Slowly, I moved close, closer to her and pulled her to mee. "I told you." Tears filled my eyes for I could not hold back any longer. "I told you I would return. I returned . . . I returned."

My words cracked with pain, with struggle, with sacrifice. I felt the tears burn from my nose to the squint of my eyes.

"By God, Edward! Edward!" She clasped her hand over her mouth, crying.

I grabbed her and hugged her, gripping her ever so tight, stronger than any gravitational pull in the universe. She breathed and breathed, gripping my arms. "I never thought you died. Everyone told me. Everyone . . . everyone told me, but you didn't. They were wrong, so wrong. You are not dead. You are alive."

"What of you? Of your sickness?"

"A miracle, Edward. A miracle happened while you were gone. I was on my deathbed a year ago with a cough, with a fever, with aches and pain. The doctor gave up on me as he said he would, for I had no money to pay him for the medicine, for his treatment.

"As I lay dying, I said no to death. In my heart, I said nay until I saw you, Edward, again. I prayed to the Lord to allow me to see your love's face once more before we parted ways for good. That night, the fever subsided, and the cough disappeared. Edward, the Lord answered my prayer—*our* prayer—for . . . or . . . for you are here! Here! I knew you were still alive from that night on, and I never gave up on you, Edward."

"I never gave up you, Rose."

I gripped her with my heart and fell into a kiss of the deepest, the truest love that no word could describe. We kissed and kissed, loved and loved, talked and talked until our famished hearts were pleased. We sat in our bed with only our white blanket to clothe us.

"Tell me, what did you see abroad?" asked Rose with an enchanting smile.

I paused with a smile and deep stare, reminiscing.

"What?" she asked, waiting for an answer.

I laughed subtly. "Well, I saw elephants."

"Elephants?"

"Yes, elephants."

"What were they like?"

"They had long noses, like this." I positioned my hand and arm to appear like a long elephant truck. Then, I puckered my lips and made a loud blowing sound. She laughed and laughed.

"What else?" she asked, excited.

I smiled. "Cheesecake, splendid cheesecake."

www.ingramcontent.com/pod-product-compliance
Lightning Source LLC
Chambersburg PA
CBHW031335020726
47499CB00005B/1273